The Main Ingredient

Margo Wilson

Ramsfield Press

Published by Ramsfield Press
18417 Argyle Ave.
Homewood, IL 60430

Library of Congress Cataloging-in-publication Data

Wilson, Margo K.
    The Main Ingredient / Margo K. Wilson

    ISBN 978-0-9838589-2-8
    1. Fiction 2. Mystery 3. Urban Renewal 4. Family Drama
    5. Women's Fiction 6. Midwest 7. Wisconsin 8. Recipes
    9. Cooking

Visit our website at www.ramsfieldpress.com.
Printed in the United States by B.C. Design, Inc.
bcdesigninc.com

The Main Ingredient

Margo Wilson

Ramsfield Press
2013

To Mom, for sharing with me the keys of reading and love.

Praise for *The Main Ingredient*

If you were to combine some of Garrison Keillor's "Lake Wobegone" characters with a collection of recipes that range from Bridge Mix to Fried Egg Sandwiches, you might come up with the combination that makes Margo Wilson's **The Main Ingredient** great fun to read. This story, which contains both humor and pathos, concerns three middle-aged women who have been friends for most of their lives. Wilson's characters prove that you can go home again, but that home will be changed and so will you in ways both surprising and charming.

— Jane E. Wohl, Author of **Beasts in Snow** and **Triage**

*Full of the surprises of love and replete with recipes for every occasion, **The Main Ingredient** is the perfect indulgence. One key ingredient of Margo Wilson's novel is her celebration of girls' and women's friendships with all their complicated challenges and joys. Another key ingredient is her exploration of the tangled hearts of mother and daughter relationships. Mix in exuberant writing and fresh imagery and Wilson's novel is delicious; it is funny, serious, and compelling. A treat not to be missed.*

—Nicola Morris, Ph.D., Co-editor of **Alchemy of the Word;** Author of **The Golem in Jewish American Literature**

The Main Ingredient is a delightful concoction, baked to perfection by author Margo Wilson. This novel, set against the backdrop of working class Weewampum, Wisconsin, left me satisfied – always the sign of an excellent meal. I particularly enjoyed the recipes at the beginning of each chapter, and how they delicately illuminated the different characters in this novel. The deepening friendship among the Fearsome Threesome, childhood buddies who originally bonded in a tree house, was delectable. This savory slice of life, served up by the smart-mouthed narration of Wendy, is truly an original creation. For a tasty treat – without the calories – read **The Main Ingredient.**

— Vivian Borger, Writer, Journalist, Educator

*M*argo Wilson gave you a book that is smart and fun just like her protagonists, Wendy, Amber and MerriBeth. Who would have dreamed the Weewaumpumite women of Wisconsin would get up to such shenanigans? Arson, breaking and entering, birthing babies and nothing less than love among the raspberries completes this book. Even the recipes are entertaining.
This tale of contemporary lives entwined with the past will snare you from first page to last. Questions are asked and answers attempted until eventually, everything falls into place like a Schaum Torte in a cold oven.
Sherry Clements, author of **The Holdouts**

Author Margo Wilson asks us to consider the main ingredient: Is it the identity of the suspect who burned down three friends' restaurant? Is it family, friends, place, ethics, love? Or is it the best beer batter fish fry in the Carp River Valley? This savory novel is about women who reunite in their hometown, open a restaurant, then try to avoid prison by solving the mystery of who incinerated their eatery. The Main Ingredient explores the dynamics of small-town politics, family bonds, and the rigors of friendship; it's a substantive main dish served with tart humor and tenderness.
—Rosemary McClure, editor and writer: *The Chicago Tribune*, *The Los Angeles Times*, University of California, Yahoo

Acknowledgements

Thank you to my parents, Elizabeth and the late Neil Wilson, and my brother, James, for putting up with me; to my late husband, Michael Kraft, ditto.

Thank you to oh, so many people – my teacher aunts Margaret and Kathryn; my Uncle Alton; my Aunt Grace and Uncle Glen; and my cousins Renee, Jorene, Brad, Randy, Gary, and Cherrie. Thank you to my mother-in-law, the late Lucille Kraft, who got us cooking. And thank you to my brother-in-law Tom, who materialized like a saint when I needed a helping hand. And thank you to my brothers-in-law Jim, Jerry, and Dan, and to my sisters-in-law Pat Williams, and Sheryl, Ginny, and Pam, for that Kraft sense of humor.

And thank you to so many teachers and friends. Thank you, Mrs. Harriet Rehder, for letting me read to the class and same to you, Mrs. Marjorie Siewert. Thank you, Mr. Richard Holzer and Mrs. Carice Griffith, for helping me peck my way through the music and Mrs. Gladys Veidemanis, for inspiring excellence in English. Thank you to my Goddard College advisor Marina Budhos, and thank you, Billy Wilder, for spending time with me. Thank you, Lizzy Wilson, my former agent.

Thank you to my "blurb" writers: Nicola Morris and Jane Wohl, who inspired me as advisors at Goddard College; to Goddard friends Vivian Borger and Sherry Clements; and to Los Angeles Times and Yahoo.com travel writer and my former editor Rosemary McClure.

Thank you, Oshkosh friends DeeDee, Ellen, Corinne, Kathy, Debbie, and the late Cass, among others; thank you, newspaper friends, including editor extraordinaire John Friedell, and folks in Wisconsin, Canada, Indiana, and California. Thanks, Sally Ann Maas and Laura Nott, who helped me stay employed.

Thank you, Sherrie of San Bernardino Unified, Betsy of San Anselmo, and Regan of Santa Monica. Thank you, Tia Shawnte of Orlando for not giving up and Jenean for hanging in there.

Thank you to my Pennsylvania friends, including Marina Agrafiotis, Madeline Smith, Marsha Nolf, and Kausar Yasmin, for being there; and Karen, Lisa, Todd, Kurt, Janet, Bill, Bill, Pat, Ron,

Alan, Jim, Pratul, Savita, Tina, Tim, Jody, Mark, Sarah, Christina, Krystia, Marianne, Peggy, Carrie, Ellie, Debbie, Kim, Michael, Bill, Bill, Beth, Karen, Tracy, Emily, Michele, Pam, Marianne, Lauren, Bob, and Angie.

Thanks to my furry kids Lulu, Mopsy, Pokey, Clawdia, Licorice, Popcorn, Blueberry, Ollie, Oreo, Moosie, Grizzly, Squeaky (Panda), Lucy, ChaCha, and Mimi.

Thanks to my publisher, Bill Moser, and his wife, Ann, for their kindness and patience.

And thank you to the Great Spirit in us all.

Chapter 1

Three Bean Salad

1/2 green pepper, chopped
2 cups green beans, freshly cooked or canned and drained
2 cups kidney beans, cooked or canned and drained
2 cups canned wax beans, drained
1 onion, chopped
1/2 cup sugar
2/3 cup vinegar
1/3 cup vegetable oil
1/2 teaspoon salt
1/4 teaspoon pepper

Combine vegetables in large bowl. In separate bowl, mix sugar, vinegar, oil, salt, and pepper.
Pour over vegetables and mix well. Cover and refrigerate for 6 hours or longer.
Serves 6.
— *Our Lady of Perpetual Need Cafeteria*

I came home to Weewampum to watch my mother die. At least that's what I thought. But Seal's still with us, holding her own. So that turned out not to be the reason.

For a while it seemed important to be in Weewampum to help Amber and Merribeth get Amberosia's off the ground. But when the restaurant went up in smoke like Christmas wrap in the fireplace, that apparently wasn't the reason, either. After that, I thought it must be my mission to hunt down the pyromaniac responsible for the dirty deed, and I did my best to root out enough evidence to get a prosecution to stick. But then that turned out not to be the reason, either.

It's ludicrous to think I'd leave a good job and a condo with a pool view just to come home to Weewampum to help Amber make one last grab at youth before the snooze alarm on her biological clock got permanently stuck. Personally, I thought she

1

was as misguided as my hometown, from which anyone with any sense had leaped aboard the last Amtrak out before they'd discontinued the route. Sure, there was a small Weewampum airport now, serving guilty escapees paying holiday visits to root-bound relatives, but fortunately, someone had had the good sense to schedule all departing flights before 9 a.m. No sense prolonging courtesy calls to the place only the natives were bold enough to dub "God's Country."

So what was I doing in a Weewampum hospital room the size of a closet, trying to help my middle-age best friend – or second best friend, depending on how you want to count it – launch another generation of Weewampumites into the world?

"Goddammit, Lars Hunssen! I'm going to kill you," Amber was screaming while Merribeth sponged our laboring friend's brow with lavender-scented water. Merribeth had prepared the balm from a shoe-deodorant sachet I'd spotted in the Our Lady of Perpetual Need Medical Center's gift shop. I'd been only too happy to take a break from our "birthing suite" to scout for something that might calm Amber down. Besides the sachet, I'd found a bag of sour lemon drops – but Amber wasn't interested in food this one time – and a stuffed gingham koala, which probably had suffered a brain concussion when Amber had hurled it against a petal-pink wall. The three of us weren't exactly presenting the appearance of a peaceful nativity tableau.

We were caged there like animals, like snapping, snarling wolves – well, I'm speaking for Amber and myself. Merribeth remained as perky as Sally Field in "The Flying Nun." We were trapped in this shoe box, waiting for a baby who was in no hurry to drop into our world. It was our sentence as women, the price of our friendship, but not the way I'd have chosen to celebrate my Christmas Eve. I even would have preferred sipping eggnog with Cecilia Dandridge Whitby, my mother, whom I preferred to call "Seal," as in "sealed shut," "My mind is made up," "black and white," "case closed."

But I guess you could say I came home to Weewampum, where

the natives choke on paper-mill air in winter and slap themselves sunburned in summer when the mosquitoes hatch out, thinking I could predict what would happen next. I figured I'd be back under the Santa Dolorosa palms mourning my mother by the time the ground was thawing in Weewampum and they were starting to tear open the earth to build the foundation for the new Our Lady of Perpetual Need Medical Center. I did manage to predict a few things that happened – like my mother hated Amberosia's, at least at first, and Lars Hunssen and Jim Hartwell proved, at least for a while, that they were still major-league, first-class jerks.

But I couldn't predict that the feelings I thought I'd flushed out like old oil when I'd moved to California 20 years ago had just coagulated in the bottom of my crankcase heart and only needed a little air and a spark to flare up again.

"Jesus Christ! Get this train off my back!" Amber was raging, but the Chicago-Northwestern's tracks were at least 10 blocks from our room.

Merribeth and I pleaded with Amber to take drugs, preferably in massive doses, until she freed her body of this infant invader. But she refused.

"I want it natural," she'd decided weeks earlier and the pain wasn't changing her mind. "It's better for the baby. Besides, I want to get in on this motherhood thing from the ground floor up. I might not do this again and I don't want to miss out on any of it," she'd persuaded us as convincingly as if we were a couple of her real estate clients, wavering about whether to buy a bigger house than our budget was ready for.

So now Amber was doing her "I Am Woman, Hear Me Roar," routine, and Merribeth and I were not eagerly joining in the chorus. Merribeth kept patting Amber's hand while I carved a groove in the brown rubber floor tiles from pacing. I'd glance out the window every five minutes, but all I could see through the old-fashioned glass panes was Lake Weewampum, frozen black and hard like a grimace.

3

I suppose I sound unsympathetic toward Amber and believe me, I was. Well, mostly. I couldn't feel too sorry for this 40-plus-year-old pal of mine, who still hadn't figured out there were other parts to her body than those she could pack inside a bustier and fishnet hose. It's not that Amber is stupid. She's one of Weewampum's leading real estate agents. It's just that she's so vivid. She gets what she wants with that flame-like hair, breasts like cream-filled pastry horns, and a booming laugh like a wave crashing on rocks along a sunny cove. It's what drew me to her –well, not the breasts, really – when she first showed up in Mr. Caesar's eighth-grade math class at Cedar Pines Junior High. She seemed such a rebel, so confident about flaunting her not inconsiderable charms. Later, I found those attributes reactionary when I finally made my Weewampum escape. And I guess my attitude hasn't changed that much since, although I do love Amber. She just tends to get on my nerves.

It's interesting that of the three of us, Amber, the most wild of our wild bunch, is the one who took root and spread her branches in our inert hometown, while Merribeth and I zoomed out like jets.

Actually, Merribeth, in her usual, reasonable, please-everyone, Merribeth-fashion, didn't zoom but drove at a sensible speed just 80 miles down the interstate and landed a job teaching the inner city kids of Milwaukee. Still, the point is, she agreed with me from childhood that Weewampum wasn't where we needed to be if we wanted to have some impact on the world.

I could always count on Merribeth like that, Merribeth, my oldest, and other best friend. She lived right next door to us. She had everything I thought I wanted and was everything I'd never be – you can start with nice. Everybody liked her. She had a good attitude. I hate good attitudes. And she was blonde, a natural enemy. But I loved Merribeth because she shared.

Mostly, she shared her family – her two brothers and twin little sisters and her mother who seemed to have stepped out of a Dick and Jane reader. She had a father, too, but when he was home, he usually went into his study and shut the door, so I didn't pay much

4

attention to him. Although the Hartwells weren't rich, they were comfortable, and Merribeth and her brothers and sisters always had the latest clothes and lots of toys and books. I lived with Seal and she was a secretary, so we didn't have much money. But then, Seal never was one to go overboard on anything, so we had even less than we might have.

One Christmas, even before we'd started school, Santa Claus gave Merribeth a gold locket shaped like a heart that I thought was the neatest thing in the world, mostly because I knew I'd never get more than white bobby socks and a candy cane from Santa Seal. You could open the locket and put two photos inside. Merribeth took a photo her mother had shot of us playing in the sprinkler and cut out her own Goldilocks-like head and put it on one side of the locket and tucked my Buster Brown-type photo into the other side. Her mother must have helped her. Then, Merribeth gave me the locket. It was the most wonderful Christmas present I'd ever received, and I wore it home like Queen Elizabeth's jewels. I proudly showed it to my mother, who made me march right back to Merribeth's to give it back. Mrs. Hartwell and Merribeth marched right back home with me. It's the only time I can remember Mrs. Hartwell coming to our house. She told Seal that Merribeth wanted me to have the locket. I guess my mother must have felt outnumbered by the three of us cajoling her, so she reluctantly backed down and allowed me to "borrow" the necklace. But Seal wouldn't let me wear it; she said I'd only break it. So I kept it in the shoe box in which I kept all my treasures, but sometimes I'd sneak it out and wear it when Merribeth and I played "Bride."

"Bride" wasn't my favorite game, cowboys and Indians was. But sometimes, if Merribeth promised me a Popsicle later, I'd pretend I was a bridesmaid just to humor her. I knew my best friend was the most generous person I'd probably ever meet. I knew if it had been my locket, I'd never, in a million years, have given it away to Merribeth. So I loved her for her generosity. But she also got on my nerves.

Naturally, Merribeth had a much more benign attitude toward

Amber's soon-to-be baby than I did.

"Oh, Wen. We'll be almost-aunts! It will be so much fun," she tried to encourage me.

But I just felt the whole matter had been so ill-conceived that all I could do was keep my mind focused on the next month or so when I'd be back in my natural habitat, sipping from a tall glass of iced tea and reading from – or at least pretending to – a paperback version of Foucault or Barthes. I guess I've always been somewhat of a quirky snob, at least that's what Seal, and later, Merribeth and Amber, told me. In Santa Dolorosa, people actually went to plays on occasion and at least some of them even read books, at least my friends in the Post-Modern Society book club did. We called ourselves the PMSers. In Weewampum, the biggest pastime is bowling. And reading from cereal boxes and the billboards along Highway 11 is what passes for contemplating philosophy or literature. OK, maybe I'm being a little bit harsh. But not much.

So, I guess you could say I came home to Weewampum with an attitude the size of the State of California that only cancer, fire, a baby, two best friends, and one stubborn mother, all working in concert, had any chance of penetrating.

"Lars Hunssen, I'm going to shove your speculum up where the sun don't shine," Amber howled as she clutched my arm like a grab bar. Lars was the perpetrator of Amber's pregnancy and also a leading Weewampum gynecologist.

Every time Amber had a contraction, she'd squeeze my arm and it was starting to turn blue. Around 11:45 p.m., when I wasn't sure how much longer my arm could hold out, nurse Nancy Bedloe trundled in, checked Amber and said, "You're in transition, honey. This is the worst part. Pretty soon, you'll have to push." Then Nurse Nancy scurried out because she knew what was coming, but poor Amber, Merribeth, and I could only gulp.

The morning had dawned cold and surly. We'd been in the birthing suite now about nine hours and it seemed like a century ago that we'd been bustling about preparing for our first holiday buffet at Amberosia's.

Amber had worked us like galley slaves those first couple months at the restaurant and it's a wonder Merribeth and I hadn't invested in industrial-sized flamethrowers to lay waste to it. But by Christmas, business was going better than even Amber had expected and we decided we'd like to host an all-you-can-eat buffet as our little holiday thank-you to the community.

Merribeth thought the food should be on the house, but Amber and I outruled her. We weren't a charity; we just wanted to make our customers feel good. We decided to charge $3 for the buffet. We'd still lose money, but not a whole lot. It was cheap enough that people would be happy, and high-priced enough that the three of us wouldn't be left with a bad taste in our mouths.

We spent the early morning getting organized and making sure everything looked nice. Merribeth had put up holiday decorations right after Thanksgiving. Seal even had some momentary sentimental lapse and let us borrow some glass ornaments and old-fashioned bubble lights for our plastic tree. The fire department wouldn't let us use a fresh fir. We lined up a fleet of tables to form the buffet line and covered them with red and green taffeta that Merribeth had discovered on sale.

Then we covered the taffeta with bowls and bowls of food. Everything from deviled eggs to herring in cream sauce, smoked salmon, boiled shrimp, tossed salad and a salad bar, hot corn chowder, turkey, ham, mashed potatoes, yams, green beans, pumpkin pie, pecan pie, a Shaum Torte, banana cream pie, cheddar cheese, and a fruit compote. Amber ladled punch into cups at the end of the line. Merribeth ran the cash register. I kept bouncing between the dining room and the kitchen to make sure our workers kept preparing more food, replenishing the buffet line and tidying up the salad-dressing overslops and clumped-together slices of smoked salmon. It was amazing what the staff could overlook. I found a chef's knife lying on the floor under a taffeta ruffle and slipped it into my kangaroo-sized, front apron pocket. Someone had dropped a melon ball into the black olive bowl, so I fished it out and popped it into my mouth. (I used a fork, of course.)

It had taken Merribeth and me days to clean and cook and get everything in order while Amber flitted in and out, tending to her real estate business and checking up on us between clients. When she felt she needed a rest, she'd sit on a chair and run the cash register and chat with some of her favorite customers, who would tell her what a great job she was doing with the restaurant. That kind of got on my nerves, too.

We arranged with some madrigal singers from the high school to stand in a corner and sing carols at our buffet in exchange for free food. When we opened the doors at 11:30 a.m., there was a line of impatient customers wrapping around the corner. Within minutes, it was standing room only inside. The customers dove like football tackles for chairs, and soon it was almost as noisy as a cramped stadium. We asked people who finished to leave so we could seat those still standing. Everyone understood and smiled and wished us "Happy Holidays" or "Merry Christmas." We stationed a waitress at the door with a hospital petition to catch folks as they were heading out and ask them to sign. We needed their signatures to push our request for a referendum over the top.

We got another 123 names on that one day alone. Amber had made Amberosia's the unofficial "Stop the Hospital Move" headquarters, and I agreed with Amber there was no need for Our Lady of Perpetual Need to move. Merribeth was uneasy about the situation. She thought the hospital should stay near downtown, but since her father had designed the new building, she was torn about backing one side over the other. She figured she'd be just like Switzerland and try to stay out of it, but it was fine with her whatever Amber and I chose to do.

Our customers were in great spirits and wished us good luck with the restaurant. The choir had just wrapped up the last verse of "The Twelve Days of Christmas," and the line for the buffet had thinned a little so there was only a 5- or 10-minute wait. By 1:45 p.m., we were beginning to think about calling it a day.

Then who to our wondering eyes should appear but Lars Hunssen and Jim Hartwell, sidling into line like some kind of vampires of Christmas Past? They took their time on the buffet line and loaded their plates as if they were anticipating a blizzard.

When Lars and Jim reached the end of the line and were near Merribeth and Amber, Lars seemed to fixate on Amber's belly and I had to ask him several times if there was anything else he wanted, just to get him to take the last few steps toward Merribeth and pay his bill. Meanwhile, Mr. H. said to Merribeth, "We need to talk." She motioned Lars and Mr. H. to the only open table in the room.

For a moment it seemed Mr. H. just might go quietly and sit at the table that Merribeth pointed out, but I guess he just wanted to make sure he got a table. After setting his plate down, he was back at Merribeth's side, insisting, "We need to talk."

Merribeth just looked at him and said, "I'm busy, Father."

Some customers still waiting in line started coughing and clearing their throats. I wanted everyone to have a good time, not remember a father-daughter showdown.

"Go see what he wants," I whispered to Merribeth and took over for her at the register. Merribeth reluctantly joined her dad and Lars.

Amber and I couldn't hear what they were saying. I had to make change and wish our customers the best of the season, and Amber felt she needed to say "Merry Christmas" while pouring the punch. I did, however, hear Merribeth say pretty loudly for Merribeth, "They're my friends and they can do what they like. I'm not going to stop them."

I glanced up from the register and noticed that Lars' face was red as the berries on the fake holly we'd strung along the ceiling, and Mr. H. looked as if he wanted to snap Merribeth open, chew her up, and spit her out like one of the tails on the fresh shrimp on our buffet.

Then he said loudly enough for the whole restaurant to hear, "This is your last warning, Merribeth. At your age, you should realize that your father and your family are far more important than friends can ever be. But if you can't see that, fine. Don't expect to see us this Christmas. Don't call us. Don't write us. And whatever you do, don't you ever open our front door or back door again. Don't you ever consider yourself our daughter again."

Most of our customers halted their chewing for a moment, then tried to pretend there'd been no interruption in their partaking of holiday cheer. I could see Merribeth's bottom lip trembling; it was so unfair. She'd done nothing to provoke her father. She'd just been a good friend to Amber and me. But that's the way her father was, arrogant, hot-tempered, stubborn. He'd always been this way and apparently the fact that we'd knocked 50 cents off his bill as a senior discount had done nothing to mellow him. He almost made me glad I'd never had a father. Merribeth blinked and stared, then bent over as if her father had slugged her. It made me so mad. Merribeth backed over to the cash register, staring at her father with tears streaming down her face. He had no right speaking to her like that in our restaurant.

I picked up a turkey bone a customer had dropped and strode over to Lars' and Mr. H's table. I told them that although it might be Christmas Eve, it didn't seem as if they were adding much to our celebration. I told them to finish eating as quickly as possible, then leave without saying another word to Merribeth – or Amber.

I should have known those two weren't likely to take direction. They figured they'd paid their money, which gave them the right to bully Merribeth – or Amber and me, too, if they so chose. But the way I saw it, $3 or not, this was my restaurant – or at least Amber's – and I didn't want those jerks in Amberosia's anymore, taking up our space and breathing our air.

I jabbed the turkey bone – it was a wing – close to Mr. H's face just to emphasize my point. I wasn't going to poke him in the eye or anything.

"Put that down, you idiot," he snarled, and then, I don't know, something snapped. Or something flared up; it must have been that brain tissue that's supposed to be the most primitive, somewhere near the nape of your neck. I remembered the chef's knife in my apron pocket, so I pulled it out and took a good long look at it. I guess Mr. H. must have thought I was going to slit his throat or something. I should have, but I didn't want to stain the carpet.

Out of the corner of my eye, I glimpsed Merribeth, her blonde curls springing into action like Slinkies, and Amber, her belly leading the rest of her body by at least a foot. They were heading my way, probably to disarm me. I slipped the knife into my pocket so they wouldn't have to get involved. When Amber was about three steps away, she paused as if considering whether to continue her advance or leave me to fight this battle on my own. Her face froze suddenly in a look of surprise, then changed to a Halloween horror mask of pain.

She gasped, "Oh, my God!"

And then, all of a sudden, it looked as if she were peeing all over her red velvet pumps with the one-inch heels.

"It's the baby!" she yelled.

Lars glanced at her with disdain and said, "It figures," then made a great show of pushing away from the table and walking toward her to play his role as the great master of medicine.

"Stay away, you bastard," Amber screamed. "The rest of you, Merry Christmas. Now, all of you go home."

Merribeth started shooing everyone out the door. And to tell you the truth, they were of no mind to stay. I was kind of mesmerized by everything and just stood with a hand in my pocket, clutching the knife handle. Then I noticed Amber slumped in a chair, so I asked her if she was OK.

"Except for the fact that my guts are being ripped out, I'm just fine," Amber growled.

11

I asked her if I should call an ambulance, but she said, "No. Just drive me to the hospital and call Dr. Deirdre."

Dr. Deirdre Smithers, Amber's gynecologist, had admitting privileges at Our Lady of Perpetual Need but her main hospital was in Pearville, which was where Amber had intended to give birth. But Amber said the way she felt, she didn't think she'd make it the 20 miles up Highway 11 to Pearville Memorial.

So we locked Amberosia's door as soon as the last straggler wrapped two pieces of pecan pie inside a Santa napkin, and then we piled into Seal's Oldsmobile and drove the two blocks to our Lady of P.N.

Amber probably could have made it to Pearville. Dr. Deirdre had warned her that first babies take time. Lars was a gynecologist on staff at Our Lady of Perpetual Need, and Amber didn't want to see him there. But Amber's pain was so intense she couldn't imagine being cooped up in a car for the 30-minute drive to Pearville. So, Merribeth and I signed Amber into the pride of Our Lady's, the birthing suite, which had all the charm of a solitary confinement cell.

Amber sat in the bed with her arms clasped around her knees, cursing Lars, doctors, nurses, sex, womanhood, and Merribeth and me. She was in agony and Merribeth and I were, too. It's not easy watching your best friend suffer, even when she's calling you an "uncaring bitch." There was nothing Merribeth and I could do but pat Amber's head and hands, massage her back and hope this thing would be over soon.

It took hours for the baby to bash its way through the tissue and bone. At one point, Amber stripped off all her clothes and sat in a rocking chair and rocked and rocked as if she could rock the baby into being.

When it was nearly midnight and nurse Nancy told Amber she was in transition, Amber was screaming as loudly as the noontime whistle on the White and Bright paper mill.

12

"Take some drugs," Merribeth begged her. "Drugs are good," I chanted. All Amber could do was howl, "No-o-o-o-o-o!!!" Merribeth and I felt helpless, exasperated, scared. We wished we could make a run for the nearest getaway car. All we could do was stand there and tell Amber that everything was going to be all right, even when everything seemed to be going all wrong. And then Amber started panting. Just when we were sure things couldn't possibly get any worse, Dr. Deirdre popped in, took one look at Amber, and smiled.

"I think we're going to have a baby," she said. I swear she rubbed her rubber-gloved hands together.

Amber growled, "No shit!"

Merribeth and I helped push Amber's bed into the delivery room. There was no way we were going to leave Amber alone at this point after all we'd been through that day. Somewhere in the distance, I thought I heard a fire engine. Or maybe it was just Amber's screams echoing in my ears. We rolled Amber's bed under a bank of lights, and Dr. Deirdre said, "OK, Amber, now you've got to push."

Amber started pushing as if she'd push herself inside out and as she did, we all heard sirens. One, two, three. Must be a big fire, we figured. Then Dr. Deirdre said, after what seemed like months, "It's crowning."

Merribeth and I looked down and there, between Amber's legs, was this round, furry thing that looked like a wet coconut. Oh, my God, what a sight. Then, Dr. Deirdre said, "Now, push just a little, not too fast."

And then Star started sliding into the world. I listened and then I heard the sirens one last time. It was as if they were heralding Star's birth. Pretty soon nurse Nancy wiped the goo off the baby and handed her to Amber. And then the new mom gazed down and touched her daughter's nose, her fingers. She moved the baby's legs back and forth. Star gazed up in the general direction of her mother and seemed willing to smile if we'd just give her one

13

good reason why.

"Well, hello, little girl. I'm Amber, your mother. Welcome to our world. So, tell me, what do you think so far?" Amber asked.

Then, a brief grin crossed Star's face, I swear it. But Nurse Nancy bundled her up and scurried her out of there so fast that all Amber, Merribeth, and I could do was just stare at each other. It was only when Star was making her exit that we heard her first cry. We listened as that sad little wail trailed down the hall while we beamed and beamed at each other.

Finally, Amber said hoarsely, "Boy, what a ride!"

Merribeth hugged Amber and told her she'd done a good job and so did I.

"But what happens now?" Amber asked, in an uncharacteristic moment of reflection, as if thinking for the first time about the consequences of what she'd done.

"Well, you'll love her and hold her and make her a good home," Merribeth said soothingly.

"Oh, yeah," Amber said kind of dazed, then sank into her pillow and looked at me as if seeking my reassurance. Not even I had the heart to tell Amber she'd made a big mistake and there were no returns or exchanges once she'd signed on for this long-term motherhood thing.

"Oh, my God," she said and gulped and stared at me. "What have I done?"

I squeezed her shoulder. "Don't worry, Amb," I told her, not thinking where my words were going. "We'll figure it out."

We? I didn't know where that had come from, but it seemed to be what Amber needed to hear. She sighed, got a smile like a mile of storm fencing, and fell asleep. Merribeth grinned at me and nodded at the door. We tiptoed out and drove into a night as crisp and cold as an ice floe with a million silvery stars glinting above. We didn't talk until Merribeth got out of the Olds. As she reached for her purse, she smiled at me.

"Merry Christmas, Wen," she said. "We did it."

But she was wrong. Amber had done it; we'd mostly just watched; but we'd been there, and that seemed important, somehow, although I couldn't explain why just right then. So I guess you could say I came home to Weewampum, expecting to jet out of here as quickly as I could. But maybe I had to learn that sometimes, jets won't get you where you need to go.

Chapter 2

Amberosia's Fish Fry

2 cups Bisquick
1 egg, beaten
1 cup beer
Seasoning salt (Frank's Seafood Pleasoning, if available)
1/4 teaspoon ground pepper
1/4 teaspoon basil
Lake perch or pike filets
(Cod is OK)
Cooking oil (A deep fryer works best. But you can cook the fish in hot vegetable oil in a frying pan.)

Pat the fish dry so the batter sticks to the fish.
Mix all ingredients except for the fish.
Dip the fish into the batter. Place in deep fryer or frying pan.
Cook until batter is golden brown and fish is tender.
— From Michael Kraft

W hen I got home from the hospital that Christmas Eve, still glowing in my status as a first-time midwife and step-aunt, Seal was waiting up for me with a peculiar grin on her face. It was peculiar mostly that she was grinning; she doesn't like to do that.

"Sit down," she said before I could tell her she was a great-step-aunt. "You're not going to like this," she said, smiling bigger than ever. "And don't you think it's about time you did something, anything, with your hair? You're like a skinny version of, what's his name? Ringo Starr."

I wasn't about to tell Seal that Ringo was no longer in the spotlight. She'd never known whom I was talking about back when Amber, Merribeth, and I formed the Weewampum chapter of the Beatles' fan club, but then we turned the presidency over to Trudy Trumbull anyway because we decided we weren't cut out to be club women. Seal dropped her smile to her usual frown as I contemplated what she was about to tell me. Probably that it was time for me to either pack up and head back to Santa Dolorosa or, at least, start looking for my own place.

I slumped into the barrel-shaped, nubby, mustard-colored chair by the TV that was the only chair in the living room where I'd been allowed to sit when I was growing up and still attempting to please Seal. I'd been staying with Seal for the past few months – just until Amber got Amberosia's off the ground and I was convinced Seal truly was on the mend.

I came home to Weewampum after Merribeth, then Amber, phoned and said Seal was ill, really ill, I'd better get home right away. Seal had ovarian cancer; it looked pretty grim. So I packed some clothes and my laptop and was in the skies four hours later, expecting the worst and praying to the Great Spirit, Mother Earth, or even Jesus Christ – whomever was on duty – to grant Seal and me a reprieve.

Even though I rushed, I reached the hospital two days after Seal had surgery. The doctor told me she'd pulled through surprisingly well. In the next few days she rallied like a bruised quarterback who glugs down some Gatorade and goes out to score a couple more touchdowns. In a couple weeks she was out of the hospital, and I was taking care of her as best I could. Mostly, we spent our time, when I wasn't at the restaurant, trying to outscore each other at Scrabble, and Seal was winning the majority of games. I'd taken a leave of absence from my food editor job at the *Santa Dolorosa Advance*, and now, Seal was telling me daily that I should go home. She didn't need me. Why was I hanging around like a hawk, waiting for the hen to topple over from old age? Didn't I have better things to do? What about my work? How could they spare me? I should get back before I didn't have a job. And I'd better not think she was going to support me after they finally wised up and fired me in Santa Dolorosa.

In the meantime, Amber had conned Merribeth and me into helping her out at her new restaurant, a move Seal didn't approve of in the least. "I didn't raise you to be a cook in a greasy spoon," she said. "Don't you forget I spent a lot of money on your education."

"It's only for a little while, to help Amber out," I told her.

You'd think I'd been nothing but a beach bum for the last 20 years. In my own little world, I was a medium-size fish in a medium-size pond. I even had freelance writers and a staff of two working for me. I was only helping out at Amberosia's because Seal didn't want me underfoot. But I didn't feel comfortable enough about her health yet to just wing on back to California.

"You'll never make it work. People here don't eat that kind of food," Seal said about our Chinese salads, vegetable lasagna, and pitas stuffed with alfalfa sprouts and free-range chicken.

Seal and I were alternating currents, jolting each other's nerves, so now I figured she'd had enough and was about to tell me to leave. It had seemed the smartest thing to do, to sleep under her roof, so I could be there if she needed me, although I'd probably have to stumble over her shivering, shaking body on the floor before she'd ever let on I might be of any use.

"Did you hear the sirens while you were out?" she asked.

"Uh, yeah, well, actually, we did," I said. "It was right before Amber had the baby. She had it, Mom. It's a girl and she weighs 7 pounds, 8 ounces and she's got curly hair like a toy poodle, and she's really cute."

"Well, isn't that nice," Seal said, not the least bit interested. "You're not going to like this, but while you were busy, Amberosia's burned to the ground."

"What!?" I jumped out of the chair. "What are you saying? How do you know? What do you mean?"

"It's gone," she said, smiling, seemingly pleased with this turn of events. "Phhht."

And then I flew out of the house and drove Seal's car to the restaurant.

It wasn't there. Ashes and chunks of burned wood like fallout from Nagasaki dotted the lot where Amberosia's had stood just hours before. As I ran up, the only thing I could see that was vertical was a lone fireman, breathing vapor into the air.

"What's going on here?" I screamed.

He responded so gratingly matter-of-factly that I wanted to slap him. "Well, what does it look like?"

Then he recognized me; it was Kenny Stokes, who used to live with his brother, Denny, over on Fourteenth Street in a house with pigeon coops in the backyard.

"Oh, Hi, Wendy," he said. "Sorry about this. It just went up in a poof. We couldn't save anything."

The stars still were glittering, but now their smirky light seemed a mocking dance along the deserted Main Street. Amberosia's had occupied the former Haskin's Drug Store on the corner of Menominee and Main. Marilyn's Bridal Boutique was next door. Marilyn's still stood there, soot-caked, the display window a black crepe veil of mourning, concealing the scalloped-necked bride's dress behind it.

It was hard facing Amberosia's, now just a charred memory. Snakes of smoke still curled into the dark sky. I remember thinking, this shouldn't be affecting me. It was Amber's restaurant, not mine, after all. But it was as if I were suffering from smoke inhalation, although the night was clear and cold. I couldn't catch my breath and gasped for air.

"Are you OK?" Kenny asked.

One tear and then another etched a trail down my cheeks. "Yeah, sure." I toed the ashes with my boot.

"That's good. Better go home and get some rest. There's nothing you can do tonight. Tomorrow, the fire marshal will be out, so you'd better start thinking about what you want to tell him."

"What do you mean?" I choked out.

"Well, when they go this fast, it always looks suspicious."

"You don't think we did it, do you?" I managed to blurt.

"Look," Kenny said. "I know owning a restaurant isn't the easiest thing in the world."

I kicked up some ashes and they rained on Kenny's boots.

"Just keep an eye on this place," I said, and now I was really crying. I ran toward the cold metal comfort of Seal's car.

I raced to the efficiency apartment Merribeth was renting and told her the news.

"Oh, my God!" she screamed, breaking into tears that matched mine. "Who do you think would do something like that to us?"

"I don't know, but I'm going to find out," I vowed. And pretty soon I started finding things out that I really didn't want to know.

***

Merribeth's and my first stop the next morning was to visit Amber, of course. A nurse brought in Star and she was quite respectable, as far as babies go. Amber practiced nursing; she couldn't quite get the hang of it.

When we told her about the restaurant, she once again screamed, "Lars Hunssen, I'm going to kill you!" insisting that Star's accidental father was the man who'd lit the match.

A nurse rushed in and swiped Star out of Amber's arms.

"First babies are the hardest," the nurse said, sure that Amber was beset with some sort of severe postpartum depression. And maybe that was part of it, but we couldn't get Amber to calm down. She was a madwoman, screaming and swearing.

We tried to tell her that Lars had too much to risk to burn down the restaurant, but we couldn't convince our friend he was innocent. Finally, the nurse stormed in and put some clear liquid in Amber's I.V., and she settled down right away.

From the hospital, Merribeth and I drove to the restaurant, but a fireman we didn't know wouldn't let us poke through the rubble. Merribeth started sobbing and walking around in circles. I was out of tears but the place looked even worse in the sun. One charred wall was half-standing and an 8-quart stainless steel pot propped up a singed rafter. On the far right corner of the lot, I spotted a porcelain sink – it looked like the one from the women's rest room – and that was pretty much all we could spot from the sidewalk.

Merribeth and I drove to McDonald's – It was the only restaurant open on Christmas Day. We ordered coffee and sank into a molded plastic booth. I was wrong; I still had tears left, and we sat and sobbed while kids all around us ate their Happy Meals.

But sitting on that unbending seat seemed to harden me after a while, and I said to Merribeth that although Amber thought Lars was responsible for the fire, maybe we should consider the unthinkable, and at least explore the idea that Merribeth's father had a hand in the blaze. After all, he was angry that Merribeth didn't try harder to get Amber and me to keep quiet about the

21

hospital move. Then, I provoked him with the turkey bone and chef's knife, even though I really hadn't planned on maiming him. Maybe he was trying to teach us a lesson now.

"That's out of the question!" Merribeth said, her voice a shaky whisper. "My father is an honorable man."

So I said, of course it could have been Lars, although he wouldn't have wanted to get his hands dirty, but he could have hired someone. Then, again, maybe it was one of Amber's many lovers, whom she'd wrap around herself like a new sweater, then discard when she spotted the first snag. Or maybe it was a customer whom we'd inadvertently food-poisoned.

All Merribeth and I knew was that someone was out to do us in.

Chapter 3

Amber's Spiced Cider

1 gallon apple cider
1-1/2 teaspoons whole allspice
1-1/2 teaspoons cinnamon
1/2 teaspoon ground cloves
1/2 teaspoon nutmeg
1/2 teaspoon ginger
2 teaspoons zest from orange
1/2 cup dark brown sugar, packed
Or skip everything above and buy a container of mulled cider spices at some upscale foodstore
1-1/2 tablespoons brandy

Combine all ingredients except brandy. Bring to a boil, then simmer five minutes.
Pour brandy into mugs. Add the cider mix. Skoal!

I charged into the downtown fire station at 8:01 a.m. on the day after Christmas to read the report on Amberosia's blaze. Fire Marshal Warren Caramel was on duty. A doorway separates Warren's office from the garage, where a 100-year-old brass fire pole is a reminder of a Weewampum that existed even before Warren Caramel, although two almost-new, blood-blister-red fire trucks dominate the room. The building is on the must-see list of field-trip destinations for the braver teachers in the Weewampum Unified School District.

A fussy kind of a guy who wouldn't seem to know what a fire pole is used for, Warren sat at a gray steel desk, running his fingers through his twig-like gray hair. He looked up only to say he was behind on his reports because Anita, the department's secretary, had just quit for a better-paying job selling mobile homes in Pearville.

The field report had been filled in by hand; it had been Anita's job to clean up these jottings and make them look official. From what I could make out from the jagged scrawl, the cause of the fire was undetermined but suspicious. The blaze seemed to have started on the main floor and spread quickly. The speed made it seem particularly suspicious. "Investigation to continue," the report said.

"So, whom have you interviewed?" I grilled Warren. "What kind of evidence did you find? What kind of fire was it? How did it start?"

But he was of no mind to talk. "It's under investigation," was all he would say; then, "When can you come back for an interview?" He said he didn't have time for me that day but he had questions for "you and your gal friends."

"What do you mean?" I popped. "You can't believe we're suspects?"

He just handed me a card embossed with an orange flame that said, "Warren Caramel, fire marshal," and said, "I'll be in touch."

He stood up then, turned his back, strode into an inner office and pulled the door shut. I tore up his card and left the shreds on his desk.

I aimed Seal's Olds toward the incinerated Amberosia's, where nothing was going on except for a starling pecking through the rubble, searching for a holiday handout amidst the ashes and burned boards. I slipped under the yellow plastic tape announcing this was a criminal-investigation site and joined the starling but was less successful. He seemed to have found a snack of some kind of black beetle that had forgotten to burrow deep into the dirt for a winter snooze. I picked up the 8-quart stainless steel pan that still was supporting a scorched wooden beam and poked my black chukkah boot into the ashes that were now held in place by about an inch of icy snow. I kicked and prodded my way through the snow and scuffed up a navy-colored plastic button with a little anchor on the front, and on the back, a plastic shank with two holes. It was possible the button had fallen off a pea coat. I pocketed it and kicked my way through the lot, feeling like a steam shovel. I had nothing better to do and found it strangely therapeutic. In the far left corner, opposite the porcelain sink, I kicked up an old plastic Oscar Mayer wiener whistle on an odd little pink-plastic-bead keychain and pocketed this, too. The sink was too heavy to lift so I left it, then retraced my steps to the car since there was nothing left to scuff up but snow.

When I got home, Seal was taking a nap. If I've forgotten to mention it before, which Seal would say is just oh, so typical of my self-centeredness, I should bring it up right now that Seal was doing the best she could with her new status as a cancer patient. She'd had her surgery on Halloween and I hadn't known about it. When I showed up two days later, the last of the autumn leaves swirled around my feet like lost dogs as I scurried into the hospital. Two weeks later, when I took Seal home, she seemed surprisingly intact from her hospital encounter – except for both ovaries that Dr. Bill Stetson had excised, along with her uterus for good measure.

My mother had weekly appointments now at which they gave her full abdomen radiation, something like firing a thermonuclear gun point-blank. This followed a bout of chemotherapy, drugs so potent that one milligram no doubt could eat through a diamond drill bit. Seal was stoic about the treatments and said they really didn't hurt – the chemo, after all, was just an I.V. It was the aftermath, though, that was the modern version of trial by endurance as these strong poisons killed everything in their path. Seal was beyond tired and spent day after day in bed, when she wasn't in the bathroom throwing up most of her meals.

She never refused, however, to let me drive her to Dr. Bill's every Wednesday at 2:45 p.m. and was adamant about not discussing how she felt with me. Dr. Bill, I have to admit, was as kind as any doctor could be who uses all the modern arsenal of treatments. I sensed he felt his remedies inadequate for the disease, but it was all he was armed with. I quizzed him about herbs – would they hurt or help? He said, at this point, probably most anything was worth a try. So I became an habitue´ of Nancy's Natural Foods and Supplements, tucked alongside Bernice's Breads and Baked Goods on Second Street.

I thought Seal would resist my efforts at playing herbalist and I

25

was right. But she was determined to heal herself, so I asked her to just think about Dr. Bill's words – herbs probably wouldn't hurt. Could she definitely say that about chemotherapy or radiation? After about a month of my constant harping, Seal must have arrived at the same conclusion, although she'd never admit it. I'd simmer up a batch of seaweed soup each morning or steep teas of white willow bark and yucca all day long. The yucca made the kitchen smell like desert dust after a rain and helped me feel not so far away from Santa Dolorosa. One day, Seal joined me for a bowl of wakami, and from then on, our kitchen was like a witch's den, with potions always brewing. I made soups and infusions, teas and inhalants. And Seal started to accept these brews I placed before her.

She drew the line, however, when I suggested she try guided imagery. I'd once interviewed a cancer survivors' support group in Santa Dolorosa who believed they were having success fighting the disease by visualizing big brawny white cells chawing away at the cancer cells, and a flood of chemotherapy drugs drowning the puny infection. I thought maybe Seal should give this a whirl.

"Don't be ridiculous," she scoffed. "I've got enough to worry about without cluttering my brain with such nonsense." So I decided I'd do her visualizing for her, but of course I didn't tell her.

She had shrunk so much there was almost no meat on her bones, just leathery, springy sinews that she resisted allowing me to help revivify with my aloe vera hand lotion. Her bobbed brown hair that so skillfully hid all the gray, fell out in clumps. Soon she was looking like a bald Nancy Reagan. Instead of getting a wig – she insisted her hair would grow back and there was no need – Seal started wearing turbans with jewels in the front. If she'd wanted to, she probably could have opened a successful tea-leaf-reading practice on our front porch, but instead, she spent her days recuperating by sleeping, drubbing me in Scrabble, and, during brief spurts of energy, cleaning and sorting and polishing the house into a new plateau of tidiness that we'd never attained before. It seemed each time she vomited, she was inspired afterward to try to scrub a wall or scour a floor. Nothing could be left out of place; everything had to have a function and be out of sight or placed just exactly where Seal felt it should be. She was distilling her life, dusting it down to its essence. I tried to understand, but my presence seemed to create a disharmony of elements in the still life that Seal was trying to compose.

We were heading out of Dr. Bill's office on our way to the parking lot three days after Christmas when Warren Caramel spotted us as he was cruising past in his official red fire department pickup. I hadn't seen or heard from him since our first encounter.

"I was just heading for your house," he yelled from the window. "See you over there." He was waiting at the front steps when we drove up.

"Been looking through the report," he said, before we even got the door open. "Funny thing, fires. No two are alike. Sort of like fingerprints. Or people."

Seal asked him if he wanted some coffee; he did. I went to fetch it. Seal asked him if he'd like to take off his coat. He didn't, but he did unbutton it. He sat in the nubby, mustard-colored chair, and I could see him and Seal from the kitchen while I brewed the coffee. They just stared at each other, not unfriendly, but not friendly, either. Neither said a word.

"Here you are, Mr. Caramel," I said and smiled, doing my best imitation of Merribeth. "Sure's a cold one."

"Yup," he said and took a big sip and swallowed loudly. I watched his Adam's apple bob in his throat.

"Well, I suppose you know why I'm here," he said, and without waiting for an answer, informed us the fire had spread much too fast. "And you gals hold the key to why that is."

Seal shifted her gaze to me. It was inscrutable, dispassionate, as always. I couldn't figure out what she was thinking, except, perhaps, that she was harboring an arsonist under her roof and could she be held as an accessory to the crime?

Warren seemed waiting for me to say something. Seal kept looking at me as if she were the Sphinx. I took my cue from her and looked back at Warren, trying to convey no emotion and not speaking a word. My mother turned her gaze on Warren, too.

In a few seconds he seemed to get a little nervous, with both of us just sitting there, watching him. He started picking lint balls off his navy blue jacket. I really didn't have anything to say to him; all I knew was that Merribeth, Amber, and I hadn't started the fire and that he couldn't have any evidence that we were guilty.

Finally, he said, "Well, what do you have to say for yourself?"

I just kept looking at him until he started jiggling his foot up and down, and then I relented a little.

"Say?" I asked.

"You know." He tried to burrow his eyes into my head, but it didn't work, and he eventually sighed and looked away.

"What did you use for fuel?" he asked.

Seal shifted in her chair and leaned forward, moving on to the next level of her cat-and-mouse game.

"Ha, that's a good one," she said. "Amber was so busy having that baby that it couldn't have been her. I've known Merribeth Hartwell since her mother brought her home from the hospital, and I know that destroying property is not up Merribeth's alley. So that leaves Wendy. Now, she tells me she was with Amber and Merribeth at the hospital. I would think that could be easily checked. I suppose the girls could have rigged up the fire before they left for the hospital or hired someone to burn the place down. But why would they want to do that? I just can't figure it out. And don't think I haven't tried."

Seal shifted again and put a hand on each knee. She was throwing her full weight – all 97 pounds – into this.

"I was sure Amberosia's would go under in those first days after they'd opened," she said, making it clear she was not just another cheerleader kind-of-mother for her daughter. "But from what I can tell, the girls somehow managed to succeed in that old barn of a building. They had a good lunch business, and dinner seemed to be building. So why would they want to burn down a place that was proving all the Doubting Thomases in this town wrong? Use your head, Warren Caramel," Seal said. Then she stood up and walked slowly but haughtily toward her room. The audience was over.

I was taken aback, almost speechless. My mother had stood up for me. Although I was teetering on the abyss of middle age, I found my mother's performance made me feel like a choked-up, 7-year-old child. Was this the same Seal who had told me from the high-chair stage on that I was too much of a sourpuss to ever expect to get anywhere based on my personality, and that my looks would scare away all but the most eccentric husband material, so if I expected to do anything with my life at all, other than be the town oddball, then the only hope I had was to find a way to use my brains – and they weren't exactly a finely honed piece of machinery? But now, Seal seemed in my corner and I was uncomfortably grateful to her and touched, although I wasn't about to tell her so.

Warren had stood up as Seal rose and seemed to be waiting awkwardly for one of us to tell him his next move. Since Seal already had disappeared inside her room and shut the door, I told Warren, "I didn't do it."

I told him to verify my alibi with the hospital. "Oh, the hard-to-get type," he said, but reluctantly headed for the door. "Maybe I should try Merribeth," he said with a last spark of hope. "She's always seemed like she's the most reasonable of you gals." So, Warren Caramel interrogated Merribeth Hartwell.

"Oh, Wen," Merribeth reported to me on the phone later that evening, "that Mr. Caramel was so horrible. How can he possibly think we would burn down our own restaurant after all the hard work and time and love we poured into it?"

"I don't know," I told her. "Just lack of imagination, I guess."

"Buzz off," is what Amber said she told him. And then we didn't hear from Warren Caramel for quite some time.

***

On the fourth day after Christmas, Amber and Star not only were home from the hospital, but the new mom had invited Merribeth and me over for a cup of holiday cheer. Amber lived on the edge of town in a glade of trees that once had been part of an unruly thicket of honeysuckle and high-bush cranberry bushes, punctuated here and there by maples. But then, a developer leveled most of the greenery for an expensive development of semicustom homes. As I drove Seal's Olds toward Amber's, I thought how strange it was that Amber was the most settled of the Threesome.

For years, she'd collected houses through her real estate business as if they were cosmetic jewelry. She owned so many properties, it was hard for her to keep track of them. While she'd been a student at Weewampum State, she'd worked part-time at Greerson Real Estate and had spun that job into a money-making machine, waiting for her upon graduation. When the economy turned sour on several occasions and other real estate agents couldn't afford to stay in the game, Amber lived comfortably off the rent from her tenants. But her passion was trying to find the perfect house for skeptical would-be homeowners. She was tenacious, I'll give her that, or maybe just overly optimistic. When she believed she'd found the right house for someone, she couldn't rest until the client believed it, too. Houses were her mission. She thought lives would change if people just had the right dining room where they could chat with their friends or bedroom where they could wind down with that certain someone. It probably had something to do with her moving around so much as an Army brat and seldom living somewhere she felt was home.

I'd always thought Weewampum had an uninspiring hodgepodge of housing, with styles from too many time periods and nothing quite matching and most everything slightly shabby.

To Amber, though, "Weewampum is just a dream buyer's market. There's such a great mix of houses here."

Her zeal for appreciating Weewampum's fading houses led her to try to persuade the City Council to take action to spruce up the turn-of-the-20th-Century buildings along Main Street. When the council told her it was up to the owners, not the city, to fix up the properties, instead of giving up, Amber simply started buying Main Street buildings. Then, in a burst of restoration zeal, she'd opened Amberosia's. She'd just show everybody how to turn Main Street around. But the restaurant was a lot of work, even more so than real estate. Amber had bitten off more than she could chew.

So she drafted Merribeth and me to run Amberosia's, and she was able to step back and enjoy the restaurant as a sort of philanthropic pursuit and hobby. Besides, if it succeeded, it would help keep up the property values of her other Main Street buildings. Now that Amberosia's was just a pile of ashes, Amber wasn't likely to want that prime corner piece of Main Street property staying idle too long. I wasn't eager to hear her plans for the lot, but I suspected that's really why she'd invited us over this evening. I didn't care; I'd just ignore what she said and play cootchycoo with Star.

Amber had bought, lived in, and sold seven or eight of her residences already. I pulled up to the latest, a one-story, white-brick number with pillars and a porte cochère. Merribeth and I called it the Temple of the Huntress – well, at least I did.

Star was sleeping when I arrived and Merribeth already was there. Amber let us peek in on the slumbering babe and we whispered, "Happy New Year," to her. Amber had apple cider simmering on the stove, in which she dumped an expensive little half-pint container of spices. She floated around in a tangerine peignoir and matching silk scuffs, looking like a citrus fruit in motion. Her one nod to motherhood was a flamingo pink terry-cloth towel flung around her neck like a boa, dotted with crusty splotches of baby puke.

"So," Amber said, looking ready for business. You'd have thought she'd still be tired from popping out Star, but she seemed as if she'd be ready for a marathon mambo contest.

"So," Merribeth and I said together, preferring to talk about Star, the weather, the pair of pantyhose Seal gave me for Christmas, anything but what we knew Amber wanted to talk about – well, in addition to Star.

"Good cider," Merribeth said, swirling the contents around in her mug. "Very tasty."

"The best," I said, nodding as if Merribeth had just said something most wise and wonderful.

"Uhmmhmmm, really good."

We sipped our cider and the house got as quiet as the morning after a shrieking snowstorm dumps 10 inches of snow on the roof.

31

Amber cleared her throat. Oh, oh. Here it comes, I figured.

"Anyone want more cider?" I asked, leaping into the crevasse of silence. But wouldn't you know, I was too late, and Merribeth let her sympathetic nature get the best of her?

"Oh, Amby," she said and fell into Amber's arms. They just stood hugging each other until I started choking when I swallowed some cider and took a breath at the same time.

Amber whacked me on the back and said, "So, we've got to rebuild."

"Wait a minute," I sputtered. I felt it best for me to sever all apron strings with any future restaurant right now. And besides, I explained, Amber couldn't proceed until she had the insurance money from Amberosia's in hand.

"What insurance money?" Amber asked, nonchalantly, and then said she'd meant to get around to it but since she'd financed the restaurant herself with some second mortgages on her properties and cash advances from her credit cards, she'd been kind of strapped for cash.

"Oh, Amber, you don't mean it?" Merribeth looked at her in disbelief. Amber just smiled and shrugged. I was not that surprised; it was a typical Amber stunt.

"How can you possibly expect to rebuild?" I hammered at her. Amber just shrugged again.

"I'll take care of it," she said. "But I'd feel better if I knew for sure why Amberosia's No. 1 burned down."

Now, here was something we all could agree upon. We wanted to find out what had happened to Amberosia's and see the firebug zapped by a lightning bolt of justice. Even Merribeth said she thought someone should go to jail. Amber thought the responsible party should be drawn and quartered. I would have settled for burning him or her at the stake.

I said I didn't know what the others thought, but Warren Caramel didn't seem to be pursuing any leads that seemed too promising to me – not that he'd discussed them with me.

"Well, we all know Lars had something to do with it," Amber insisted.

"Maybe not," Merribeth said.

"Who else would do it?" Amber asked, but Merribeth just shrugged.

"Lars had the motive – to wear me down, drive me off, get me to stop the 'Stop the Hospital Move' campaign, maybe even drive me out of town so he wouldn't be reminded he has a daughter," Amber said.

"Oh, come off it, Amber," I said. "I've only met Lars Hunssen once or twice and each time, he seemed too interested in preserving his Fabio image to want to risk melting his hair mousse over something as hot and dirty as a fire."

"Oh, blow it out your back side, Wen," Amber groused. "You're always such a know-it-all."

"Stop it, now," Merribeth interceded. "We're all friends here now, aren't we?"

"Yeah, sure," Amber said and made an ape face at me and scratched under her arms. Honestly, for a middle-age new mother and real-estate agent, Amber acts like a reform-school girl out on a weekend pass most of the time. But she did manage to force a smile out of me.

"Yeah, maybe we're friends," I conceded. That gave Amber all the encouragement she needed.

"So, like I was saying," Amber continued, "Lars doesn't want Star around, the inconvenient consequence of his rampaging dick. He doesn't want the Threesome around, keeping him from his dreams of a medical empire along the highway."

Merribeth gently countered that if Amber prospered at the restaurant, Lars wouldn't have to pay as much child support.

"What child support?" Amber exploded.

"Oh, Amber!" Merribeth said. "Isn't he helping you out at all?"

"Fat chance," Amber said. "But, hell, who needs him? I tell you, he burned down Amberosia's."

"I don't know, he just doesn't seem the type," Merribeth replied. "I noticed he ate everything on his plate at the buffet. He couldn't have hated the restaurant that much."

"Trust me," Amber said.

"Well, what do you think we should do?" I asked. We discussed the possibilities. They ranged from strapping Lars to a two-by-eight and staking him in the lot where Amberosia's used to be, our own version of the pillory, to burning down his house, to taking the high road and waiting for cosmic justice to find him (Merribeth's solution, naturally).

Of course, we had no solid proof that he'd done anything, except turn his back on Amber and Star. Amber insisted that prison would be too good for him, but that once he was there, at least it would be safe for us to open Amberosia's again. She felt that reopening would make a statement that we couldn't be scared off, that we felt we had as much right to be in Weewampum as anyone. Merribeth and I weren't so sure. After all, we'd been handling most of the day-to-day operations, not Amber. To me, it seemed the restaurant was one of Amber's toys, and therefore, she should be the one spending the most time playing with it.

Merribeth and I had our own lives. Merribeth had taken a leave from her teaching job because Amber had begged her to come help launch Amberosia's. I planned to return to Santa Dolorosa but didn't want to make any decisions, any commitments, until I knew that Seal was all right. I couldn't kid myself that as food editor, I was making much of a mark on the world, but as Seal had pointed out, she hadn't spent good money on my education for me to wind up peeling potatoes in a Weewampum greasy spoon. Didn't I tell 100,000 readers each week how to lighten their load in the kitchen? It wasn't much, but it was something, better than coaxing a handful of reluctant Weewampumites into testing our fruit soup or sampling our Thai chicken wraps. And although I was skirting the edge of the half-century chasm, I hadn't tumbled over the precipice yet. There still was time. I could probably even line up a job as the editor of some small paper, or at least, as features editor somewhere, if I looked hard and long. Then, I could be in charge, make things happen, maybe even promote a little social change in the community where I wound up – and with a little luck, that town would be hundreds of miles from Weewampum. There, I wouldn't have to take orders from my floozy friend. But really, I couldn't even think about this now, not with Seal's health so precarious.

Well, OK, I thought about it a little. And I just felt Amber, Merribeth, and I had grown so far apart that we shouldn't try to force our friendship. True, we'd taken the Fearsome Threesome Vow of Perpetual Friendship when we were 12, but we were all different now. Or maybe, we were just a little more the way we'd always been, and it just seemed too much to ask for us to overlook our oppositions and contradictions and work in peace and harmony like all those hands on one of those Indian divas.

Amber pressed cup after cup of cider upon us that evening, and the *pièce de résistance*, a bundt cake that a client had given her for New Year's. Amber wasn't Weewampum's leading real estate agent for nothing. She persuaded us we shouldn't rush into making up our minds about the restaurant. Seal wasn't back to full strength, yet, so I wouldn't be jetting off to Santa Dolorosa any time soon, and Merribeth's leave was good for a year, Amber pointed out. We had time to think about the restaurant, and, in the meantime, didn't we owe it to ourselves to find the culprit responsible for the fire? And, besides, Amber and I had started the petition drive for the referendum on the hospital move. Didn't we need to see our efforts through?

Sometimes, Amber makes more sense and is more organized and driven than she first appears to be. I don't know what was in that bundt cake, but the cider was pretty potent. Amber knew just what she was doing. At some point around midnight, she got us to repeat the Fearsome Threesome pledge:

> All for one and one for all.
> If Wendy doesn't whomp you
> And Merribeth doesn't maul,
> Then Amber will offend you
> Like mold in a bathroom stall.

It wasn't pretty and it was pretty stupid. It always had been, and the years hadn't added a patina. But after we took the pledge,

Merribeth and I didn't stand a chance. By the time we left for home, Merribeth and I had agreed to stick around at least until we celebrated our victory after the referendum forced Our Lady of Perpetual Need to stay downtown where it belonged. And we wouldn't give up until we found the arsonist – if Warren Caramel wasn't going to do the job right. Amber was sure we'd collect enough evidence to permanently nail Lars to that 2-by-8.

Chapter 4

Our Lady of Perpetual Need's Sugar Cookies

1 cup butter
2 cups sugar
3/4 teaspoon soda
1/2 teaspoon salt
1 teaspoon vanilla
1/2 teaspoon almond extract
3 eggs, beaten
3-2/3 cups sifted flour
2 teaspoons baking powder

Cream butter and 2 cups sugar with soda, salt, vanilla, and almond extract. Add beaten eggs and beat until smooth. Sift together flour and baking powder and add to creamed mixture, mixing until smooth. Chill dough until firm enough to roll out on a floured cutting board. Use cookie cutters to cut dough into shapes. Place the "cookies" on greased baking sheets and bake at 450 degrees for 8 minutes, or until cookies are golden.

Cream Cheese Frosting

1/2 cup butter
1 8-ounce package cream cheese, softened
1 teaspoon vanilla
1 pound powdered sugar, sifted

Combine butter, cream cheese, and vanilla in large bowl and beat until well-blended. Add sugar gradually, while continuing to beat. If frosting is too thick, add milk until frosting is spreadable. Frost the cookies and decorate. Leave cookies out until frosting starts to set up, then store cookies in air-tight container overnight, with cookie layers separated by wax paper. The next day, the moisture from the frosting will have permeated the cookies, turning them from crisp into moist.

If it ain't broke, don't fix it was pretty much how Amber, Merribeth, and I felt about the proposed move of Our Lady of Perpetual Need Medical Center. From what I could tell, location was the main reason the hospital board had voted to move the building. The board figured that if the hospital were along Highway 11, then people from all around would be lured there like ants to a store-bought cake because they wouldn't have to drive all the way into downtown Weewampum. But that's sort of like saying more people would visit the state capitol if the state abandoned the historic domed building in downtown Madison in favor of a concrete box along the interstate.

It didn't make much sense to me. There were Weewampum doctors' offices and florist shops that had grown up near the hospital. They would all have to pack up and move to the highway, too. We at Amberosia's and other Main Street merchants benefited from the hospital staff and visitors dropping in. It seemed a shame and a complicated task to disrupt all those habits and traffic patterns.

Amber was the most outspoken of the three of us in insisting the hospital should stay where it was. Several years ago she'd been asked to join the hospital board before anyone knew her politics and was only envious of her real estate acumen. They hadn't kicked her off the board yet, although her term was just about up and she hadn't been asked to serve another term. She had become the lone vote against the move and the other board members resented her lack of team spirit.

Amber owned four buildings downtown, including those housing Pearl's House of Yarn, Andy's Fish, Swaggart's Music, and an empty brick three-story on the corner of Main and Sweet that formerly was Armand's Tuxedo Boutique. The hospital added to the business climate downtown, Amber argued. Weewampum should be doing what it could to build up Main Street, not taking steps to dismantle it.

So far, Amber, Merribeth, and I had offered more talk than action in our efforts to stop the hospital from moving. Sure, we'd circulated petitions from Amberosia's and tried to get support from our customers, but that was about the extent of our actions. I found it curious that I seemed to care whether the hospital stayed put or not. I guess I was influenced by logic – the move seemed unneeded – and also because Lars Hunssen and Jim Hartwell so ardently supported shutting the downtown facility that I naturally gravitated to the opposing side. Besides, the hospital issue was shaping up as great winter sport in Weewampum, and God knows, I welcomed all diversions. Surprisingly, Seal and I found ourselves on the same side of the Our Lady battleground. It was probably the first time in history we could expect to vote the same way.

Seal still was kind of tired from her treatments, but her longtime friends Dottie Wentzell and Florence Schmidt were out knocking on doors, trying to rally the troops. Actually, only Dottie knocked on doors. But Florence helped tally the petitions and strong-arm holdouts via the telephone tree she'd organized. Dottie had been raised in Weewampum; Florence had moved here as a young woman. They both wrapped themselves in Weewampum's affairs as if in a favorite frayed blanket. They could see no need to disrupt the status quo by moving the hospital. They were on the phone daily with Seal, plotting and planning and sniping at the opposition. Dottie expected to have canvassed all of Weewampum by the end of the following week.

It was a Thursday in mid-January when I answered the phone and Dottie insisted I put Seal on the line immediately.

"Huh. OK, then," Seal said in her usual minimalist fashion and hung up the kitchen phone before I'd even had a chance to find a spot where I could listen in.

"What did she say?" I quizzed Seal.

She raised her eyebrows slightly. "They got the signatures. There'll be a referendum," Seal said and then trooped out of the kitchen to scour the bathroom sink.

The referendum was scheduled for Feb. 14. Amber rallied Merribeth and me to go door-to-door and pass out fliers, urging people to vote. I wanted the fliers to say, "I Left My Heart at Our Lady of Perpetual Need," but Merribeth thought that was too graphic since Our Lady did have a pretty good cardiac unit and she didn't want us to reflect too negatively on the pulmonary care doctors. Finally, we agreed on the simple "Save Our Lady. Save Downtown. Vote Feb. 14" and drew a heart around everything.

The only reason we had any hope a referendum might halt the hospital move was because the city would have to spend money to put in water and sewers and pave roads at the new site. If we could just persuade voters the move was coming out of their pockets and they owed it to themselves to help save their downtown, then maybe our side had a chance.

I guess someone on the hospital board must have seen our fliers because a couple days after we distributed them, there was a story in the *Weewampum Bugle*, announcing the board was holding a public information meeting to show the new plans for the hospital and discuss why the move to the highway was important for Weewampum.

They held the meeting in the high school auditorium because they were expecting a big crowd and they were right. Every seat was taken and people were standing in the aisles and sitting on the floor, although it was against fire safety rules – but this one night, no one cared. As we filed in, the hospital board members, except for Amber, sat on the stage, facing us like a hanging jury. Lars Hunssen – whom Amber had eagerly welcomed to the board, then changed her mind about – stood on a dais, the board's designated spokesman. When we all were seated, candy-stripers in their pink-and-white-striped pinafores, working from hospital food-service carts, started passing out pop cans and little plastic trays of snacks to the audience. On each snack tray there was a bag of peanuts, an apple, some cheese and crackers, a little cup of butterscotch pudding, a sugar cookie, a Peppermint Pattie, and a small plastic spoon. It was as if the auditorium had suddenly transformed into a 747 and we were taking a slow flight to the new hospital site.

"I'm so glad you all could make it," Lars boomed into a microphone, wearing an insincere grin and a surgeon's white coat, like a theater costume, over his expensive gray suit and blue regimental tie.

"We're so happy to have this opportunity to share our vision for the future with you tonight."

Amber leaned over. "There wouldn't be any sharing going on

here if we hadn't started the petition drive," she hissed.

I tried to smile at Amber, but the woman next to me, Emma Swanson, a checkout woman at Tom's Super Valu, had doused herself in Obsession perfume, so the most I could manage was to roll my eyes.

When I'd taken my seat, Emma had said, "Wendy! Are you back in town? I guess I'll never forget what you did to those photos. People still talk about it, you know," and then she'd clicked her tongue and scowled.

She was referring to one of my unfortunate experiments with artistic liberty many moons ago when I'd shot some photos of my high school classmates, then altered them in unflattering ways. It was an incident I'd prefer to forget, chalk up to youthful indiscretion, but it was a story that lived in the memories of more than a few unforgiving residents.

"Now, we're pleased that in our audience tonight, we have the man responsible for designing our exciting new building, Mr. James A. Hartwell, head of Weewampum's leading architectural firm. Jim, Jim, where are you? Jim, would you take a bow?" Lars went on.

Lars had to know where Mr. H. was sitting; after all, Mr. H. was in the front row. Mr. H. stood up, turned, and faced the audience and took a sweeping bow.

"Thank you so much, Jim," Lars continued like a game-show host. "And now, Jim, would you come on up and show us the hospital that's going to put Weewampum on the map?"

Mr. Hartwell bounded up to the stage and took the helm of a computer, set on a TV cart draped in a spider's nest of wires. Without a hitch, he revved up his 3-D architectural software and breezed us through the brown, nondescript front doors of the hospital and on a virtual warp-speed ride through the surgery wing, the pediatrics unit, and the gift shop.

"And there you have it," he said, beaming. He bowed again.

"Wow!" two women in the second row with their necks craned back gasped. I think it was the speed of the tour, not the beauty of the building, that left them breathless.

"Slow down," Amber shouted. "Do it again. And take it nice and slow."

Someone tittered.

"Yeah," piped up an elderly man in a brown suit, whom I didn't recognize. "I wasn't wearing my specs."

Mr. Hartwell sighed but sensed the audience would welcome a repeat performance. He fired up the program again, and this time, we toured his masterpiece at a more leisurely pace. The building was L-shaped and looked like two Saltine boxes fused to a Quaker oatmeal container and coated in a textured beige coat of Gunnite.

Amber, who'd opposed the plans when they'd been presented to the hospital board, muttered fairly softly, for her, "That building's got as much character as the county highway garage."

"Oh, Daddy," Merribeth murmured so only I could hear. "How could you?"

I'm not sure if Mr. Hartwell heard Amber. He certainly gave no indication he had. He proudly walked and talked us through the lobby and the radiology lab, the emergency room, and the basement, equipped with the newest in air and water purification systems and a solar heater backup unit.

By the time he'd finished, I'd say at least half the audience was smiling as if they were jolly burghers who'd just hosted a successful Oktoberfest. Just to reinforce those good feelings, the candy-stripers passed out pens with little angels perched on the caps and "Our Lady of Perpetual Need Medical Center" emblazoned down one side.

"How cute." "Isn't that darling?" "How sweet," the audience buzzed.

Lars shook Mr. Hartwell's hand heartily and then explained how hard it was for out-of-town patients and visitors to get to the existing hospital. By moving the facility to the outskirts along the highway, we'd be helping Our Lady vault into the ranks of the major medical centers of the nation, or at least Central Wisconsin. Weewampum, Wis., could become as well-known as Rochester, Minn., for its cutting-edge medical prowess. It was necessary for the city's growth, the next step we had to take, our children would thank us and put flowers on our graves for having so much foresight as to approve the move. Then Lars opened the floor to questions.

Eleanor Owsley, the organist at First American Lutheran Church, stood up. "We just want to tell you how impressive we've found your presentation and how proud we are that Our Lady is part of our community," she cooed.

At least half the room applauded and Eleanor smiled and blushed the same pink as the stripe in the candy-stripers' uniforms, then sat down.

Dottie Wentzell rose next. Dottie was not an imposing-looking woman. I'd always thought she looked kind of like a frog. She had big, round glasses; short, straight gray hair, and she moved quickly, in little spurts and jumps. But Dottie's relatives from a few generations back were among the founding settlers of Weewampum. This, alone, not to mention her position as reference librarian emerita of the Weewampum Public Library, made Dottie an authority on the city's history, and she took pride in her know-it-allness.

"For the life of me," she said, turning her head left and right until she had everyone's attention, "I don't understand why we have to uproot tradition and move out of a perfectly fine building and wreck our downtown in the process. You all know full well that another big vacant building isn't going to do one bit of good to make our downtown a tourist destination. That's what this town needs – tourists. We've got plenty of old, fine buildings that we could turn into cute little shops where people could spend an afternoon. The hospital's been part of our downtown for years and years and helps hold it all together. Put it out along Highway 11 and what have you got? Not atmosphere. Not history. Just a pile of concrete blocks and wood that you can't tell apart from the Outskirts Outlet Stores and Emil's All-Night Bowling Lanes."

The audience was quiet. Many seemed to feel Dottie had hopped upon a lily pad of truth.

"Let's face it," she said, "Weewampum's never going to be a major medical center, at least, not in my lifetime. But we could be a fun little spot folks visit on the weekend, known for our gift shops, restaurants and bed-and-breakfasts on the lake. Tourists don't come because you've got a new hospital. They come because you've got cute fudge shops and sportswear stores and maybe a few good bars."

Jerry Finch, the John Deere store owner, and Wally Eskridge, an electrician, snorted. Dottie had earned a reputation over the years for being outspoken. For years, she'd recommended books to students that had more of an adult slant than perhaps their parents would have liked. She'd kept *Catcher in the Rye* and *Lady Chatterley's Lover* on the shelves when there'd been pressure to hide them in the locked bookcase. When I was researching the coccyx for a "Parts of the Body" science report in fifth grade, Dottie showed me a most enlightening medical encyclopedia from which I learned about much more than just a little bone in the spine.

"If we move the hospital, our downtown will dry up. Unless we want to charge admission for having our very own ghost town, leave Our Lady of Perpetual Need where she is," Dottie said. She snapped her mouth and eyes shut and plopped into her seat.

Before anyone had a chance to react, Amber shot up, her face and hair shooting sparks.

"One thing I've noticed that no one's talked about so far is that your new building is plug ugly."

You could hear the audience breathe in collectively, then there were some embarrassed giggles, a guffaw or two, and much throat-clearing.

Chester Sands, who runs the concrete block business along the highway, stood up. "Come on, now," he said. "Let's be fair. I think Jim Hartwell and our hospital board have done a lot of good work and we should compliment them, not be picking their plans apart."

A couple people clapped. "I think the building is OK," Chester said. "You know how modern architecture is."

Then, Merribeth stood up, which surprised me considerably, because Merribeth likes to keep out of the spotlight. Her face was bright red, her eyes kind of glazed over; she obviously was upset.

Her voice quavered.

"I've been listening to all of you," she said. "And like you, tonight is the first time I've seen the plans. And now that I've seen them, I'm wondering if some of you have totally taken leave of your senses."

Her eyes darted here and there across the audience. I was afraid she was going to flee. But she pushed forward.

She said the old hospital has Doric columns and patterns in the brickwork, that it's neo-classical and looks so stately. She asked how the new building could duplicate the charm of the old one, how it could replicate the fountain of Mary and the baby outside the front doors and the statue of Jesus and the little lamb in the lobby.

"And what about those rosy marble floors?" she asked. "Are you sure you want to give all that up for a plain little box?"

The audience gazed at Merribeth as fascinated as if they were cruising past a car wreck on Highway 11.

"I don't care if my father designed the building or not," she said, her face glowing crimson. "I think it's ugly. I think the plans should be put in a drawer. I don't care. I've got to say it. I just really think Weewampum deserves better."

She looked at her father, embarrassed, and said, "I'm sorry, Daddy, but it's just not up to your usual standards."

I couldn't see Mr. H's immediate reaction, but Merribeth looked sick, as if she'd just hit a big deer with her Toyota. I couldn't argue with her. From my standpoint, probably the best structure Mr. H. ever designed was our tree house in Merribeth's backyard. It was simple and functional, yet provided us a place to dream about a world far away from Weewampum, so unlike this deadly beige medical facility. Maybe if Mr. H. had spent more time in the tree house, he'd have designed a more inspiring building.

***

The first time I noticed something going on in Merribeth's backyard, I was up in my bedroom, weaving pot holders. My mother had really splurged for my birthday that year and given me a pot-holder-weaving kit and a pop-bead Little Princess jewelry-making kit, when what I'd really wanted was a palomino. But the way I figured it, maybe I could weave enough pot holders and sell them to buy a horse. Even I was bright enough to realize I couldn't make a dime selling pink or blue pop-bead necklaces and bracelets.

I couldn't believe Mr. Hartwell was building a tree house for Merribeth. It seemed so unfair. I'd begged and pleaded with Seal to let me build a tree house in our big maple tree in the backyard, but she'd said, "I'm not going to have you whooping and hollering out there like some kind of wild Indian. That tree deserves more respect. And so do I."

I tried to persuade Seal the tree hardly would notice I was there, but her answer was final, no matter how much wheedling I did. Now, Merribeth was getting a tree house and it just wasn't right. She got everything she wanted and more, like fun toys and clothes and a nice mother and even a father who was beginning to look as if he might not be so bad.

He seemed to be doing a pretty good job on the tree house from what I could tell. I watched him for a couple of days from my upstairs window. I saw him take an old bathroom door and paint it taxicab yellow. There weren't any taxis in Weewampum, naturally. But I'd been to Milwaukee, and they had plenty there. I wished I could ride in a taxi. Maybe when we were in the tree house, I could pretend to take a ride. A limb could be a stallion, a cab, or a swift-moving dugout canoe. If Merribeth and I paddled hard enough, maybe we could even fly.

The day that Mr. Hartwell finished the tree house, I was weaving my 23rd pot holder, over and under, over and under. I saw Merribeth sitting on the ground, waiting to hand her father his tools if he needed them or run to the refrigerator to get him an iced tea or Michelob.

I thought Merribeth was too willing to be a good helper to her father. Her big brother, Joey, wasn't helping one bit. He was bouncing a tennis ball against the apple tree's trunk, thunk, thunk, just waiting until he could climb into the tree house.

Although I didn't like pot holders much, I didn't like Mr.

Hartwell even more, so I was staying home, out of his way. It's not that Mr. Hartwell ever had done anything to me. And maybe that was it. Every time I was in the yard and he saw me, he'd just look the other way. I didn't think it was anything personal. I just thought he wasn't very friendly. Anyhow, I figured I was better off up in my bedroom, watching the action, than pressed into service helping Merribeth hand Mr. H. his tools while dodging Joey's tennis balls.

Finally, through my screen window, I heard Mr. Hartwell yell, "All right, Joey. You can come up."

Well, what about Merribeth? Mr. Hartwell gathered his tools from the tree house's deck while Joey scampered up.

"Wow! Neat!" Joey said.

Merribeth looked up and smiled.

"Can I come up?" she asked.

"Ask your brother to help you up when he's ready," Mr. Hartwell said as he climbed down the tree house steps.

Boy, if I'd been Merribeth, I would have been boiling to not be invited up after all my hard work. But Merribeth just smiled at her father as he walked past her. He was her father, so I figured that, naturally, she liked him better than I did.

"Thank you, Daddy. It's a really pretty tree house," she said.

I couldn't understand how she could be so nice to him. Mr. Hartwell patted her on those blonde, bouncy curls that I envied and walked into the house. Merribeth had some jacks in her pocket, and I watched her pull them out and start to play as she settled in to wait out her brother. I knew she must be dying to go up in that tree house. I sure was.

Joey stretched on his back on the plank in the apple tree and closed his eyes. If I were Merribeth, I would have thrown the tennis ball at his head right about then. He made me glad I didn't have any brothers or sisters. He made no effort to move, and Merribeth kept playing with her jacks. At this rate, it would be days before Merribeth and I got up there.

It seemed I'd been waiting forever, watching Mr. H. sand and paint the door and hammer it into the tree. I'd been waiting so long, I'd had time to count all the apples in that tree. I'd had nothing better to do, really. I was truly sick of pot holders.

There were 537 apples that I could see. I didn't count the rotten ones on the ground. Five-hundred-thirty-seven was as high as I'd ever counted. But now that the tree house was finished, I had more immediate things on my mind, like how to get up there.

Joey looked as if he was prepared to hog the tree house for the rest of the day. So we had to get him out of there or change his mind or something. My mom always was lecturing me about how I was a spoiled brat being an only child. She said I needed to learn about sharing.

Maybe here was a chance to practice. I didn't really think this out clearly but somehow I knew that if I gave Joey something, he might give us something back – like time in the tree house. It was worth a shot, I figured. But what would I give Joey? He wouldn't want a pot holder. And I didn't want to give him something really good, like my mechanical pencil or roller skates. I started walking through the house, looking for something he'd like. I passed the cookie jar and grabbed a Lorna Doone. Suddenly, that cookie seemed to speak to me.

I grabbed a fistful and flew over to Merribeth's. This would work. I knew it would work.

It worked like an intricate plot in an Ellery Queen Jr. novel. Joey wanted all my cookies, but I made him come down to get them. He was so busy chowing down that Merribeth and I raced up to the tree house. Joey didn't seem to mind that much; he seemed to feel he'd gotten something for nothing, as far as I could tell.

When he'd gobbled down those cookies, he clambered up the tree house steps, and we all sat up there and looked around our neighborhood. It was so liberating on that bathroom door, as if we'd transformed into birds or butterflies. We could see everything that everyone was doing – well, almost – for blocks around. It made me feel like a fairy godmother or Tinkerbell to have this kind of vision.

I pulled an apple off the tree and bit into it. I guess I expected the apple would be transformed, somehow, too. But it was as

48

green and hard as ever. I could see Merribeth, and especially Joey, thought I was nuts. I told them I'd counted 537 apples in their tree. They looked at me round-eyed. Who'd be nuts enough to count all the apples in a tree? Maybe I really was nuts.

I decided I'd show them how nuts I was, especially Joey. Maybe if he thought I was really crazy, he'd leave Merribeth and me alone in the tree house for a while. So I grabbed another apple and ate it. Then, I grabbed Nos. 3, 4 and 5. By No. 6, I was starting to feel queasy. But it was Joey's eyes that egged me on. He was looking at me with a kind of weird admiration that he'd never shown me before. It was as if he were seeing me for the first time and admitting that I wasn't just his little sister's sappy friend, but a crazy and kind-of-brave kid. And that was really something.

So I grabbed another apple and bit down. By No. 8, I knew I couldn't eat another bite, so, of course, I grabbed No. 9. That did it. I started throwing up all over everything. I tried to lean over so I wouldn't hit us or the tree house. Joey tried to scramble to the ground. I didn't mean to, but I showered his head with the remains of my breakfast Cheerios and the undigested apples.

Joey ran into the house and Merribeth and I just looked at each other, and then we started to laugh. We laughed until we were afraid we'd have to run inside to go to the bathroom.

Somehow, my throwing up that day did the trick, and Joey never really spent much time in the tree house after that. Merribeth acted as if I were ingenious, as if I had planned everything from my bedroom window. She said I was really smart and brave, and I wasn't about to tell her any differently. I probably agreed after she started going on and on. But I'd been acting on instinct, going apple by apple, moment by moment.

What I really learned that day was the value of the bold stroke, and also that Merribeth hadn't been as pleased as I'd thought when I saw her handing her father his tools and waiting for her brother to have his fun. What I learned that day was that if you want something, then you need to go after it, and that if people think you're crazy, then it gives you a kind of power.

***

So now, Merribeth, who'd never been crazy, was embarrassing her father before this crowd, and Mr. H. wasn't taking it very well. He stood up in the audience, turned around, and glared at Merribeth. And then, she just kind of fell apart. She hurled herself into the aisle and raced out the back door. The audience shifted around in their seats uncomfortably. Mr. Hartwell stood with his arms folded, just glaring and glaring, as if defying anyone else to speak against his creation. While Mr. H. tried to stare everyone down, Lars signaled to the candy-stripers, who worked their way down the aisles, passing out Payday candy bars.

I felt I should run after Merribeth and see if she was OK. On the other hand, I wanted to see what happened next. Merribeth was a grown woman; she could take care of herself. Before I could decide what to do, Amber popped up again.

"If you want people to laugh at us, then go ahead and build that hospital," Amber warned. "But, if you want my opinion, I think that building looks like a dead duck with broken wings."

The audience would have gasped but their mouths were stuffed with Paydays and it was just too difficult. Amber propelled herself over a pair of tennis shoes and some pointed-toe high heels and pushed her way to the aisle and out into the fresh air.

In a show of solidarity with my friends and also because I was starting to feel seriously nauseous from Emma Swanson's perfume, I, too, launched myself over a minefield of boots and knobby knees and left the manufactured town meeting. Later, I learned that by not staying till the end, I missed collecting a calendar filled with scale drawings of the Our Lady building plans, as well as a written message from Sister Omega, the hospital president, and a coupon for 15 percent off any item in the new medical center's gift shop.

Chapter 5
Weewampum Knights of Columbus Tom and Jerries

4 eggs beaten
1 heaping Tablespoon powdered sugar
¼ teaspoon ground cloves
¼ teaspoon ground cinnamon
¼ teaspoon ground nutmeg
2 Tablespoons vanilla
½ teaspoon cream of tartar
4 cups (1 quart) of milk
4 jiggers brandy or rum

Combine eggs and sugar in double boiler pan. Beat slowly over medium heat about one-half hour. Add cloves, cinnamon, and nutmeg. Add vanilla and cream of tartar. Heat the milk to boiling in separate pan. Pour a jigger of brandy or rum into four mugs. Add the hot milk so the mug is about 2/3 full. Top off each mug with the egg batter. Garnish with a dash of nutmeg. Serves 4.

The war was on. The hospital was pulling out all the stops. They advertised incessantly in the *Weewampum Bugle*. They even bought commercial time on the three Green Bay TV stations that attempted to give us our local TV news. Our Lady leafleted our neighborhoods with fliers and pounded our mailboxes with wave after wave of direct mail. We got letters with the personal stories of grateful patients whose lives had been saved over the years at Our Lady and who now thought they had no choice but to support whatever the hospital wanted to do. But there also were enclosed pot holders, memo pads, pencils, and combs to help us not forget Our Lady of Perpetual Need's needs.

Merribeth, Amber, and I joined Dottie Wentzell going door-to-door on our side's behalf. We plastered posters and banners on every building that Amber and any friends and acquaintances owned. Yet, we were outspent and outmaneuvered at every move. That is, until I suggested we stage a sit-down strike in front of the hospital with people staking themselves on gurneys and in wheelchairs with signs saying, "Hell No, We Won't Go."

Merribeth added a creative touch. She suggested we ask protesters to either dress as hospital patients, nurses, or doctors, or else in old-time clothes to demonstrate their ties to Weewampum's roots. Then we made posters of the faces of some early town settlers, using photos and sketches that we found at the library with Dottie's help. We created quite a show on the sidewalk in front of Our Lady. We got top billing on Channels 2, 5, and 11 for two nights running and a story and updates in the *Weewampum Bugle* every day.

All we needed was to keep up our momentum; the referendum wasn't that many days away. It looked as if the vote was going to be close, that we had a fighting chance. Of course, we hadn't counted on the weather, which soon turned violently wet, cold, nasty, and germ-filled. Our ranks were decimated by the common cold and icy, cutting snow like surgeons' blades. But even so, we remained optimistic that at least we were doing the best we could. And when the clouds dissipated, which they did after a couple of days, we returned in full force to the walks outside Our Lady.

***

It was true that Amber had a financial motive for wanting the hospital to stay downtown. It also was true that she believed in Weewampum probably more than Merribeth and I ever had.

When Amber first moved to town the year we all were in eighth grade, Merribeth was the one who'd introduced this torch-haired girl to our tree house. It was the night Mrs. Hartwell insisted that Merribeth invite Amber and me over for supper, even though my best friend next door had been sulking because I'd been monopolizing my new best friend for myself ever since she'd shown up in Mr. Caesar's math class. That night at Merribeth's, as soon as we'd finished slurping down our pasta, my oldest best pal ran out to the backyard. Amber and I followed, curious, until we all stopped at the base of the apple tree.

Amber looked up and said, "Oh, wow!"

Merribeth scampered up to the tree house and Amber wanted to follow, but since she'd lived all over the world at Army bases and in civilian housing but never in America, she hadn't mastered the art of tree-house ascent. We had a rope dangling from a branch and a couple of two-by-twos nailed up as steps, and between the two, Merribeth and I always managed to pull ourselves up.

Amber put her right foot on the lowest step and grabbed onto the rope for dear life, and I did my best to push her up to the next two-by-two while Merribeth tried to haul her up from above. With lots of pushing and pulling on Merribeth's and my part, Amber scaled the tree and flopped on the yellow bathroom door.

She lay gasping like a beached muskellunge for a few moments but finally sat up and looked around. Merribeth and I hadn't been up in the tree house for a while. Instead of wanting a bird's-eye view of the world these days, we were starting to think about looking at life and maybe a boy from the back seat of some beat-up old Chevy.

But that day, Amber, Merribeth, and I abandoned any thought of maintaining our adolescent cool attitudes as we looked around the world from inside the umbrella of leaves.

"Whoohoo," Amber shouted. "I can't believe I'm really here." She laughed a big, deep laugh like a piano in the lower registers.

"All my life," she said, "I've wanted to know girls like you and live in an American town like this and have a bike with streamers on the handlebars and a store nearby where I could buy Hostess cupcakes and Twinkies."

I didn't know what had possessed Merribeth to run out to the backyard; maybe it was a test she was putting Amber through. But when Merribeth saw how elated Amber seemed up there in the leaves, she gave our new friend a hug and told us not to go anywhere.

Then Merribeth flew out of the tree and into the house and emerged in about two seconds with a bottle of Pepsi and an opener and some brownies her mother had baked that morning. After Merribeth rescaled the apple tree, she shook up the bottle of Pepsi. She pried off the lid and held the bottle over Amber like a fountain and our new friend held her head back, closed her eyes, opened her mouth, and started chug-a-lugging.

"Welcome to our tree house," Merribeth said. We were just

starting to learn Spanish so she added, "*Mi casa es su casa.*"

I grabbed the bottle away from Merribeth and raised the bottle and toasted, "Here's to the Fearsome Threesome."

Then I took a glug and passed the bottle to Merribeth, who sipped at it, then passed the bottle to Amber, who chug-a-lugged until I felt I had to prevent her from drowning and yanked the bottle away.

This was how we began. Merribeth later said we became a trinity of sisters. I thought we were more like gorgons, but it's all a matter of perspective, I guess. We lay back on the bathroom door and looked up through the leafy limbs until they spun overhead and then faded into deep black and the stars peeked out among them.

So, although Merribeth and I loved Weewampum, and especially Merribeth's backyard and the tree house because it was ours and it's what we'd known for years and years, Amber loved Weewampum because it matched a dream she'd carried with her while living in apartments in Karachi and Kenyatta and Katmandu. She'd longed to be an American girl like in the Dick and Jane readers, amidst a loving family and friends and a world painted in cheerful primary colors. Which is just another way of saying that Amber loved Weewampum the way she found it, and she wanted to protect it and improve it and make her dream last as long as she could and not really ever have to wake up and move to another outpost where she was an outsider again. Which is another way of saying, Amber wanted the hospital to stay put.

But always, there were Amber's financial reasons for wanting the hospital not to move. Her tenants in her downtown storefronts couldn't pay their rent if Main Street withered into a place where no one ever went. As I was thinking along these lines, it occurred to me that if Amber had her monetary motivations for wanting Our Lady to stay where it was, so, too, the hospital-move-backers probably had their own financial reasons for supporting the move.

Amber insisted Lars was behind the move because she opposed it. But Lars was a prominent gynecologist with a flourishing practice. He wouldn't jeopardize his monthly cash flow if he didn't think the move might bring in even more birth control, pregnancy, and hysterectomy cases. What Merribeth, Amber, and I needed to explore was what made Lars tick financially.

Amber agreed it was essential we check out Lars' economic situation. Merribeth wasn't so sure; she felt people's financial affairs were their own business. But Merribeth finally caved in after Amber insisted she should regard Lars not only as the warped guy who'd knocked up Star's mom, but also as an enemy of the people for supporting the hospital move and a potential arsonist, too.

With the approval of Merribeth and Amber, I started tracking down property records at the courthouse and found they all were on microfiche. I had to sit in a dark, windowless room in which pale-skinned lawyers and their clerks pored over records that no one but them ever looked at. But then I started hitting pay dirt. The microfiche showed that Lars not only owned a house on Cardinal Court and a rental on Appian Way, but he also owned two acres of land along Highway 11 that just happened to be right next to where the hospital was supposed to be built. He had paid $100,000 for it back in 1999 and it was worth a lot more now, even though it still was undeveloped. And guess whom Lars had bought the land from back in 1999? Well, forget about guessing. To get to the point, Lars had bought the property from Mr. James A. Hartwell, who still owned the parcel where the hospital was supposed to go up.

And Merribeth's father, I discovered, also owned about half the property in town. Well, maybe not half, but he owned a lot. Like Amber, he owned several buildings downtown – a small professional office building, a shoe store, and a C.P.A.'s office – as well as a mini-mall, some lots and the property that was Van's Prime Autos, all along Highway 11.

The evidence seemed to be pointing equally toward Lars and Mr. H. as possible firebugs. After all, they might have reasoned that torching Amberosia's would be one way to shut up the hospital-move opposition and thereby pave the way for them to start reaping whatever riches they could from the land they owned around the new medical center. When I told Amber about

55

my discoveries, she insisted I meet her at the hospital one dreary afternoon at 4:30. As a hospital board member, Amber had access to much, and theoretically all, of the hospital's business.

Amber was only five minutes late for our appointed rendezvous. We strolled into the business office, where we started pawing through the vendor files while trying to act nonchalant. No one objected because Amber was a board member, although I did notice the executive secretary with the pink pearlized fingernails whispering into the phone shortly after we walked in.

What did we find? Well, for one thing, the hospital referred some emergency room patients to Lars, and he billed the hospital for his services, which meant we found some numbers in his file: his taxpayer I.D. number, state medical license number, Social Security number, and driver's license number. We were going to be able to get a pretty good picture of Lars' financial activities.

Eileen, the secretary, kept asking, "May I help you find something?" but we were doing pretty well without anyone's help, especially Eileen's. When it got to be 5 p.m. and Eileen was ready to go home, she said, "It's time for us to be going," and Amber said, "Well, good night."

Eileen said, "I need to lock the door," and Amber said, "We'll pull it shut when we leave," so Eileen shrugged and looked at us as if we were some disgusting moles who'd tunneled into CIA headquarters. But she was powerless to stop us, so she grabbed her black plastic purse and fled.

Amber was totally focused on Lars' file, but I decided that just for curiosity's sake, I'd look under "H." And there I discovered that Mr. James A. Hartwell's architecture firm had been receiving design fees from the hospital for years and years. Everyone knew that Hartwell and Associates had been chosen to draw up plans for the new hospital building. But I'm not sure everyone knew how much design work Mr. H. had been doing for the hospital over the years – everything from turning a linen closet into a patient's room to reconfiguring the cashier's station in the cafeteria. It would seem he might have had an unfair advantage when the hospital board was seeking architects for the new building. The records showed he'd been receiving a $5,000-a-month retainer fee for years just for being a good old boy, I guess, and willing to render architectural services when asked. This retainer was in addition to his bills for redesigning the cashier's station and all the rest. Our Lady of Perpetual Need was kind of Mr. H's own, personal, trust fund. And of course, in looking through his file, we found some more identification numbers.

***

When we finally left the hospital about 6 p.m., I was convinced we needed to act fast on this information. All my training and experience as a reporter made me believe that people need the facts to make voting decisions. Weewampumites had a right to know that Mr. H. and Lars would profit from the hospital move. This news could help our side win the election. As we left the hospital, I told Amber I thought we should take our discoveries to the *Weewampum Bugle* the next morning. I was sure she'd agree.

She looked surprised.

"Are you sure you want to do that?" she asked, much more cautiously than I would have expected from my flame-haired friend.

"You really could wreck Merribeth's old man with that stuff," she said. "And her family."

Like most reporters, I really hadn't thought through the repercussions of what I wanted to see in the paper.

"I thought you wanted the hospital to stay downtown," I said.

"I do," Amber said. "More than you do. Hey, look, you've got to do what you've got to do. But I'd run it by Merribeth first."

We got into our cars and drove away; Amber to her sprawling home, where a new housekeeper, Marta from Romania, was staying with Star; me to Merribeth's efficiency.

A big smile spread across Merribeth's face when she opened the door and saw me stamping my feet to stay warm.

"How great to see you, Wendy," she said. "I was just going to have some cod and wild rice. Won't you join me?"

I phoned Seal and told her she was on her own for dinner. How could I refuse my best friend's offer of a meal packed full of most of the essential food groups? I volunteered to make a run for some mocha almond fudge ice cream, but Merribeth said, "Oh, we don't need that. I'll poach us some pears."

She seemed so delighted with this solution for dessert, I decided to let her have her thrill and not confess that my heart would sing out ever so much more happily if it were treated to a bowlful of saturated fats.

I didn't mince any words, however, about what Amber and I discovered while rooting through the hospital files.

"Your father owns the property they're going to build the hospital on," I told her. "He's been getting a $5,000-month retainer for years. He's going to really clean up with the new hospital. I'm going to the *Weewampum Bugle* tomorrow morning to tell them. This could make a difference in the election. I know he's your father, but . . ."

Merribeth's face drained to the color of the cod.

"That's out of the question!"

Before I had a chance to argue, we heard someone pounding on the door. It was Amber and Star.

"I decided I should be here," Amber said, appropriating the kitchen chair I'd been sitting on. "I don't think we should go to the *Bugle*."

Star cuddled against Amber, but her eyes were on me, big and unblinking.

"Why not?" I shot back.

"Because," Amber said. "If we do, Merribeth will probably have a hernia."

"I will not," Merribeth snapped. "But I can't imagine why you'd want to ruin my father's reputation."

"He just needs to be held accountable for all the secret little things he does in this town, all the strings he pulls," I said.

"Don't go to the *Bugle*," Amber said. "We're not done poking around yet. If either Lars or Mr. H. burned down the restaurant because they wanted us to shut our yaps about the hospital move, just think about what they'd do if they find out we've gone to the newspaper. I've got my Little Sweetie to worry about," she said, planting a kiss on Star's right ear.

"Please don't do it, Wen," Merribeth pleaded.

"I thought you wanted the hospital to stay downtown," I fired at Amber.

"I do," she said. "But we can defeat those cocksuckers in the election without having to destroy Merribeth's whole family to win. If we find out later that Mr. H. burned down the restaurant, we'll make sure he's sentenced to wearing one of those cute little orange convict jumpsuits. Lars and Jimbo know we're fighting the hospital move, but they don't know the kind of dirt we're digging up on them. We've just got to shovel up some more before we're ready. You know yourself that we don't have enough evidence to convict them in court of the fire. You're just used to exposing people in the newspaper and making them squirm there. I'm not defending either of these assholes, but we're talking about Merribeth's whole family. If we want to see these creeps locked up, then we've got to know we're totally in the right and that we're going about this the right way."

I've said it before and I'll say it again. Sometimes, Amber knows more than I'm inclined to give her credit for, and she can be quite persuasive. But it was like leaving my fingernails impaled in a chalkboard to back down from my journalistic crusade and admit that at least in this case, I didn't feel the public's right to know was as important as placating my friends.

***

Amber, Merribeth, Dottie Wentzell, and I pounded on our last doors on the sleety Monday evening before the election. Then we caught a few hours of sleep and were up at dawn. Well, Merribeth and I were up at dawn. I'm not sure about Dottie. I think Amber slept in.

It was snowing that Valentine's Day Tuesday. The polls opened at 7 and I was there early, No. 4, when they signed me in. Merribeth, always thinking of others, had volunteered to drive those needing transportation to the polls. I drove myself to vote at the 100-year-old Jefferson Elementary School – a building that cried out for a new paint job – then headed home, making sure I took the byways and avoided the most direct route down Main Street. Two enterprising entrepreneurs, Bill and Stan Lemmert, were converting an abandoned Thom McAnn shoe store into a microbrewery and restaurant a block from the ashes of Amberosia's, and I didn't care to witness right now the outward manifestations of these brothers' probably doomed hopes and dreams. When I arrived back home, I crawled into bed.

Seal started rumbling around at 8:30, so I got up for good and made us a breakfast of oatmeal with brown sugar, dates, and walnuts. Seal even said, "Not bad."

She wanted me to drive her to the polls – she still wasn't driving yet. On our way, she asked me to stop and pick up Dottie Wentzell and Florence Schmidt.

I'd been able to breeze in and out of the polls earlier, but now, there was a line from the school hallway where the voting booths were, down the hall to the door of the principal's office.

On our way home, Florence said she was glad there was such a big turnout and that must mean our side was going to win. But Dottie reminded us the Our Lady's board was throwing a big party that night at the Knights of Columbus hall and the public was invited.

"Lots of folks might vote for the move just so they don't feel too guilty helping themselves to the deviled eggs and cupcakes tonight," Dottie said.

Florence conceded Dottie had a point, and we all agreed it was too hard to predict who'd win.

Merribeth, Amber, and I gathered at the Temple of the Huntress to watch the election returns on TV. When we turned on the tube about 10, we had to wait until the end of the newscast, naturally.

And then, right after the news about the Bucks losing another game and while Amber was up checking to see if Star was asleep, Brent Butler, the anchor who wore trendy wire-rim glasses, intoned, "And in other news, Weewampum voters defeated a measure that would have halted plans for construction of a new Our Lady of Perpetual Need Medical Center along Highway 11. The vote was close, 7,867 in favor of the new hospital and 7,805 to defeat it. Up next, 'Does Your Dog Need Dentures?'"

"Oh, shit!" Merribeth yelled, perhaps for the first time in her life. Amber came running in to see what was the matter, but by the time she reached us, it was time to flip to another channel.

"Fuck, fuck, fuck!" Amber yelled and fell into her well-padded mauve Lazy Boy.

"It's Weewampum. What do you expect?" I said. "Just another reason why I'll be so glad to blow this place."

"Oh, Wendy," Merribeth said. "A lot of people voted to keep the hospital downtown. You know they really outspent us in the campaign."

"We should have told *The Bugle*," I said.

"Bullshit," Amber blasted me. "We did the right thing. We've just got to get all our ducks in a row. If we're going to aim our guns at Lars or Jimbo Hartwell, we've got to make sure we don't miss.

"Besides," Amber added, "who needs a hospital with a lot of sick people, anyway? We'll rebuild Amberosia's and then revive the rest of downtown without any help from some old hospital. We'll show them we can make downtown work."

I rallied briefly. "We don't need to prove anything to anybody," I said. "Why do we even care what happens to downtown and all those old, abandoned buildings?"

"We care," Amber said, getting up and walking toward me as if to drive the point into my brain, "because we live here. At least, I do. And you're going to, too."

"No way, Jose," I said.

Merribeth cleared her throat, took a breath, then proceeded.

"Uh, Amber, Wendy," she said in almost a whisper. "I've been meaning to tell you that, uh, my district called and asked me if I could cut my leave of absence short. They really need a second grade teacher at my school, and I said I'd help them out."

"Merribeth!" Amber exploded. "It's just like you to wimp out when the going gets a little rough."

"I am not wimping out," Merribeth said huffily. "I am a teacher. This is what I do."

"Don't you owe it to yourself to find out if your old man burned down the restaurant?" Amber argued. "I still think Lars did it, but you've got to at least consider that maybe Old Jimbo was somehow involved."

Merribeth's peaches-and-cream complexion flushed Pepto-Bismol pink. "I just can't accept that," she flared.

"Merribeth," Amber said, "you've got to face it. Your old man's a real asshole."

Merribeth just glared at us, but maybe it finally was starting to register that we might have a point.

"Merribeth," Amber said, "let's show Jim Hartwell, Lars Hunssen, and any other shithead with dollar signs in his eyes what three determined women can do when challenged. Help me prove there can be another vision for Weewampum, that the town can thrive if we just build on what we've got."

Merribeth just sat on Amber's black velour couch, staring at Amber but not saying a word. But you could see something was going on behind those turquoise eyes of hers, as if they were lakes fed by underwater currents.

Chapter 6

Seal's Company Coffee

4-5 Tablespoons cheapest ground coffee
Coffee percolator
Tap water
2 percent milk

Fill plastic coffee percolator to just above the lower part of the coffee pot spout.
Place 4-5 Tablespoons ground coffee (to taste) in coffee percolator basket and place basket on post that fits into percolator.
Place basket and post inside percolator.
Plug in coffee pot.
When it's done perking, pour coffee into cup.
Leave room for milk and pour in milk until coffee is tan-colored.

The morning after the election, I woke to the sound of Seal pounding on my bedroom door.

"Phone," she said and stomped into her room and slammed the door.

I shuffled out to the kitchen and barked, "Yeah?" into the receiver. It was Amber.

"I've been thinking," she said. "You were right. We should have gone to *The Bugle*." She said we might have stopped the hospital project with an article about Lars' and Jimbo's property wheelings and dealings. Maybe we should go there this morning and tell them what we knew. We might not ever find out enough facts to convict Lars or Jimbo of starting the Amberosia's fire, but at least, maybe we could still stop the hospital.

"Weewampumites have spoken. They want a new hospital," I reminded her. "You were right. If we want to convict Lars or Jim, we've got to do things right, get all the facts. Good-bye."

"Wait, Wen," Amber yelled before I could hang up. "I figured you'd say that, so I've got another proposition."

She said she'd had a brainstorm. The quickest way to find out if Lars or Jimbo had burned down the restaurant was to search their houses for any incriminating evidence, like kerosene or other flammables, and that while we were there, we should also pore over their checkbooks, credit card bills and other documents to see if we could figure out how they'd spent the last few days before the blaze.

"You've been watching too many cop shows," I told her. "We're not the F.B.I."

"Yeah, I used to think it would be cool to be a Charlie's Angel," she laughed, "but now I'm kinda hooked on 'Columbo' reruns. But really, Wen, I think we could pull it off."

She told me then how she always kept a key to the houses she sold. She did it as prevention; she didn't know how many times new homeowners locked themselves out and called her, and the only way she could help them was with her set of duplicate keys. That meant that although Lars didn't know it, Amber could unlock the big colonial house she'd sold him on Cardinal Court, not to mention about a quarter of the houses in town.

"But I'm not going to his place by myself. No way," she said. The Threesome, however, could pull off a successful covert operation, she felt. The best time to go would be Tuesday. That was prime time for Lars to be yanking out some poor woman's fibroids or uterus.

"I know he burned down the restaurant," she said. "And I know we can get him."

"Sorry," I told her. "I've got an appointment on Tuesday to color my hair."

I'd never been much into the hair scene, but the hairdresser at Lucille's Locks and Wigs had promised the auburn color I'd tentatively chosen would cover up where my bulldog-brown spiked tresses were corroding to gray baling wire – not that I really cared. I just figured the red hair would make a statement to whomever had burned down Amberosia's that I wasn't someone who was going to fade without a fight.

"Aw, come on, Wen," Amber egged me on. "What's a few gray spots here and there? We can nail him. I know we can nail him. We'll be a great spy team."

64

"Sorry," I said.

"The Tuesday after, then?" she proposed.

"I think I'm supposed to go back for a toner then," I said.

"Oh, all right, two weeks from Tuesday, but that's final. We've got to get moving on this."

"No way," I said without really thinking about my answer. But after I'd said it, I realized I didn't want to risk getting caught pawing through Lars' unmentionables by some overzealous Weewampum patrolman.

"What do you mean, 'No way'?" Amber asked.

"I'm not going to do it," I said. "And you shouldn't either. Did you ask Merribeth?"

She hesitated, then said, "Yeah," kind of softly.

"Well? What did she say?"

"'No thank you' and 'Don't do it,'" Amber admitted. "Jesus Christ. What good are friends if they won't take a few little risks?"

"Good-bye, Amber," I said and started to hang up, but Amber was too fast again.

"No, wait, Wen," she said, her voice kind of trembling. "I know he did it. We can prove it. I know it."

"Good-bye, Amber," I said and jammed the phone into its cradle.

If I were a better friend, or dumber, I might have gone with Amber just like that. She's the kind of person who, once she gets an idea, just as once she latches onto a real estate prospect, just won't let go.

Instead, I kept my hair appointment. I should have gone with Amber. Lucille used too much peroxide and my hair turned the color of yams.

When I walked in Seal's front door that Tuesday afternoon with my hair lit up like a Union 76 sign, Amber was sitting in the mustard-colored chair and Seal was on our moss-green mohair sofa. They were just staring at each other, not saying a word, Seal's typical manner for entertaining the bold vacuum-cleaner salesmen and Jehovah's Witnesses enterprising enough to blaze a trail past our threshold.

I knew when I walked in that Amber had been to Lars'. She was jiggling her leg up and down, and her hand-painted, ceramic ankle bracelets were pinging against each other. It occurred to me she was doing it on purpose to annoy Seal, but that was more like something I'd do. I decided to give Amber the benefit of the doubt; her jiggling probably was unconscious.

"Well, here comes Pumpkin Head," Seal said as I walked toward them. I didn't want to sit on the couch next to Seal, so I flopped on the floor next to Amber's bracelets.

I expected Amber to say something about my hair like, "Hey, cool," which would irritate Seal. But instead, Amber leaped up, looked around, confused, then dropped back into the chair. Her face flashed from red, to white, to red again in about five seconds.

"Oh, my God, Oh, my God," she said. She wasn't even looking at my locks.

"What's up, Amb?" I asked.

"Call Merribeth," she said. "We need a powwow."

"You went over to Lars', didn't you?" I asked.

Seal raised her eyebrows disapprovingly, ready to sit in judgment on Amber's latest escapade and confession.

But Amber wasn't playing Seal's game. She opened and shut her mouth a couple times like a sturgeon. It was unusual for Amber to be so quiet.

"What did you find out?" I asked.

"Just call Bethy," she said. "I didn't want to phone her until you got here."

"Go phone her," Seal said to me, annoyed. "She wouldn't tell me a thing." Seal stood up in a huff and walked to the kitchen. "I suppose you'll be wanting coffee," she said.

"It's OK, Mom," I said, but Seal slammed around with the coffee percolator. She nearly always feigned disinterest in my affairs, so I was as surprised with her reaction as with Amber's. I'd given her a Mr. Coffee machine years ago and a coffee grinder, but she insisted on using the old percolator, which she said was good enough for her.

Amber just sat and stared at me. She seemed kind of in shock.

"Are you OK, Amb?" I asked.

She nodded and asked, "Is Merribeth on her way?"

So I phoned Merribeth, who couldn't resist a plea for her assistance and she was ringing Seal's doorbell within 10 minutes.

"What is it, Amby?" Merribeth asked as soon as she rushed in and gave Amber a quick hug.

"Well, you know where I was this morning," Amber said.

Merribeth lowered her voice to a whisper. "Oh, Amber, you didn't really go over to Lars', did you?"

Seal was hovering at the kitchen door. Amber glanced over at her and said, "Look, can we go outside or something?"

"Oh, honestly," Seal said and sniffed like an empress who'd just smelled dead worms in her tea rose garden. She stalked across the living room and into her bedroom and banged the door shut.

"She still hates me," Amber said.

"She doesn't hate you," I said. "That's just Seal." But Seal had never liked Amber. She'd never let me sleep over when Amber had slumber parties. She rarely let me invite Amber over. She said Amber's parents were too lax – and they were – and Seal said, like parents, like daughter, and maybe she was right.

But a lax friend was just what I'd wanted at the time. I knew Amber's parents did spend a lot of time at the officers' club at Fort Snowcap. That meant Amber was home a lot by herself, and to Seal, that spelled trouble. Merribeth's mother took an entirely different approach, however, and tried to include Amber in many Hartwell family activities. That was fine with me, because I spent as much time as I could at Merribeth's, so Seal never really succeeded at keeping Amber and me separated.

With Seal out of the way now, Amber seemed to relax slightly, and the three of us headed for the kitchen.

I poured Amber a cup of coffee. Merribeth asked for a glass of juice. Amber drained about a half-cup of generic roast before she finally blurted out, "I can't believe it. I just can't believe it."

I set out a plate of Oreos.

"What? Amber, what?" Merribeth wanted to know. Merribeth was all ears, even though she'd opposed Amber's illicit exploration of Lars' house.

Amber loves to be in center-stage position. She sipped some more coffee to draw out the suspense, then tossed back her hair. I noticed her leg was still jiggling. She seemed more agitated than usual. But then she launched into what sounded like a typical Amber escapade.

"Wel-l-l-l," she said, letting out her "l-l-l's" like a lasso, luring us into her tale of espionage. "I parked my car a block away from Lars' house – I was wearing my cute khaki suit – and I walked up to Lars' back door with a rake in my hand. I figured if the neighbors saw me, they'd think I was just coming to loan him some garden tools. The door opened s-o-o-o easily, I couldn't believe it, so I just slipped inside. I don't think anyone saw me, and if they did, I really don't give a damn."

Amber was watching Merribeth and me for our reactions. For a second, I got the feeling she was trying to cover up something more serious with her chatter, but like Merribeth, I wanted to hear what our cat-burglar friend had discovered inside Lars' abode.

"What he's done to the inside of that house is simply criminal," Amber said, severing an Oreo in half with her front teeth. "It used to be in warm wood and earth tones."

I wasn't interested in either Amber's fashion choices or Lars' decorating tastes so I asked her, "Did you find any old checks paid to explosives experts or telephone bills with long-distance calls to match vendors?"

Amber opened her eyes wide at me as if she were struggling not to tell a state secret, then blinked and proceeded in a close-to-everyday voice, as if I'd just complimented her on her choice of outfits for her breaking-and-entering escapade.

"He's painted all the oak woodwork white, can you believe it? And the walls are a deep, military blue. It just makes you want to salute, but Lars Hunssen is the last person I'd want to give that kind of recognition to."

Amber said she thoroughly scouted the place before entering, just to make sure Lars wasn't lurking in some dark corner.

"It wasn't easy going into that house again. I wish you'd come along," she said, looking at me as if she were a betrayed Irish setter.

I didn't feel guilty, if that's what Amber intended. Maybe she was just making a simple statement. She said Lars has set up one bedroom as an office and has a high-tech desk with a glass top and gray steel drawers. The drawers were locked, but Amber managed to pop them open easily when she found the hidden lock on an inside desk panel.

"Oh, God, he's so boring," she said, rolling her eyes and laughing kind of nervously, almost as if she had to pretend to be the blasé Amber we knew so well. She provided us with an inventory of the contents of Lars' desk. No old letters, photos, squirreled-away chocolates, unusual rocks, old coins, loose keys, or maybe a bottle of bourbon as she had expected.

"At least, that's what's in my desk," Amber said. Lars had computer paper in the top right drawer, nothing else. He kept paper clips, pencils, and rubber bands in the second drawer down. The big bottom drawer on the right held nothing but a ruler, a scissors, and a black, felt-tipped pen. The desk didn't have any left-side drawers.

"I guess he doesn't need them," Amber said, shrugging.

Amber proceeded from the desk to the closets but found little of interest, except a crocheted afghan in patches of yellow and orange. That was tucked inside a black plastic bag on the top shelf of a guest bedroom, the only swatch of brightness in an otherwise drab house.

Amber paused in the kitchen and checked out the knife drawer, where she discovered Lars has an extensive collection of knives with blades of every dimension.

"Oh, my God, can you imagine how scary that was? Every minute I was thinking, 'What if he comes through that door?' But, thank God, he didn't."

She advanced to the garage. She was postponing the master bedroom until last. Lars' house is one of those new ones built on a slab so it didn't have a basement where he could conceal the tools of his trade as an arsonist. The garage was immaculate; there wasn't a drop of oil on the floor. There also were no paint cans, pipes, lumber, old boxes, rags, cobwebs, yellowed newspapers, or any of the items that Amber has stuffed into her own garage. There was a lawn mower and a snow blower. She also noticed a rake.

But there were no containers of kerosene, just a gallon can of gasoline, and no bombs, firecrackers, or other incendiary devices that she could discern.

"I went back to the kitchen. I just wanted to take a pause to refresh, you might say, you know, gird my loins, before heading for that master bedroom. There's only one door in and out of there. I wanted to be absolutely sure that Dr. Asshole wasn't heading home for an early lunch.

"I opened the refrigerator, just to stall a little. There was a pear, half a head of brown lettuce, and one Roma tomato. No salad dressing. In the freezer, there was a Weight Watchers linguini dinner, frozen hard like a brick. I looked out the greenhouse window, which is just above the sink, and it was then I realized that Dr. Shithead has turned his backyard into a cemetery for plants.

"The bastard's ripped out the rose bushes, pulled up the phlox, dug out the daylilies, and dumped dirt into the pool. I think he's going to fill it in."

When she saw that dead garden, that's when she knew Lars could be capable of anything and when she really got scared. She knew she was free to leave, but she also felt the bedroom would be the most likely place Lars had hidden any evidence.

She squared her shoulders, took a breath, walked into Lars' bedroom and looked out the windows. The coast was clear but Amber wanted to hurry as much as she could.

She searched Lars' closet and found nothing of interest. No charred shirts or cinders dirtying the toes of his white running shoes. She checked his dresser drawers and found nothing. She looked under his bed and didn't even find dust balls. She checked his nightstand. It was as empty as a nightstand at the Holiday Inn, but there was no Gideon Bible. Lars did have a Physician's Desk Reference on the top of the nightstand, as if prepared for any emergency late at night.

70

"It's a shame it took me so long to realize he's a guy with zero signs of a personality," Amber sighed.

I couldn't agree more.

The only room Amber had left to search was Lars' bathroom. She made a quick sweep through it and found nothing. Like the rest of the house, it was just another dark blue room, but since it was a bathroom, it was tiled.

"I mean, you can only take so much blue," she said, her voice high. "I mean, the house called out for some buttercup, rose, mint, lavender. It needed some life, some oomph."

She said the medicine cabinet was well-stocked with bandages, salves, Thera-Flu and an economy-sized bottle of aspirin. She had struck out. She could never even prove Lars existed as a person from her snooping session.

She walked out of the bathroom and just had passed the king-sized bed that sat on a black metal base when she glanced toward the hallway.

"And there stood Lars, looking like Darth Vader if Darth went blond."

Oh, my God, Amber can get herself into some scary spots.

"He just braced himself in the doorway, his hands on his hips, so cocky-like, his eyes cold as sabers. I know I jumped but I tried not to scream."

She credited her relative poise to a stint playing Penelope when Mrs. Nowacki's senior drama class at Weewampum High adapted *The Odyssey* for the stage. She'd had to fake how excited Penelope was when that gadabout husband, Ulysses, had shown up after 20 years of carousing around the globe.

"I just pretended that walking out of Lars' bathroom was the most natural thing in the world and that I was s-o-o-o glad to see him."

She welcomed Lars with, "Ah, there you are," before he snapped, "What the hell are you doing here?"

At this point in the tale, Merribeth grabbed Amber's hand and squeezed it. I was impressed that Amber was sitting here, telling this story, without any visible bruises, gashes, or broken teeth.

71

"God, Amber," I said. "We told you not to go."

"Yeah, shit. I just felt I had to. I was so sure he'd burned down the restaurant."

Amber frowned, then picked up the story. She said she guessed she was lucky she'd found no evidence and that her hands were empty, except for her black, crushed-leather Gucci purse, which she started swinging like a pendulum at Lars.

He didn't budge from the door frame. "He looked as mean as a jailer who's just busted up a prison break. I decided I'd better smile."

Amber had to think fast so she told Lars, "I've got a client I told about your house. If you want to sell, I think you could get a real good price."

"Cut the crap," Lars replied.

He walked into the room and reached for the telephone, which, unfortunately, was out of Amber's reach. He told her he was calling the police because he doesn't like burglars. Amber told him, "That's a good one."

She said she couldn't help thinking about those steel-edged knives in his kitchen drawer. Then, because Amber just never knows when she should keep her big mouth shut, she blurted, "Well, I don't like liars. And I don't like rapists. And I don't like arsonists."

Sometimes, I think Amber is one of the most self-destructive people I know. Or maybe it's just that she's never really learned to think before she acts. But whoa, wait a minute. What had she just said?

"Rapists?" Merribeth gasped. "What do you mean, Amber? What are you talking about?"

Amber stopped, blushed, trapped by her words. She looked at us as if she were a rabbit about to bound out of sight. There was silence. Merribeth and I watched Amber intently and finally she tossed her hair back. "Well, you know how I get carried away," she laughed, kind of tentatively.

"Amber!" I yelled at her. "What did he do to you?"

"Uh, look," Amber said, rather shakily at first but gaining

volume with each syllable. "OK, maybe sometimes I stretch the story just a little teensy bit. But would you just SHUT THE FUCK UP AND LISTEN?"

Merribeth and I exchanged worried glances. We'd learned that once Amber held the floor it was best not to stop her. We'd grill her once she ground to a halt.

"All I could think of was my little Star and of how she needed me," Amber said. "I was sobbing, really; just shaking and shuddering.

"Then Lars rushed at me and slapped his hand over my mouth and held me close to his body. I stopped crying. I got cold all over. I still was shuddering. 'Think, Amber, think,' I told myself. 'Do something.'

"I tried to bite him, but he cupped his hand over my mouth. I kneed him in the groin, just as my father, Mr. Macho Army man, taught me. Lars winced but drew me closer, till I was pressed into him like a rib-eye steak. His belt buckle filleted a strip of skin off my stomach, even though I had my clothes on.

"I really started struggling then. I stomped on his feet and tried to shove my palm up his nose as my father had demonstrated, but I wasn't getting anywhere. Lars started laughing. I had to get the hell out of there.

"Somehow, my purse still was dangling off my arm like a bowling ball on a chain. I grabbed the strap and swung my purse up and hit Lars on the head. This time, he stumbled forward. I squirmed out of his grasp and he fell on to the bed. I ran for the door.

"He sat up.

"'Amber, wait,' he yelled, and like a fool, I did. I braced myself in the door frame this time. He stayed sitting on the bed and demanded, 'I deserve an explanation of what you're doing here.'

"'If you want to talk, we can do it in court.'

"'I don't think you really want me to press charges.'

"The gall of him. HIM pressing charges against ME?!!" Amber yelled at us, grabbing the edge of the kitchen table and shaking it so my mug and Merribeth's juice glass wobbled.

"You bastard," Amber screamed at him.

"Tell me," he insisted, "What are you doing in my room?"

Amber told Lars it shouldn't be hard for a guy with his education to figure out what she was up to. She had lost her restaurant and the fire marshal thought the fire had been set. Who was her biggest enemy in town?

"Take a guess. Some people call him, 'Dr. Lars Hunssen.' But I call him, 'Dr. Asshole.'"

Then Lars totally bewildered her.

"Despite what you may have convinced yourself of, I'm not your enemy," he said. "Despite what you may think, I have better things to do than burn down your diner."

"When he called Amberosia's a 'diner,' that's when I really flipped out. I started thinking about those knives again and where I could use them. I could cut off his ears with that paring knife and pierce his tongue with the steel rod knife sharpener. With the steak knife, I could slice off his fingertips and with the butcher knife, I could whack off his dick. That would feel so good. Just to hear that little thunk."

"Amber, really!" Merribeth objected and then pleaded, "You've got to tell us what he did to you!"

"Just listen, Merribeth," Amber yelled. "That's all I ask of you."

"Well, you just really seem to hate him. I just want to know why and that you're safe and sound," Merribeth said, hurt.

"Just listen, OK?" Amber insisted, galloping on with her story. Merribeth and I had no choice but just to hope Amber reached the finish line soon. Amber said she told Lars she understood that he couldn't stand that she wanted the hospital to stay downtown so he'd decided to turn Amberosia's into cinders to keep her quiet.

"But he just stood there smirking like the fucking Cheshire cat. Then he looked up at the ceiling, like only he and God could share the joke."

Lars told Amber that if he had burned down the restaurant to keep her side of the hospital issue silenced, then he hadn't been very successful. Her side had been pretty vocal and he felt his side had won the referendum fair and square.

But Amber persisted. She said Lars had burned down Amberosia's because he was hoping she would "just shut the fuck up, go away, forget about the hospital, this town, and his being Star's father."

And then, he said, "Well, maybe there is something that will make you shut up."

"By now, I was wishing I'd remembered to make out a will," Amber said. "I know what he can do."

"God, Amber! What did he do to you?" I screamed at her, but she ignored me.

"I could have run out the door. He wasn't holding on to me. But it was like he made me feel I was in his trap."

"Amber!" Merribeth and I both shouted at her. "What did he do to you?"

It sure didn't seem that Amber was just enjoying telling this story to see our reactions. Amber plowed on, "Well, he just reached deep down into his pants pocket. I figured maybe he had a stiletto down there or a long, thin nylon rope."

"Amber!" Merribeth and I cried.

"But he just pulled out this blue passbook and tossed it at me. It fell on the floor and I bent to pick it up without taking my eyes off him. But he didn't move, so I opened it."

She glanced at the total: $33,587.92.

"So, big deal," she told Lars. "You'd think a big-shot doctor like you would have more money than this."

Then, she happened to glance at the name on the book: "Star Moore."

"Well, my mouth dropped open wider than a laundry chute. 'What's this all about?'" Amber asked.

Lars said, "Just get out of here now. And drop that bankbook on your way out."

So Amber dropped the passbook and backed down Lars' hallway. He didn't follow her although she was afraid he would. And when she reached the door, she ran all the way to her Lexus, not looking back even once.

Amber finished her story, almost gasping for breath. She pushed her chair back and grabbed for the coffeepot. It was empty and she was going to make some more brew. I snatched it from her and got the coffee perking myself.

"What else happened?" I demanded. "You seem pretty upset to have just learned your daughter's an almost-rich girl."

"Well, tell me, Wen, just what do you think that bankbook's all about?" Amber asked, her voice quavering.

"Well, maybe he's going to pay you support after all," I said, more calmly. "What do you think?"

She slumped in the chair.

"I wish I knew," she said. "He says he didn't torch the restaurant. And who would have thought he'd have that bankbook? But that still doesn't explain how he treated me."

Merribeth had been listening to Amber this whole time, and except for a few outbursts, had sealed her mouth as tightly as a No. 10 envelope. But now she spoke, and Merribeth wasn't going to be silenced until Amber gave her a satisfactory answer.

"What did he do to you, Amber?" Merribeth demanded in her low, controlling, Ms. Hartwell the teacher voice, which she uses on us only on rare occasions. "You're not leaving this kitchen until you tell us."

Amber looked around skittishly. "Is there somewhere we can go, some place more private?" Amber asked. This was so unlike Amber.

"It's private here. Seal's sulking in her bedroom, if that's what you're worried about," I told her.

"You know she never liked me," Amber said. "And she won't like me even more if she gets a load of this."

"How about a walk?" I proposed.

"No walks. I don't do walks," Amber said. "You know that. What are cars for?" she said, trying to make light of what was beginning to look like storm clouds ahead.

"A drive, then," I said.

"Can we take the coffeepot?" Amber asked. "And the cookies?"

"Oh, come on. Let's go to my room. We can close the door. I don't think Seal will press up against the door with a glass against her ear," I said. I grabbed my cup and the coffeepot and led my fading Musketeer pals to the bedroom that was temporarily mine. There was a single bed, a desk, a chair and one unopened suitcase that I'd left standing in the middle of the floor. With some squeezing, we'd all fit on the bed. I shut the door.

This Motel-6-style bedroom of mine was definitely a Seal room, with its white chenille bedspread with no distinct pattern to the nubs and ribs. The walls were off-white, the lone curtain, beige. The dresser had five drawers and gold-plated, horizontal bar drawer pulls. There was a picture of Seal and my father, Rex, on the wall. Seal was wearing a square-necked, beaded dress with pointy-edged, butterfly sleeves and a veil spraying out in all directions, attached to what looked like a mobcap. It was a "singular" outfit, to put the best possible spin on her wedding raiments, although "peculiar" would be closer to the truth. My father wore a boxy suit that was in vogue at the time, I guess, and he looked rather detached from the whole wedding process but, nevertheless, quite debonair. He was a head taller than Seal, had dark, straight hair, clipped short, and eyes that reflected back the light and were hard to get behind.

We squeezed onto the bed like the "Hear no evil, See no evil, Speak no evil" monkeys, but we were all ready to hear, see, and speak everything.

"OK, Amber, go," I said. Amber cleared her throat and stared at the wedding picture.

"Christ," she whispered. "Everybody and his brother and sister has one of those." She gazed wistfully at Seal and my dad. "Even Seal."

"Oh, honey, your time will come," Merribeth said, patting Amber's wrist. "You've had plenty of chances."

"Yeah, sure," Amber said. She fingered her hair. "OK," she said, "let me tell you a little about why Lars Hunssen and I will never tie the knot."

She said she never had really told us what had happened because she figured she could handle it.

"Besides, Wen," she said, "You'd only tell me, 'Get a handle on your hormones.' I didn't want to hear it again."

She said she already was a member of the hospital board when

Lars had moved to town and was asked to serve on it, too. She was smitten with him from Day One and had even dropped 10 pounds and gotten down to a size 12 to catch his attention. But he never seemed to notice.

She plotted and strategized how to get him to take her out. She advised him over and over that a big, influential doctor needed to make a statement that he had arrived in this world and that the best way to do it was by purchasing a big, swanky residence. Finally, Lars took the bait and asked Amber to show him some houses.

Amber showed him house after house. Actually, there weren't that many nice homes in Weewampum that would convey the impression of wealth and success that a prominent gynecologist would want to project. Finally, she persuaded him to buy the big, expensive house on Cardinal Court and then she talked him into celebrating with a victory dinner. She had wanted to take him to the Water's Edge Inn, but Lars insisted he was paying, so they wound up at the Heidi House, everyone's second choice. Amber ordered halibut; Lars, sauerbraten. After dinner, Amber asked Lars if he'd like to see his new house by moonlight.

She was kind of surprised when he agreed because he'd been as remote as Neptune during dinner. She said her plan was that they'd tour the house quickly, maybe linger in the garden and then, perhaps, wind up at the Temple of the Huntress for sherry, maybe a soak in the spa and ... But when they arrived at Lars' new place, he insisted they inspect the bedroom to see if his bed would fit or if he'd have to buy a new one. Amber was hunting through her purse for the little tape measure that she always carries, when Lars walked up behind her and grabbed her breasts.

"You've been waiting for this, haven't you?" Amber said he growled, kind of low and soft.

Merribeth gasped, "Oh, he didn't really?" Amber assured us he had. It seemed such strange behavior for the suave, if somewhat banal, sophisticate that Lars appeared to be.

"I was going to tell him to stop acting so immature, but before I had a chance to even open my mouth, he pushed up my skirt and pulled down my pantyhose and undies and I couldn't even elbow him before he jammed himself into me from the back. I couldn't even see his face," Amber said, starting to cry.

"What? Amber! Oh, my God!" Merribeth yelled.

Amber said she would have screamed more and struggled if she'd fully understood what was happening. But she was so surprised that she needed a few seconds to think.

"He grabbed me so close I could hardly breathe, and then he bent his knees into mine and pushed me to the ground. I started crying and then my brain finally clicked in. Why was I never, ever, in control, even when I thought I was?"

Amber continued weeping. Merribeth and I both reached for her. She said she thought she'd been acting the part of a professional real estate agent just seconds before, and then, there she was, being attacked on the floor. She thought if she was going to be treated like a dog, then she'd act like one. She tried to crawl away but couldn't because Lars was clenching her around her waist.

"I tried to kick him where it hurts but I only kicked the air. I bit his arm, he yelled, and suddenly I broke free. I scuttled like a dachshund across the carpet to the bathroom and locked myself inside."

She said Lars pounded on the bathroom door and asked what was the matter. It seemed he was surprised that Amber would choose to hole up in a barren bathroom rather than in a bedroom filled with him. But Amber said "there was no way in hell" she was going to open up. She huddled on the toilet seat for what seemed like hours. The power was off in the house and the only light was from the moon spilling through a clerestory window on one wall.

She looked at the floor. There was a stain she hadn't noticed before. Finally, she heard Lars stomp down the stairs, start his car and drive off. Then she slipped out. It was only after she got home and stripped off all her clothes and stood under the shower that she realized she was bleeding.

Jesus, Amber gets herself into some spots that I don't even want to imagine being anywhere near. Why had she never told us about this before? I guess it's a good thing she hadn't. I would have tested those knives out on Lars myself.

Amber was shaking and sobbing as she finished telling us about Lars. I found a spare blanket and wrapped it around her.

Merribeth just kept telling her, "It's all right, Amber. It's all right. You're safe with us, honey. Everything's going to be all right."

Finally, I asked Amber, "So how did you have enough nerve to go back there today?" Amber just looked incredulously at me, as if baffled why I couldn't grasp this.

"I just had to," she said. "I knew he burned down Amberosia's. And I knew it even more this morning when I woke up. It just felt like today was the day. I wanted to get the proof. I should have taken him to court before for being Star's old man, but I felt we could win this time if we just dug up enough dirt on how he set the fire."

Sometimes, I guess, I'm not the most nurturing friend in the world, but Amber's behavior often mystifies and scares me.

"Why risk your safety?" I yelled at her. I don't know if I was most mad at her for putting herself in Lars' path once again, at me for not going with her, or at Lars for being emotionally dead. "Why didn't you explain to us why you suspected him and why you wanted us to go with you?"

"I don't know. Would it have made a difference? Would you have gone with me if you'd known?"

Amber seemed all wrung out and I really didn't know the answer.

"I didn't want us all to get busted for breaking and entering," she said. "Besides, I thought I knew what I was doing. And I never thought he'd show up. There was nothing in the refrigerator, for one thing. Why would he come home for lunch?"

Amber pulled the blanket tighter. Merribeth patted our foolhardy friend's hand.

"So what do you think now, Amber?" Merribeth asked in soothing tones. "Do you still feel he burned down Amberosia's?"

Amber looked at Merribeth for the longest time.

"I just don't know what to think, Bethy," she said. "I still think Lars is an asshole. But now I'm wondering whether I may have egged him on, given him a false impression that night I went to his house with him. What do you think?"

"I think he treated you like dirt," I snapped. "Don't you forget that for one second."

"I don't forget it," Amber said softly. "Not ever for one second. But I'm confused. I thought he'd torched the restaurant, but now I don't know. That bankbook makes me kind of think maybe he's not the one."

Chapter 7

Amber and Marta's Chef Salad

1 head iceberg lettuce, washed and chopped into bite-sized bits
1 head Romaine lettuce, washed and sliced diagonally from each edge into bited-sized bits
1 head escarole, endive, or red leaf lettuce, washed and chopped into bite-sized bits, or a bag of mixed field greens, washed and chopped into bite-sized bits
3 carrots, scrubbed and shredded
1 cup or more cooked chicken or turkey, sliced into julienne strips, or 1 cup or more cooked, julienned ham
1 cup or more cubed cheese – choose what you like: cheddar, Swiss, Colby, pepper jack, Monterey jack, mozzarella or ... You might mix two or more if you'd like. You might prefer to shred the cheese.
1 can black olives, drained and washed. You might prefer green, stuffed olives. That's OK. Maybe you'd like to use both.
Florets from one medium head broccoli. You might like to use florets of cauliflower.
Go right ahead. You might like to use both. That's great.
4 hardboiled eggs, cut into quarter wedges
1 green pepper, washed, with seeds removed, cut into strips
1 cucumber, washed, and cut into circular slices
1-2 large tomatoes, washed and cut into small wedges
1 can garbanzo beans
1 bag shelled, salted sunflower seeds

Dressing. Buy this at the store. We don't have time to make our own. Good Seasons puts together a pretty good packet of Italian seasonings that you can mix with vinegar and oil. Or make your own. Do what makes you happy.
Wash and chop lettuce first on a cutting board with a nice quality chef's knife. Good tools are important.
Dump the chopped lettuce into a big metal mixing bowl.
Mix in the shredded carrots.
Arrange the meat, cheese, olives, broccoli, eggs, green pepper, cucumber, garbanzo beans, and tomatoes in an eye-appealing fashion.
Sprinkle sunflower seeds over top.
Use salad tongs to place some salad in individual salad bowls.
Add dressing to individual bowls.
Serves many.

Warren Caramel was as much a part of Weewampum as the rusty Civil War cannons in the herb garden of the Weewampum Municipal Museum. It seemed Warren always had been at the fire department, serving his town, part of the landscape, stern and sober. He was a good ol' boy by default, not one to laugh at his own jokes because he never made any, nor at the jokes of his buddies because he didn't quite grasp the concept of laughter. But neither was Warren one to spread tales about Mrs. Zingler, who ran away with the water filter salesman, nor about Stevie Rubidoux, who smashed his car into a pallet of plywood at Danton's Lumber and killed himself after he was fired for stealing a hollow-core oak door. Warren was implacable, unflappable, think "Calvin Coolidge" and you've got Warren, and it seemed he was moving about as quickly as a dead president to solve the Amberosia's fire case.

Warren had his own methods and worked in his own way, and I'd hate to give him credit for actually having developed a theory about the fire, but it seemed Warren had deduced that the Threesome, either as a group, or acting individually, had cremated Amberosia's. Now it seemed Warren felt all he had to do was set a trap to catch us and sooner or later we'd fall into it, and then he could move on to more interesting things, like giving orders at garage fires or supervising fire-truck polishings.

For about a week now he'd been following us around town in his red Ford pickup, not even pretending to conceal himself or his truck, just slowly, patiently, tailing us. I don't know what he thought he'd see. If one of us was walking, he'd chug a few paces behind us. If we turned to wave or to glare, he'd just drive slowly, not acknowledging us but not about to be scared off, either.

I'd see him every so often in the produce aisle of Tom's Super Valu or pumping gas at Clyde's 76 Station.

"Hi, Warren," I'd say. "How's it going?"

"Wendy," he'd say. Then he'd turn his full attention to a head of iceberg lettuce or to the little numbers flipping around on the gas pump. So when Amber reported that Warren had cornered her and interrogated her while she was showing a new couple in town an expensive house out on Stokeley Road, I was a little surprised that Warren was escalating his surveillance from just watching us to actually talking to us, but I figured he'd have to speak to us eventually, before he was convinced it was time to move on to the real arsonist.

On the last day of February – it was leap year – Amber decided to give herself the day off from real estate because the day was like a free one, she felt. She invited us over for lunch and gave Marta a day off from watching Star so that Marta could prepare our meal. Merribeth and I would have been happy to have met Amber at a restaurant to spare Marta this extra labor, but Amber wanted to spend the day at home with Star. So now Marta was storming around the kitchen as she prepared the chef's salad that Amber had requested for us. Normally, I would have asked her to set to one side the ham and cheese she was so vigorously dicing, but her whacks of the knife were so emphatic that I held my tongue, then thanked her profusely when she announced, "Eat now."

Amber told us Warren had followed her when she went to meet the new manager of the Happy Clown Potato Chip factory, Bob Tuohy and his wife, Fay, at a big brick Cape-Cod-style house and show them around.

"He waited out front with that old red truck of his rumbling while I showed Bob and Fay around inside," Amber said. "They loved the house, so all I had to do was talk them into agreeing that a carport's just a hell of a lot more convenient than a three-car garage. So, we're standing in the doorway when Warren strolls up and says, 'Miss Moore, how much did you stand to gain by burning down your restaurant?'

"Jesus Christ, talk about a deal-killer. Old Bob and Fay took one look at each other, made a mad dash for their BMW, and peeled out of there like Richard Petty."

Amber was more than a little perturbed that Warren had come between her and a sale so when he started asking her again where she'd been the night of the fire, she was in no mood to try to charm him into leaving her alone.

She tried to unlock her Lexus and just drive away from Warren, even if he followed her. But Warren stood inside the door opening after Amber eased herself into the car, and she would have had to slam him into a sandwich to make her escape. For once, she calculated the potential effects of her actions and decided she'd be better off if Warren couldn't arrest her for assault and battery, as well as arson. So she was trapped in the driver's seat while Warren took his time questioning her about the blaze.

Where had she been the day and night of the fire? Amber was pretty exasperated since we'd already told Warren how she'd been at the hospital delivering Star and it was easy enough for him to check it out. Warren said that didn't mean she couldn't have planned the fire in advance, and Amber said, how could she have known when the baby would arrive? And Warren said she could have had a general plan that she could have activated when she felt herself going into labor.

"Christ Almighty, like I was going to think about anything as insignificant as a fire when my body was being torn in two by the pain?!" Amber complained, while spearing big chunks of lettuce and talking and chewing all at once. She was wearing Star in a baby sling and Star was trying to nap as stray pieces of lettuce and carrot shreds tumbled from Amber's mouth.

Amber said she told Warren to watch some "Columbo" reruns if he wanted to learn how to conduct a real criminal investigation. At that point, Warren reached into a jacket pocket and pulled out a subpoena for Amberosia's ledger.

I must say Amber did maintain good financial records, primarily because she had Edna's Accounting Service handling the books. I know the accounts showed the restaurant was slightly in the black each month. The restaurant didn't earn enough to support Merribeth and me at the salaries we'd been earning at our old jobs. But Amber wasn't forced to borrow any more money after she opened Amberosia's, and she paid all the bills every month. That's pretty much as successful as you can expect to be at a new small business, I figured. If Warren was looking for proof that Amberosia's was in financial hot water before the fire, he wasn't going to find it.

"So I said to him," Amber continued, "'Look, Smokey the Bear, if you want to find out who did it, go ask Lars Hunssen what he was doing Christmas Eve.' But instead, do you know what he said?

"'What do those gal friends of yours have against you? Why would they do it?'

"So I told him, 'Just buzz off, you old buzzard.'"

Merribeth set down her fork, gaped at Amber and said, "Oh, you didn't really?"

"You bet your bikini I did," Amber said.

Star stirred in the baby sling and started twisting, then pummeled her mom on the chest with her tiny hands. Amber unbuttoned her blouse, popped a breast near her baby's lips and Star latched on all in one smooth motion. Amber had mastered the knack of nursing since her first bout at the hospital and now unselfconsciously provided lunch for her daughter. Marta, who was slowly cleaning up, glanced over and thwacked the chef's knife extra hard on the cutting board, then stalked out of the kitchen. Apparently she and Amber had differing views about breast-feeding etiquette.

"What did Warren say then?" Merribeth prodded.

"He just asked if you or Wendy were having financial problems."

"Oh, honestly," I said.

"I told the asshole you didn't do it," Amber said. "I told him Merribeth won't even have a gas stove in her place for safety reasons and that you, Wen, prefer me and Merribeth to a lot of other people in town. I told him, 'She hasn't torched your house lately, has she? So why would she burn down my restaurant?'"

Warren just stared at Amber so she told him that if he wanted to do some real detective work, why didn't he look into the background of Lars Hunssen and Merribeth's father? Was Warren aware that Jimbo Hartwell had an argument with Merribeth at the restaurant the very day of the fire? And did he know that Jim Hartwell – not to mention Lars Hunssen – owned the land around the new hospital?

"Go check it out, Columbo," Amber told him.

Star had finished her lunch by now and was groggy. She was

such a good baby; she seldom cried.

Merribeth shifted nervously at the table. I suspected she wasn't as comfortable watching Amber's public nursing as she was trying to let on. I had to give Amber a hand for taking her motherhood role in stride, acting as if it were no more of an imposition than taking in a stray kitten. I never would have adjusted as well to momdom, especially considering Star's father. I wouldn't have been able to help feeling resentful and would have been about as warm and loving as "Mommy Dearest." But then, I never would have allowed the matter to get so out of hand. After all, abortions had been legal since 1973.

But having a carbon copy of herself seemed far more important to Amber than to me. And then, of course, Star hadn't been Amber's first experience with the joining of sperm and egg. Maybe if it hadn't been for that first experience, Amber wouldn't have so readily welcomed No. 2 into the world.

The first time was when Amber fell head over her sling-back pumps with a visiting botany professor whose specialty was fungus and spores and who had a one-year appointment at Weewampum State. Amber met Frederick Morton on his first day in town at Clyde's 76, where they both were pumping gas.

Frederick said he was new to Weewampum, and Amber liked his cowlick so she offered to show him around town. After a tour, dinner, and a walk along Lake Weewampum – on special occasions, Amber made exceptions to her no-walk policy – Amber and Frederick wound up at the Temple of the Huntress.

The day after their encounter, Amber was on the phone with Merribeth and me, telling us how spores were not Frederick's only area of expertise. They'd spent an invigorating night in Amber's sleigh bed, and Amber was convinced they'd be an item forever, or at least until Frederick found out if the university would convert his one-year appointment into an assistant professorship, or if he'd have to leave before summer sessions.

Amber and Frederick were inseparable for weeks. Then one day just before spring break, Frederick's wife, Izzy, drove into town in a beat-up Subaru pickup with a patchy Airedale named Weevil and a skinny, 5-year-old kid named Thornton. Frederick was gone the next day. He didn't even say good-bye or wait for the details of his professorship.

Amber was pretty broken up. How could he have left her? How could he have led her on? It wasn't that she was totally opposed to having an affair with a married man, but she expected him to be upfront about it, not to so thoroughly conceal the rest of his life from her. A wife was something you should have the courage to own up to.

"Open your eyes, not your legs," was about the only advice I could think of giving Amber, but I didn't tell her that, although I was tempted. I think I did tell her that somebody else would come along. It had been my observation that the longest Amber had been minus a male companion was about two weeks. Although, come to think of it, she'd not dated anyone since Star had been born, although I was sure that any day now, a new Mr. Wrong was sure to pop up in her bed.

Anyway, the curtain rose on Act 2 of the Frederick Morton matter a few weeks later when Amber phoned Merribeth and me and this time, Amber was really upset. She was pregnant. She was throwing up almost on the hour, and she was determined she was going to have an abortion.

I encouraged her to hurry up and do so. Merribeth advised caution and really thinking through her feelings about ending a life.

"The kid's coming out," Amber insisted. But then she did nothing. She just kept phoning Merribeth and me every night.

"Just hurry up and do something," I told her one night and hung up the phone. I was applying a verdigris finish to a metal bookshelf and didn't welcome her interruption. The next morning, Merribeth called me at work during her recess break.

"Did you hear about Amber?" she asked, her voice tearing apart. "Yeah. She called last night. Nothing's changed. Why?"

"Well, this morning around 5, she had a miscarriage," Merribeth said. "She's OK now, but I think she's pretty shook up."

I phoned Amber at Our Lady of Perpetual Need, where she was

supposed to spend a couple days resting.

"God's punishing me," she said. "I know it. I had scheduled the abortion for today at 9 o'clock."

She said she awoke to a feel of something giving way and tearing apart and then blood swooshed all over her bed. Amber said she felt as if she were being shredded by tiger's teeth. She called 911; she was out of her head with pain. She lost her baby in the ambulance before she got to the hospital.

"My poor baby, my poor baby," she cried while I tried to console her, but after about 30 minutes, I said I had to go and hung up. Why did Amber always have to learn about love the hard way?

I had to admit, though, that her lessons about Star so far seemed more joyful than painful. Star was dozing now in her little sling. Amber smiled down at her and whispered to Merribeth, "Do you want to hold her for a while?"

Normally, Merribeth would have welcomed the chance to cuddle with Star, but now she averted her eyes. It had to be Amber's still amply-exposed breast.

"No," Merribeth said icily. "I have to go."

Amber buttoned up, slowly realizing that maybe she had somehow offended Merribeth.

"What's your rush?" Amber asked.

Merribeth started to stand but then apparently changed her mind and spread her arms across the table like a ice-hockey goalie defending her turf and glared at Amber.

"It's just . . . It's just . . . " Merribeth said, her voice rising in pitch if not in volume. Then she said in one breath, "How could you? Why would you? I can't believe you'd try to get Warren Caramel to pin the blame on my father when you have no real evidence. You have no right."

Merribeth gasped for air.

"Ha!" Amber said, seemingly surprised at how perturbed Merribeth was, and actually, I hadn't found Amber's words to Warren anything to get too excited about, either.

"I have every right," Amber insisted. "I saw how he treated you that day in Amberosia's. I know what he's like."

"You don't know anything about him, not really," Merribeth said like a proud, albeit aging, child, defending the omnipotent grandeur of her parent.

"I know what he's like," Amber said, softly enough for Amber. "I learned about him a long time ago."

Merribeth continued to glare at Amber but finally took the bait. "What do you mean?" she asked.

"I've known about your old man since that summer after our senior year."

Then, Amber proceeded to tell us about one warm summer night when she was working as a waitress at the Heidi House and "It was as hot and muggy as an armpit and the air conditioner wasn't liking it one bit."

She said she'd been filling up the water pitchers when Jim Hartwell walked into the restaurant. The hostess seated him in the corner station and that meant Amber was the one designated to take his order.

"He looked at me like he'd never seen me before. I'm sure he didn't recognize me. I mean, I'd been over to your house, like, how many times, Merribeth? Fifty, maybe. And this big doofus, excuse me, your father, starts staring at me like I was more than just his daughter's good buddy. He put his hand on my left hand that was holding my order-taking pad and said, 'Just bring me the wiener schnitzel, honey.'"

Merribeth got up now and carried her salad bowl to the sink.

"That's enough, Amber," Merribeth said in her Ms. Hartwell voice. "I am leaving right now. And I'd appreciate it if you would stop exaggerating."

"This is the truth," Amber said, filling her bowl with another helping of salad. "And it's about time you heard it."

I thought Merribeth would walk out right then, but instead, she turned the water up loud and washed out her bowl. But Amber had a voice that could carry above a three-engine locomotive hissing steam and she wouldn't be silenced.

"I placed his order and brought him his dinner when he had his mouth stuffed with a breadstick so he couldn't talk," Amber continued. "I asked the busboy to do most of the dirty work – clearing the dishes, filling the water glasses. But as the waitress, it was my responsibility to take him the check."

Amber said she tried to slip the check on to the table when Mr. Hartwell turned his head when the front door opened. But she wasn't quick enough and he clamped his arm around her waist.

"'What time do you get off work, babe?'" he asked me, "just like he thought he was some sophisticated dude, not just your old man, out for a quick squeeze."

"That's enough," Merribeth snapped. "I know you're making up at least part of this."

"I am not," Amber insisted. Merribeth walked over to the pantry and opened the door and stared inside as if searching for the other side of the story.

"I tried to calmly place his arm on the tablecloth. I didn't say a thing. I just stared at him. Two could play this game, I thought. But his eyes looked like they saw everything I had on underneath my waitress uniform."

Amber admitted she was the first one to blink in the stare-down contest she had with Mr. H. But then the busboy strolled over to rescue her and asked if Mr. Hartwell would like more coffee.

"The spell was broken," Amber said. "I slipped away." Merribeth slammed the pantry door.

"Oh, big deal, Amber," she said. "He didn't really do anything to hurt you."

"Would you just listen, Merribeth?" Amber insisted. "I'm not finished." Amber said she had walked to work because The Heidi House was only a few blocks from her house, and it was in the days before she'd sworn off walking. "But when I left the restaurant, that creep, excuse me, your father, followed me in his car."

Merribeth now stood with her back to the pantry door, lightly bumping her head against it.

Amber said she didn't want to go home with Mr. H. following her because the chances were good that her parents were out. She had to do something so she decided to head toward my house and Merribeth's. Mr. H. trailed her all the way to Hubbard Street.

"I thought he'd be too embarrassed to tail me down his own street, but I was wrong. I was starting to get really scared. There was a dark patch with no streetlights before your house, Wendy, and I didn't want to get trapped there in the shadows."

Amber darted up a driveway and Mr. H. pulled in after her. She cut across some backyards, then into some shadows on the far side of my house. She watched Mr. H. pull his car into his own driveway, get out, and walk slowly and deliberately toward the darkness where she hid.

"I sprang out of the shadows and ran around the back of your house, Wen, and up your front porch and jerked open the front door. Luckily, it wasn't locked and I ran inside. There you sat in a corner of the living room reading Kierkegaard or some godawful thing, and your mother was watching Mary Tyler Moore on the tube."

As Amber talked, I remembered that night vividly, how Seal and I were shocked to see Amber suddenly charge into our living room, panting, her hair flowing in a thousand directions, her eyes darting like lizards looking for the nearest rock to hide under.

"Amber!" we'd shouted in unison. All she could do was point to the door. Seal and I glimpsed Mr. H. slowly walking up the front steps of his own house. I just stared at him. I didn't know what was going on. But Seal asked, all mean and snarly, "So, what did he do now?"

I remember thinking that Seal was being rather uncharitable towards Mr. H. We'd never had any problems with him that I knew of. Amber was almost hysterical and was trembling and shaking. Seal walked toward her and told her to sit down and asked her, "Are you all right, Amber? Is there anything you'd like? Anything you'd like us to do?"

It was probably the most charity Seal had ever displayed toward Amber, whom she usually tried to not encourage in the least. Amber finally told my mother and me that she was fine, really, and nothing had happened, that she'd just gotten scared when Mr. H. had followed her in his car. Seal phoned Amber's house and there was no answer. So my mom made up the sofa especially for

Amber and told her she was going to stay with us that night, no ifs, ands, or buts.

Merribeth had stopped knocking her head against the pantry door.

"Why didn't you ever tell me this before?" Merribeth demanded. "You've both known about this for years."

I just shrugged but Amber said, "Oh, Bethy, he's your father, and we know how much you love him."

Then Merribeth walked to the table and slumped into her chair.

"He's my father, and I love him," she said, as if some kind of machine. But then Merribeth looked Amber in the eyes and said, "But you're my friend and HE HAD NO RIGHT!" She pounded her fist on the table and Amber's salad flew out of her bowl and a clump of lettuce hit Star, who started to cry.

"It's OK," Amber told Star and then Merribeth. "He didn't really hurt me." Star simmered down more than Merribeth.

"I don't care," Merribeth said, almost choking on the words. "There are some things you just don't do. And this is one of them. If he could be that out-of-control then, maybe he still is. Maybe he really did burn down Amberosia's."

She looked at us kind of shocked then, as if belatedly realizing what she'd just said.

"I'll get to the bottom of this," she vowed. "I promise. And if my father burned down our restaurant, then he'd better have a nice, big, fat insurance policy on that brand-new, fancy hospital of his."

Amber and I exchanged amazed glances. Star just whimpered a little. Was this our Merribeth talking?

"Don't get me wrong," Merribeth said, noting our surprise. "I mean, I wouldn't do anything after they moved all the patients in – just before. I mean, I don't know if I'd do anything but just wish for a flood or something to knock that building down. I mean, I don't know what I mean. I don't know what I'd do. But first, I need to find out what he did."

"Way to go, Beth-a-weth," Amber said, clapping Merribeth on the back. I squeezed Merribeth's hand and she squeezed mine even tighter. "We're here for you," Amber said. "We're behind you

100 percent."

"OK," Merribeth said, quite a bit more softly now and swallowing hard. "OK. Well, I guess I'll tell them to look for a different second-grade teacher for the rest of the spring," she said, barely audibly. "I guess I'll tell them I'm busy." She looked at us uncertainly and tried to blink away her tears. "Well, OK, then."

Chapter 8

Merribeth's Cappuccino Brownies

2 cups vanilla wafer crumbs, lightly packed
1 14-ounce can sweetened condensed milk
1 teaspoon instant coffee powder dissolved in 1 teaspoon boiling water
2 Tablespoons unsweetened cocoa
1/2 cup chopped chocolate chips
1-1/2 cup chopped walnuts
Powdered sugar

Preheat oven to 350 degrees. Butter an 8-inch square pan. In a medium-sized bowl, stir together vanilla wafer crumbs and sweetened condensed milk. Blend in dissolved coffee powder and cocoa. Stir in chocolate chips and nuts. Spread batter evenly in pan.

Bake 25 minutes, or until done. Cool.
Sift powdered sugar over top and cut into squares. Makes a panful of brownies. Cut them as big or little as you'd like.

M erribeth waited until a Sunday morning when her family was away at church. Then she sneaked into her family's home, the one that her father had told her never to enter again, and headed straight for his study. She figured any incriminating arson evidence would be in his room, with its old-fashioned, wide-slatted venetian blinds that always were drawn. She told us about her exploits that evening, after she'd invited us over for her version of a yard sale. She'd boxed up all her possessions, expecting she'd be moving back to Milwaukee for that second-grade job, and now that she'd decided to stay in Weewampum longer, she realized there were some items it didn't pay to unpack. She was going to give us an extra set of dishes, some surplus towels, and a macramé flowerpot holder if we'd just come over and get them. She even baked some cappuccino brownies and brewed a big pot of peppermint tea. If it had been Amber, she would have tried to sell the stuff. I would have tossed it on the curb. But Merribeth was all about sharing, so Amber wound up with a set of china with delicate pink and gold freesias hand-painted around the fluted edges. I got the flower-pot holder, which Merribeth had macraméed years ago when she and her now-three-years-decamped ex-spouse Charlie lived in the little brick house in Milwaukee, with its view from the bathroom window of Lake Michigan. Marta had agreed to babysit Star that evening if Amber would bring home the tulip-and-daffodil silk flower wreath that Merribeth also was unloading.

Charlie had always hated that wreath, thinking it too sissified – which is why Merribeth had clung to it after the divorce and had hammered it on her front door, like a flag of liberation. But now she had decided it was time to move on. She was tired of having any connection to her once-true-love, whom she'd caught on the night of his loan company's Christmas party in the back seat of a red Subaru belonging to his workmate, Sheila Tate. When Merribeth discovered them, Charlie was wearing nothing except the reindeer tie Merribeth had surprised him with that morning. The tie was more than Sheila was wearing.

Amber and I were surprised how quickly Merribeth dispatched with Charlie. We figured she'd give him another chance – not that he deserved it – but she didn't. By New Year's, Charlie was out the door and by the following Christmas, Merribeth was a free woman, although she didn't act like one. She immersed herself in teaching, signing up for every extra class and convention during the school year and enrolling as a full-time student in a master's program in education during summer vacations. She confessed to us in phone conversations how lonely she was and how hard it was to work with kids who didn't want to learn. And they had parents who could care less if their children came to school at all, and then there were the administrators who didn't provide enough of the basic supplies, like books and pencils and paper, and would just shake their heads as if she were some kind of troublemaker if she did anything except smile and tell them that everything was oh, just so fine. That's why I wasn't too surprised when she'd taken a leave to help Amber with Amberosia's. Merribeth must have been totally burned out and in need of some R&R.

But as we munched our brownies and Amber gloated about the

expensive dishes that now were hers, I had a hard time pretending to be patient until Merribeth got around to revealing what she had unearthed about her father's arson proclivities. Finally, she pulled up a folding chair to our table and perched on the chair's edge like a chickadee, ready to take flight at the slightest noise or movement.

Her voice was soft as feathers as she told us, "I was worried my family would get back from church the whole time I was there. I'd given myself just the hour I knew they'd all be gone. I'm not sure what I was afraid would happen if they got back and found me still there; I suppose a scene with my father. Even though he'd banned me from the house, I knew my mother would be happy to see me."

Merribeth said she'd meet her mother for lunch on occasion and that her mother kept telling her not to cross her father, to apologize, to mend fences.

"But I was beginning to feel it was my father, not I, who had some serious apologizing to do," Merribeth said, her face and body looking more angular than usual.

I guess I really hadn't realized how deeply Merribeth resented her father's involvement in the hospital move project nor how crushed she was by her banishment from her family home.

She said her father's study "was the only place, really, that I needed to search. The rest of the house was our family's space, but the study was totally my father's territory.

"The door was closed just as it always was. It fit tightly against the carpet and I had to push it open with my knee. When I got inside, the room was as familiar as ever, quiet, the air not moving. I know it's silly, but I always felt like a trapped bird in that room."

Come to think of it, I'd never been in Mr. H's study, although I'd practically lived at Merribeth's house when we were small.

"It was just like this, too quiet, a little bit too warm, that first evening my father called me into his room when I was six and it was just before Thanksgiving," Merribeth said, not looking at us, almost talking to herself. Then she glanced at us, surprised at what she'd just said.

She blushed and smiled. We smiled back.

"Good brownies," Amber said and reached for another one. Merribeth blushed.

"So, what did you find in there, Merribeth?" I prompted her. Merribeth rolled her eyes.

"I'm sorry," she said, embarrassed. "It's silly to bring this up. You know, talk about how my father used to be."

"No, it's not," Amber said. "Wendy complains about Seal all the time."

"I do not," I said.

"Oh, right," Amber said. "Well, you used to. You still do. We just don't hear about it as much with you hiding out 2,000 miles away."

"Stop it, now," Merribeth said. Amber asked, "What happened in that room, Merribeth, you know, with your father?"

"Oh, nothing. That's just where I learned to read."

"Well, that's a good thing," Amber said, washing down the brownie with a mouthful of tea.

"I guess so," Merribeth said, fixing her eyes on the far wall.

"Sister Mary Violetta at this boarding school in Tangiers taught me to read," Amber said, grabbing for brownie number three. "The wicked witch. She'd slap our fingers with a ruler every time we fucked up."

Merribeth pursed her lips at Amber but then focused on the wall again and started talking in a monotone about how excited she was the day that Miss Norton, our first-grade teacher, gave us our first primer. It had a soft cover and about a dozen different words in it. "Run, Dick. Run, Jane. Run, Sally. Run, Spot."

Amber and I joined in. "'Run, Spot, run. See Spot. See Spot run.'"

Amber strode over to the refrigerator, grabbed a carton of mocha almond fudge ice cream from the freezer and scooped out a big bowl for herself.

"Want some?" she asked. We shook our heads no.

Merribeth said she was eager to read and felt she was doing well in class. Amber plopped onto her chair and said between mouthfuls of mocha almond fudge, "You know, Merry Sunshine, come to think of it, maybe you could tell us some other time about what you were like when you were six. Did you dig up any dirt on your old man?"

Merribeth stopped, sat back, and stared at Amber until Amber paused with her spoon in midair and looked back at Merribeth.

"I'd really like you to listen now, Amber," Merribeth replied in her Ms. Hartwell voice.

I'd heard Merribeth use that voice on Charlie on occasion, not that it had done much good. I knew in the classroom, Merribeth must be steel.

"I've never told you this before," Merribeth said, "and I'm not sure why it seems important to tell it to you now." Her voice wavered a little but still sounded quite firm. It was a voice that made Amber and me feel as if we were six years old and that we couldn't do anything else but listen to Ms. Hartwell.

Merribeth said that night in November, when her father had summoned her into his study, "I walked in and stood looking around. I kind of felt like I was with a student tour group at the Weewampum County Museum. I wasn't allowed in his study, except to vacuum or dust, and then I would be so busy pushing things out of the way and hurrying to get out of there before my father returned that I'd scarcely look around. So now, this was one of the first times I'd seen the room at night and without having to hurry or with a vacuum cleaner in my hand. It was the kind of room where you were careful not to break anything and where it was hard to catch your breath."

She looked at us. I shrugged. Amber kept eating ice cream. Merribeth sighed, as if seeking something from us that we weren't providing, but then she pressed on.

"There were books from floor to ceiling on every wall, dark leather books with rigid spines. They seemed to be guarding the room, you know, like sentinels. They were dark, masculine colors – black, burgundy, and navy blue. My father sat in a burgundy leather chair that was on wheels and behind a large mahogany desk with a glass top cut to protect the wood. There was a piece of green felt beneath the glass. It was like a real office, and my father was the boss, and maybe he wanted me to be his errand girl. I thought when I could read all the books in this room, I would be as smart as my father, maybe. I wondered if it were even possible to read so many books, and I wondered how long it would take.

"My father said, 'Don't stand there gawking. Come here. Let's just see how you're getting along.'"

Merribeth walked to her father's side and he pulled her onto his knee. He had a book on his desk, a big architecture book with lots of numbers and words.

"His arms circled me like a tight barrel. I liked him holding me, but it scared me just the same. There was no danger I could slip off, but that wasn't it. It was just that I knew I could only read Dick and Jane, and then, not really, and this was an architecture book and I couldn't read one word. My father held me there, in his world of words and leather and numbers. I wanted to read for him, and he wouldn't let me leave until I could put row after row of words into patterns."

Merribeth paused for breath and glanced our way.

"Pervert," Amber said, her spoon dinging as she scraped the last drops of ice cream from her bowl.

"Shut up, Amber!" Merribeth blurted.

"Go on," I urged Merribeth.

"I stumbled over the words," she said. "I could only read the 'thes' and 'ands.' It was so embarrassing for me. My father expected I could do much, much better. I felt the tears coming, and I knew my father wouldn't want to see them, so I plowed ahead as best I could. I wanted to show him how smart I was, but I really wasn't, and that's what he saw. I couldn't read the words, and the ones that I could made no sense to me at all.

"'I can't do it, Daddy,' I told him.

"But he said, 'You could if you didn't spend so much time running in and out of this house and over to Wendy's.'

"I hadn't realized until then I was spending a lot of time running in and out of the house, but I was too afraid to say anything. Then my father said, 'Well, Rome wasn't built in a day,' and stood up. I slid off his leg and almost fell but I caught my balance. He didn't seem to notice but I do remember him trying to shake the creases out of his right pant leg."

Amber stretched her arms. "Perverted asshole," she said.

"He is not!" Merribeth snapped. "He's just a little scary." She paused.

"So, uh, maybe it might be possible he had something to do with the restaurant," she nearly whispered. She started trembling. "He hates it that I'm against the new hospital," Merribeth said before breaking into sobs.

Amber patted Merribeth's shoulder. "We're here for you, Beth-a-weth."

Merribeth tried to pull herself together. It wasn't quite working.

Not being the most sympathetic soul on the scene, I prodded, "Did you find anything in his room this morning?"

Merribeth snuffled, then looked at me as if I'd caught her daydreaming at her own arson trial. Her tears dried remarkably quickly as she told how she had opened her father's middle desk drawer, where he kept all the household bills. She hadn't seen anything unusual. The electric bill needed to be paid for the month, but it wasn't overdue and everything else seemed paid up to date. She'd found another checkbook in a bottom drawer; it looked like her father's business account, although it just had his name and nothing else printed on the checks. It looked as if the entries were for utilities and office supplies and such.

"I wasn't sure what I was looking for, and I didn't find it," Merribeth said.

She said the top of her father's desk was bare, but she had found some family photos in silver-plated frames stacked on top of one another in the second desk drawer down on the right.

Merribeth paused, then got up to brew us another pot of tea. I wished she would just hurry up and tell us what she'd found.

When she returned with the full pot, she said her wedding photo was in the stack of pictures, as well as a photo of her father, barbecuing, and one of her brother, Joey, on leave from the Army at Christmastime and posing with the rest of the family in front of the Christmas tree.

"You know," Merribeth said, "Joey always was my father's favorite. But maybe because he was a boy, my father felt uncomfortable, that he'd seem too soft, if he focused all his affection and reading efforts on Joey, so that left me, a girl, the next in line. I read to him in there for eight years."

"You are a damn good reader," Amber pointed out. "Merribeth, don't try to figure the creep out. What else did you find?"

Merribeth said she didn't find any incriminating evidence in her father's desk, but there was a closet in his study that she'd never looked inside before. All she discovered there, however, were some suits in plastic garment bags, more books, and a dress hat. She felt there must be some telltale sign in his room of something her father was doing that he shouldn't be. On a hunch, she pulled some books off the shelves in the study, but all she found was a thin layer of dust. She put the books back and tidied up the desk so her father wouldn't suspect she'd been rifling through his things. She glanced at her watch. It was 11:27. Her family would be home in about 15 minutes. Then Merribeth had an inspiration.

"I'm not sure where it came from," she told us. "I could have sneaked out of there without leaving a trace. But I walked to the windows and debated whether to open the blinds wider. Instead, I tugged the cord and pulled the blinds to their top-most position. They rose so smoothly; they almost seemed to flutter up there. The sunlight poured into the room and the gilt titles on those books just glowed. I saw *Tom Sawyer, The History of Architecture, The Vision of Louis Henry Sullivan*, the Bible. I'd read all those books, although I couldn't remember them very well now, except for the Bible. I know that pretty well. It seemed a shame those books should just glitter all by themselves in this room. The sunlight splashed off the glass top of my father's desk. It made rainbows and prisms on the carpet and walls."

Merribeth paused and took a breath. She glanced at us, embarrassed, that she'd gotten carried away just from opening a venetian blind. She told us she'd looked again at her watch. It was 11:35 a.m. Time to go. She backed out of the room, watching the glowing titles and bobbing colors. She hadn't discovered anything more about her father. But she wondered what he would think when he got home and walked into his room.

Merribeth giggled, then laughed by herself until Amber and I joined in. It was funny thinking of severe Mr. Hartwell coming home to this happy, cheerful room.

"So where does that leave us?" Amber finally asked. "How do we prove your old man burned down Amberosia's?"

"Maybe he didn't," Merribeth said. "I couldn't find any proof. Maybe there isn't any."

"Maybe you just didn't look in the right place," I suggested.

Merribeth jerked her head back a little. Maybe she thought I was proposing I could have done a better job, and who knows, maybe I was. I was exasperated that Merribeth was obeying her father's edict to stay out of the house and that she felt she had to sneak inside and not just fling open the front door and stride in, proclaiming she was ready for Sunday dinner. On the other hand, Merribeth couldn't very well search Mr. H's study with him there, so maybe it wasn't so dumb that she'd sneaked in.

Merribeth and Amber looked at me.

"What do you mean?" Amber said.

"Well," I said, "we haven't checked out everything. We found all those identification numbers. They could lead somewhere. And maybe there are police records. Maybe there are things we don't know about."

"Well, no shit, Sherlock," Amber said. "But if we don't know about them, how are we going to investigate them?"

"The way a reporter does," I blurted, not thinking, just responding to Amber's sarcastic tone. Sarcasm was my specialty, not hers. Investigation was my specialty, not hers. Why did she feel she needed to challenge me? I knew what I was talking about. What was I talking about?

Amber and Merribeth stared at me skeptically.

What was I proposing? I didn't really have any more tricks up my sleeve than Amber or Merribeth did.

"OK," I said. "Maybe I can figure some things out, look into more things. I've got the training, you know."

"Fine," Amber said. "You just go right ahead, Wendy. Nobody's stopping you. And if you find something to pin on Lars or Mr. H., I'll give you the Amber Moore Merit Badge for Shit-Kicking Journalism."

"Oh, Wendy," Merribeth said. "Don't do anything I wouldn't do."

"Yeah, right."

Why on earth had I spoken up? Some latent need to prove my superiority over my friends? I was always ready to blame Amber for having such a big mouth, but maybe it was time I started accepting that mine wasn't exactly Size Petite.

Chapter 9

Spatz Burger

1/4 pound black Angus ground beef, shaped into patty
1 sesame seed bun, sliced in half
Butter
Seasoning salt
Pepper
Shredded iceberg lettuce
1 tomato slice
2 slices of onion
1/8 cup sauerkraut
Thousand Island dressing
Ketchup
Mustard
Pickle relish
Dill pickle spear (uncooked)

Place beef patty and onion slices on a hot grill or in a medium-hot frying
 pan, coated
with a tablespoon of vegetable oil.
When the blood has burned off and the color has turned a grayish-brown,
flip the
burger.
Use a spatula to keep the onions from burning.
As the second side of the patty cooks, butter the bun, then toast each half
on the grill.
The bun can be kept moist if placed on a lettuce leaf on the grill.
When patty is starting to get goldeny-brown, it's done.
The onions are done when they start turning brown.
Remove patty, onions, and bun from grill as each gets done.
"Butter" inside of bun with Thousand Island dressing.
Place patty on bun.
Add lettuce, onions, tomato, sauerkraut, ketchup, mustard, and pickle relish.
Serve with dill pickle spear.

I'd set myself up, so now I felt I'd have to root out some evidence
so I could utter a few brilliant deductions about Mr. H's and
Lars' guilt before locking my lips tightly and stashing away the key
in a safety deposit box. I didn't know where to go next.

There was the police station to check for old reports, I supposed, and there were birth and marriage records. Then there were state Department of Motor Vehicle records, state and federal tax filings, credit reports, telephone bills, and library book and video checkout records. The more I thought, the more that popped to mind.

It made me tired just thinking of the work that lay ahead. I'd never enjoyed anything remotely resembling investigative reporting. It was hours of drudgery for usually slim results, as well as a lot of manipulation of potential sources or outright confrontation with them. Give me a feature story any day about the man who grew a record-size kumquat or the kid who played his violin with the local symphony at age 7. Come to think of it, just give me the kumquat man. The kid makes me queasy, makes me question myself too much, like what was I doing at age 7 besides throwing apples at Merribeth's brother? Or at age 14 or 21 or 35, for that matter? Come to think of it, I really didn't like reporting all that much – always writing someone else's words, listening to the person brag. I was a reluctant public servant, not temperamentally suited for it, but nevertheless, I did it fairly well. And one of the things that any good journalist learns quickly is how to cut corners, how to avoid doing all the work.

So I phoned my friend Sonja Hunt, the police reporter in Santa Dolorosa, to see if she had any contacts who might help me out. I knew she was dating a hunky police captain, who lifted weights and took muscle-mass supplements. They'd met at the gym after Sonja stopped smoking Camel straights and replaced them with every candy bar and chip entree the vending machine at the *Santa Dolorosa Advance* offered and then needed a flab-busting antidote.

Over the phone, Sonja and I exchanged what passed for wit between us:

"Hey, Sonja, still lusting after that guy in uniform?"

"Hey, Wendy, still loafing around Cow Country?" And then I asked Sonja if she could ask El Capitain for some suggestions or outright help in checking out Lars and Mr. H.

"Say no more," Sonja said. "I'll call you back when I've got the dirt."

Sonja phoned the next day. I think her captain, George Holmes, was trying to impress her with his investigative speed. "George really got into it," Sonja reported. He'd phoned a buddy in the Highway Patrol; another at the Department of Motor Vehicles, and that person knew someone who knew someone in the sister offices in Wisconsin. A friend in the California state attorney general's office knew an examiner in the regional IRS office who knew someone who knew someone and then it was Bingo! We had about as much information on Lars and Mr. H. as we probably ever were going to get. I could always ask Dottie Wentzell to pull the library cards of our two suspects, and I knew she'd do it for me because Seal was my mother, but I also knew she'd immediately tell Seal. And Seal probably would have told me I was being ridiculous and wasting my time, but that wouldn't have stopped me. But I decided to wait until I got the scoop from Sonja before asking Dottie to help me out. Then, after I heard from Sonja, I kind of lost my enthusiasm.

Sonja said Lars and Mr. H. both had reported the property they owned in Weewampum as business deductions, but neither guy seemed to have any vast holdings that we hadn't already uncovered ourselves. Their lives mostly were contained by Weewampum's city limits and neither was extraordinarily wealthy. They were just well-to-do bourgeoisie, plundering their city: good citizens, enthusiastic capitalists, nothing unusual. They were doing fine; there didn't seem to be any compelling financial reason for them to burn down the restaurant. Neither had a criminal record nor any substantial driving or credit problems. No DWIs, no mental commitments, no anything. It was a real letdown. So unless there were police records squirreled away somewhere not readily accessible or there was other incriminating evidence in someone's secret cupboard, it didn't seem likely that Lars or Mr. H. had put his hand to a match.

If they had burned down our restaurant, their motivations would have been totally emotional, and although each of these guys had enough quirks to be a lifetime meal ticket for any therapist bold enough to treat him, neither guy would seem to have been so threatened by us that he'd have turned Amberosia's to ashes. That meant either some customer we'd poisoned or one of Amber's amours might have done it, but the more I thought about that, the more unlikely it seemed. The only other people with emotional ties to the place were the three of us – and possibly Seal, Mrs. H., and Amber's folks because of their family ties to us – but I knew the Threesome had been otherwise occupied and to suspect our elders, with the exception of Mr. H., was about as farfetched as blaming Dottie Wentzell or Florence Schmidt, or Warren Caramel, himself.

I was stumped, stymied; more investigation seemed hardly worth it.

So when Sonja said our boss, Irma, wanted to talk to me and asked if it was OK to put Irma on the line, I didn't try to wriggle out of a conversation with the Boss Lady. As might be expected, Irma wanted to know when I was returning. She had been remarkably understanding – for her – to let me take the time off to be with Seal, but I knew her patience must be wearing thin as the ice on Lake Weewampum in early April.

"So, how's your mother doing?" she asked, trying to sound as if she really cared.

"Oh, fine," I said. "She's getting stronger all the time."

"So, then, you'll be coming back soon?"

"Sure, I guess so," I said before thinking.

"How's two weeks from Monday? Can I put you on the schedule?"

"Sure. Why not?" I said before considering carefully the ramifications of resuming my post amidst the Avocado Council's press releases and the free olive oil samples that cluttered my desk.

After I hung up, though, I felt I'd made a good decision, that I needed to get back into my groove. Next morning, over our Cheerios, I told Seal I'd be back at work in two weeks.

She grabbed my cereal bowl from me although I was only half-finished, dumped the contents into the sink, and turned on the garbage disposal. When she'd rinsed out the bowl, she said, "Don't you need more time to get the best airplane rate?"

Then she stalked out of the kitchen and into her room and bammed the door shut.

I wiped some drops of milk off the kitchen table with a paper towel. The telephone rang before I could decide if I should follow Seal to see if she was truly upset or leave her alone since she might just be tired, or she might just be Seal.

Merribeth was on the other end and her voice kept fading in and out like a car alarm whose battery needs replacing, as if she were unsure how she felt. She said Warren Caramel had just left her apartment and she'd told him "everything I know about the fire and more. And he still thinks one of us did it. I hate to even bring it up, but he's the kind of man who really makes me uncomfortable."

"What do you mean?" I asked her. I poured myself another cup of coffee. This might be a long chat.

"Oh, you know. The way he looks at you. It just makes you want to confess, even though you haven't done anything."

"What did you tell him, Merribeth?" I asked. I hoped she hadn't inadvertently said something dumb that would steer Warren down a totally wrong track pursuing her.

"Oh, nothing. Well, he seemed so sincere and firm about wanting to solve the case that I wanted to help him, although I'm not sure why. When I offered him some tea and a muffin with blackberry jam, he almost seemed to sneer at me."

"That's Warren for you, a real Prince Charming," I said.

"Oh, he's not so bad, I guess," Merribeth said. "Anyway, he just sat on my kitchen chair and just stared at me, so to get him to leave, I tried to help him think of some places he might check as evidence."

Even though I felt now that solving the case was mostly hopeless, I told Merribeth, "I hope you told him he needs to unearth all possible records about your father and Lars."

"Well," Merribeth gulped. "I sort of did. Now, I'm feeling kind of guilty, but I told him about what we found out about them."

Huh. This was a real step forward for Merribeth. Normally, she never would have considered speaking ill about anyone to a stranger like Warren, even if that anyone were Adolph Hitler or Atilla the Hun. Not that her father or Lars was in that category. Well, they were in their own category.

"So, what did he say, Merribeth?"

"At first, he didn't say anything, he just laughed this strange little laugh. I could tell he thought I was being ridiculous and possibly that I was just trying to take the spotlight off myself. He kept asking me over and over what kind of money problems Amberosia's was having, and I kept telling him we were making a small profit, we were doing all right. I kept telling him over and over that we'd worked so hard to open the restaurant and keep it running that we wouldn't have had the heart to do anything except take care of it.

"But he didn't seem to believe, not even for a second, that we would be running Amberosia's for any reason except making money. And since we weren't making a whole lot, he was absolutely positive we'd just want to turn our backs on it, go on to other things. It just made me so angry that he couldn't see that we had worked so hard that we'd have no reason to just burn away all our efforts. I was just so upset that I insisted he should seriously investigate my father's background. And do you know what he said?"

Merribeth had been rushing through her words as if she were trying to flee a burning building, but now she had to stop and gulp for a breath.

"Do you know what he said?" she demanded of me.

"No. What?" I replied. I could imagine Warren wasn't likely to buy Merribeth's line of reasoning because Warren Caramel played golf with Merribeth's father every Saturday morning in summer. "What did the big guy say?"

"He said my father was an honorable man and it was a shame he'd been burdened with such ungrateful children. That my brother Joey had broken my father's heart by going off to Vietnam instead of to college and that now I was even worse. I was the worst possible daughter, and it was no wonder my father had cut his ties with me. After all my father had done for me, how could I possibly accuse him of arson?"

At this point, as probably could have been predicted, Merribeth burst into big, whopping sobs that sounded sort of as if you turned an electric mixer off and on, off and on.

"Merribeth," I told her. "Warren Caramel is not worth crying about. If you want to cry about something, cry about Afghanistan, cry about the short span of a human life, cry about us still being stuck here in Weewampum. But don't cry about some dolt who's not willing to do his job and follow up on the clues you've dumped into his lap. You've done absolutely nothing wrong."

It was hard to make out what Merribeth was saying as she cried over the phone. But I did hear, "I've betrayed my father," to which I said that from what she'd told us, it sounded as if her father had betrayed her every night of her life by taking advantage of his power to intimidate her.

"Oh, maybe you're right," she said between sobs. Actually, she seemed to get over the crying part pretty fast. "They're all in this together. All these men. They control everything in this town. We'll never solve who set the fire," Merribeth said as the crying tapered off but her voice still wavered. "They won't let us. Just what are we trying to do here, anyway? These men could be dangerous. They are dangerous."

"Well, I don't know, Merribeth. I don't know if we'll ever solve it. We're not Columbo. And I don't know if it really matters all that much if we do. We've got our own lives. Maybe we should just put this in back of us and move on."

"I just don't know," Merribeth said, her voice still wavering. "I just don't know what we're supposed to do. Did you find out anything more?"

I told her I hadn't.

"I just don't know what to think," Merribeth said. "I just don't seem to know anything anymore."

In my opinion, this was not a new condition in which Merribeth found herself. From my perspective, she never seemed to know how to choose the smartest path. Maybe it was new for her to realize she didn't know what was in her best interest. But it wasn't new that she seemed to base so many of her life's critical decisions on what someone else thought, on what might please someone else, on what was expected, and not on what she wanted to do.

She'd married Charlie because that's what he'd wanted and what her parents expected, and she'd been dating him for so long, since our freshman year in high school, that by the time we'd graduated from college and Charlie and Merribeth were still an item, it seemed it was the next logical leap to make.

Merribeth's wedding was when I'd finally decided there was no way in the world I could ever be happy in Weewampum or any place within a 500-mile radius. Not that Merribeth actually ever lived there again after college, either, but she lived in Milwaukee, which was close enough to not totally escape Weewampum's sphere of influence.

I just had a hard time accepting that Merribeth would be willing to throw her life away on a loser like Charlie. I guess it's not fair to call him a loser; it's just that he was more unfocused than Merribeth, Amber, and I were – which was quite a feat in itself – and seemed to have the personality of a metal bolt. His father owned a Weewampum hardware store, and Charlie didn't want to work there when he got out of school. Charlie studied business in college but had no clue what he'd do once he received his diploma – if he got that far. He was nice enough in a wishy-washy sort of way, but engine coolant, not blood, seemed to chug through his veins. He was just always the same temperature, calm, pleasant, bland. If Merribeth had to get married, then I wanted her spouse to be an astronaut, an archeologist, an artiste. But Merribeth assured me that Charlie was her perfect match, so similar to her, so sensitive. I wanted to make Merribeth understand that she was far, far the better person than Charlie, but I just couldn't get through to her.

Merribeth scoured every bridal store in the Upper Midwest until she discovered the most dead-fish-looking color of chartreuse that I'd ever seen in my life. Chartreuse was the color of my maid-of-honor dress. I sulked about being my best friend's maid of honor – although I suppose I would have sulked even more if she

114

had asked Amber, not me, to do the honors. Merribeth thought chartreuse was a nice accent to the lemon-yellow, dotted Swiss bridesmaid dresses that Amber and Merribeth's twin sisters wore. I felt like a walking gherkin, but if that's what Merribeth wanted for her wedding, then I wasn't going to object this one time.

Just before the main event, I was sitting in my chartreuse, smoking, on the stone steps of First American Lutheran Church, thinking about Merribeth and Charlie and what a mistake this was going to be, when Merribeth's father stormed out of the church in his tuxedo and jerked me to my feet as if I were his valet, sneaking a smoke. He towed me inside and shoved me into the wedding party line, even though there still were five minutes until the "Wedding March" got underway.

Mr. H. put me in an even fouler mood than I'd been in. I didn't enjoy being treated like his chattel. I also was feeling like a hypocrite and traitor for being part of this pageant in which Merribeth would lose her freedom. Then I spotted Amber doing the Frug with her partner, Bobby Russell, across the church's limestone floor. Although the bridesmaid dresses had rather modest scoop necklines, Amber had somehow discovered a Wonder Bra before they became really popular and was displaying the most remarkable cleavage that even she didn't possess.

It just fueled my irritation to see Amber exhibiting herself in that yellow dress like some overgrown marigold, ready to pluck, so when Randy Seccombe, my appointed escort, sidled up and took my arm, I just rolled my eyes and looked away, which I guess hurt his feelings, but I could have cared less at that point.

Seal had tried to get me to go out with Randy Seccombe for ages. He was the only boy in the Greater Weewampum area of whom she approved as a potential suitor for me. He'd been the only boy at Cedar Pines Junior High who'd taken ballroom dance lessons the year when Merribeth, Amber, and I signed up for a stint at Mr. Julian's School of the Dance. Amber and I teased Randy about having to watch out or he'd become another Rudolph Nureyev and have to wear tights to work every day for the rest of his life. But Randy just ignored us and kept dancing. He seemed to enjoy it much more than we did. If Randy had stuck with dancing, I could have tolerated him as my wedding escort, I guess. But sometime when he was in high school, Randy found the Lord. And now Randy was locked away in some desolate Lutheran seminary in Iowa, studying to be a pastor.

Seal thought I'd make the perfect pastor's wife. But that was so far away from my thinking, on another planet, in another solar system, that I'd been rude to Randy for years, just to not encourage him. After Mr. Julian's, Randy asked me to go with him to the junior prom, and I turned him down, of course. I told him I didn't believe in proms, and he'd been so understanding that I'd felt bad, but that didn't change my mind. Randy told me he could respect my beliefs, but, nevertheless, I should accompany him to the prom because it might be fun, and we both knew how to dance. I clung to my position as if to my own, personal cross and refused, under any circumstances, to go and tried to avoid Randy after that.

The wedding ceremony went as well as could be expected, I guess. The bouquets of daisies and gladioli that Merribeth had arranged in baskets along the center aisle and at the base of the altar were overpowered by the 40-foot plastic cross that dominated the front of the church. It looked as if it were made from that same hard, molded plastic that fast-food restaurants, liquor stores, and car washes use as their main signs outside. It stretched from floor to ceiling and must have had two or three dozen fluorescent tube lights inside. I guess it was supposed to be showing us the light. I thought it might have looked kind of campy in the parking lot, but it was a definite taste faux pas as the major art element in the church's sanctuary.

Pastor Esker droned on about marital responsibilities so long I was sure I'd fall off my chartreuse, died-to-match, satin high heels as we, the faithful wedding party, stood freeze-framed and smiling at the altar. Finally, Pastor Esker reached the exchanging of vows. Charlie breezed through his part just fine. But Merribeth froze and couldn't get out more than two words at a time. I felt sorry for her, but I could understand she might be having second thoughts.

116

She just kept smiling sheepishly at Charlie, and he just kept staring at her, as if she were some kind of sideshow attraction, not helping her one bit, so I decided to go to the rescue of my friend and help her out of her immediate jam into a much bigger one.

I stepped to her side and after Pastor Esker would say a phrase like "to have and to hold," I'd whisper one word at a time into Merribeth's ear and she'd say that word and wait for the next prompt from me. We made it through, although it probably was the longest pledging of troths in the history of First American Lutheran Church. Pastor Esker pronounced Charlie and Merribeth husband and wife. And wouldn't you know, Merribeth started crying when Charlie tried to kiss her in front of the congregation?

Then, Merribeth and Charlie ran down the aisle toward the front doors as if Pastor Esker had turned into the Holy Ghost, himself, and was chasing them down the aisle and rattling his chains. I had to laugh. The ceremony had gone much better than I'd expected; I'd thoroughly enjoyed its theater-of-the-absurd elements.

By the reception, Merribeth had recovered from her shell shock and stood like a delighted princess welcoming the guests who'd turned out for her spring ball. Randy Seccombe and I danced a couple times, a waltz and a polka, to the music of Rollie and the FlimFlam boys, a five-piece polka ensemble much in demand in Weewampum for weddings, graduations, and company picnics. I had to admit Randy was a good dancer. If he hadn't signed on to be one of God's spokesmen, I might have tried to carry on a conversation with him that night. But before the band even took its first break, Amber and Bobby came whirling up to Randy and me and said they were going to take a walk along the beach; did we want to come along? I said sure, because I wasn't looking forward to chitchatting with Randy all night.

Merribeth had booked the reception at the Water's Edge Inn, the most upscale restaurant in Weewampum, which is to say they used cloth napkins and two forks. Outside, in back, the restaurant had its own dock, and one dilapidated rowboat, sitting right-side-up on some rocks. Amber headed for it as if it were a lighthouse beacon.

"Oh, let's go for a ride," she bubbled. "It would be so much fun." She stepped inside the boat and plopped down on the plank seat. The boat was just inches from the lake. Bobby pushed the boat into the water and laughed and Amber giggled. Then Bobby jumped in and held the boat in place with the oars dug into the sand.

I don't know why I did it. I guess I just wanted to get away from the reception and didn't want to be alone with Randy and didn't want to make conversation with all the guests and be pleasant and pretend that I was happy for Merribeth. Anyway, I jumped into the boat, and then Randy, out of some kind of misplaced sense of chivalry, jumped in after me to make sure I and everyone else would return safe and sound.

It was a lovely June night and the moon was full, and once we got away from the dock, Lake Weewampum smelled less like rotting seaweed and dead carp. There were gentle waves, nothing alarming, the air was kind of cool. It was liberating to be away from the party and kind of funny to be sitting in our wedding clothes in a rowboat.

Amber pulled off her shoes and hiked up her dress and tried to dangle her feet into the water.

"We should go skinny-dipping," she said, laughing. "We should give those people at the reception something to toast."

I was beginning to regret going out in the boat with Amber. She seemed giddier than normal and much happier than the situation called for. She was trying to dip her toes into the water, and our boat was tipping way too far towards her side.

"Knock it off, Amber," I said. "Sit on your seat and row and burn off some of that excess energy."

"Oh, Wendy," she said, "you're always such a big party poo..." and then I'm not sure what happened, but a big wave came along. It bounced our boat up and slapped it down, and somehow in the process, Amber tumbled out.

Her yellow dotted Swiss dress floated out like a parachute. Amber started bobbing up and down.

"Help!" she yelled. "I can't swim." Her dress was totally wet now and starting to sink beneath the water. Amber was thrashing around, probably 10 feet from our boat. Bobby stretched an oar out to her, but she was too far away to reach it. She was slapping the water and swallowing big mouthfuls. I started pulling off my shoes. I had to get to her. Before I could wriggle out of my chartreuse dress, Randy stripped to his BVDs and dived over my head into the lake.

He tore into the water like a heat-seeking missile and reached Amber in a couple strokes. He wrapped his arm around her and used a sidestroke to drag her back to the edge of the boat. Getting them in was the hard part. They almost dumped the rowboat over but then managed to flop inside. Bobby and I rowed us back to shore.

Amber was shivering. So was Randy. I knew Seal kept a blanket in the trunk of her car for winter emergencies out on the road. As I hurried Amber and Randy to the parking lot, Mr. Hartwell was out there, shaking hands with some guys in suits.

Randy was just in his wet underwear and it didn't leave too much to the imagination. Amber, well, you could see through her soaking wet dress. We had to walk past Mr. Hartwell to get to my mother's car. When Mr. Hartwell saw us, he pretended he didn't know us.

Wendell Krohn, in his powder-blue leisure suit, observed to Mr. H. and his other pals, "Ah, youth."

They all snickered kind of low and dirty. "Nice ass," one of them said. I think it was Pete Traeger, the Allstate salesman.

"Tits like loaves of French bread," said George Flacon, a personal-injury lawyer.

The men snorted some more and slapped George on the back. Mr. H. didn't speak up, just stood there smirking. And then Amber seemed to see them for the first time and shook her wet hair back and strutted to the car, shaking her butt. It was kind of funny and gutsy, and I was proud of her for that, but nevertheless, I wanted to kill her for risking her life and humiliating us and playing her part in this Weewampum farce.

"Forget the girl," one of the men said. "Did you see the guy? Hung like an elephant."

Randy Seccombe just kept marching toward the car, as if he truly were walking in God's footsteps.

I turned to those creeps and yelled at them, "Just shut the fuck up! They could have drowned."

That really cracked them up, but we made it to the car. I wrapped Amber and Randy up like bedraggled puppies in my mother's emergency blanket and drove them home and then I returned to our house and crawled into my bed and cried.

That night, I vowed to keep my distance from Weewampum. Mr. Hartwell and his buddies seemed to represent everything I hated about this small, unforgiving place. And Merribeth and Amber were part of it in their own ways because they didn't really reject it, not the way I did. I saw myself as just an observer and judge of Weewampum life, and I found it guilty of bad taste and gladly sentenced myself to a life spent far away. I felt I was destined to a life lived more deeply. I thought I could find this through my work and a change of location. Amber had flaunted and made a joke of her brush with the deep, and Merribeth had been oblivious to what was happening to her friends as she whirled away the evening in the cage of Charlie's arms. So now, as Merribeth finished telling me what Warren Caramel had said to her just minutes ago, I longed to get back to my life in Santa Dolorosa, where the people were a little more sophisticated. I felt the same kind of estrangement from her as I had years ago at her wedding.

"Merribeth, you did the right thing," I assured her, impatiently.

"OK," she said. "I guess you're right. Oh, Wendy, you'll always be my best friend. I love you, Wen."

"I love you, too, Merribeth," I said and cut her off with a click of the phone.

For about 30 seconds, I felt like the biggest heel in the universe for feeling so alienated from Merribeth and from Amber, too. And then the phone rang. It was Amber.

She reminded me the Lemmert brothers – Bill and Stan – had opened their new restaurant and microbrewery, Spats, over the weekend, and Amber was dying to check out the competition. Actually, so was I. By all reports the new establishment, a block from Amberosia's ruins, was doing blockbuster business. I phoned back Merribeth, and we all agreed to meet at Spats for lunch.

Bill and Stan had built wooden booths along both walls of Spats, and there was a wall of long windows facing the street where the brothers had crowded in some high-gloss-finished oak tables. The copper brewing pipes and tanks in back gleamed like a shiny jungle gym. The menu was strictly sandwiches and beer, and the place smelled like the brewery it was, and it was packed. Even Amberosia's on its best days had never been this popular. The floor was wood planks and covered with sawdust full of peanut shells from the free bucket of peanuts Bill and Stan provided at each table. I kept thinking of all the saliva and germs on the floor from those shells, and it kind of took away my appetite.

We'd heard that Spats was busy at lunch, so we arrived at 1:30 p.m. The place still was jammed, but we only had to wait five minutes for a booth to clear. Amber brought along Star in the baby sling, wearing her like a bauble she expected everyone to admire. Amber and Merribeth ordered burgers, fries, and iced tea. I just stuck to an order of onion rings and some Springtime Red Ale brewed on the premises. Star was napping. She really was a good kid.

Her mother shouldn't bring her to a bar. It could predispose her to follow in her mom's footsteps.

"I can't believe you'd bring your daughter to a tavern," Merribeth observed.

"Gotta start 'em young," Amber replied, kind of edgy. "Why do you think they'd go for that peanut gimmick even more so than for our homemade tomato bisque soup or peanut-butter fudge cheesecake?" she asked, surveying the spilling-over Spats crowd.

"It's just Weewampum," I said like a reflex. "What do you expect?"

Merribeth didn't say anything, but Amber replied, "Aw, c'mon, Wen, give the old town a break."

The waitress brought us laminated menus with pictures of the items so we could point to them.

I expected Amber to say something snide about the menus but, instead, she said, "We could do this, too. You know, show them what a crêpe or sun-dried tomato pasta looks like."

Merribeth seemed amused and smiled at Star, who was snuggled inside her baby sling, fast asleep.

"You heard that Warren paid a call on Merribeth?" I asked Amber.

"No shit!" she said and looked at me. "You're next."

Then Amber was all ears to learn what Warren had said and concluded, "The man's not playing with a full deck. But never fear, the Fearsome Threesome are going to help him out. So, what did you find out so far in your snooping, Wen?" she asked, looking at me full on, not being sarcastic at all, just expecting I'd truly unearthed some revelatory arson information.

"Well," I said, drawing down the ale the waitress set before me in a chilled mug. "Well, it's like this. I found out just about absolutely nothing."

Amber smiled at me as if to say, "Ha-ha, hotshot," but maybe I just was reading that in.

Merribeth patted me on the arm.

"Well," Merribeth said, not taking her eyes off Star. "Don't feel so bad. Maybe my father and Lars really didn't do it."

"So who does that leave?" I asked my ale mug.

"Don't look at me," Amber said.

"Or me," Merribeth added. They both looked at me.

"Well, I didn't do it," I said huffily.

"We know that," Merribeth said. "Don't get so defensive," Amber said, chug-a-lugging some iced tea. She was trying to remain alcohol-free while she nursed Star. I guess I shouldn't have been drinking in front of her, but, oh well, I was.

"It would have been easier for you to just tell us to go to hell than to burn down the restaurant. I know that," Amber said, rubbing Star's head so her few red hairs stood up straight from the friction.

Our entrees arrived. Amber and Merribeth bit into their burgers. I whirled an onion ring around my right index finger.

"Amberosia's burgers were better," Amber said and put her burger down, then picked it up again. "But I gottta hand it to them. This ain't bad." She sank her teeth in and chewed.

"We could do something like this when we're up and running again – you know, have a burger menu just as a sidelight."

"Uh, Amber," I said. "Merribeth. I talked to my boss. I told her I'll be back in two weeks. I'm sure Amberosia's II will be a real smash, Amb."

Amber must have breathed in and chewed at the same time. She started coughing and Merribeth jumped up to pat her back. Star woke up all panicky and started crying.

Tears streamed down Amber's face as she coughed but she didn't seem in immediate need of a Heimlich maneuver. She waved off Merribeth, who sat down and turned to me, flustered.

"You can't go back now," Merribeth said, her voice high like a bursting bubble. "I'm going to be here at least until September. I thought you'd be here with us, too."

Amber had stopped coughing and was trying to comfort Star and take a long drink of iced tea to settle her throat at the same time. I was afraid we'd have a repeat performance of the coughing episode, but Star simmered down and Amber didn't choke and Amber's success at doing two things at once seemed to infuse her with adrenaline.

"I thought we'd agreed we were going to open up again!" she said, her voice almost restored to full power. She seemed genuinely surprised. "I thought we had a great time at Amberosia's."

"We were having a good time, but we never said one word that we were staying forever, Amber," I told her. "You know that. And now there's no restaurant, so..."

"She's right," Merribeth said, gently.

"There is, too, a restaurant," Amber insisted. "I can't help it that you can't see it right now. But it's there. And you know it."

"Aw, come on, Amb," I said. "What business do any of us have running a restaurant? We don't know that much about the business and it's a whole lot of work."

"You learn while you go. What's so hard about that?" Amber asked. "We were doing all right. No we weren't. We were doing great."

"But I have a job," Merribeth pointed out. "So does Wendy. We were just helping you out for a little while, Amby."

Star looked fretfully at Merribeth and me.

"But both of your jobs suck!" Amber said, bringing her fist down on the table like a gavel. "I was trying to help you out. I thought you both knew that."

Star whimpered, and Amber looked as if she might start crying any minute. Merribeth was teary-eyed, and my throat tightened as if Amber had squeezed it. To tell you the truth, it never had occurred to me that Amber would think she was doing us a favor by giving us a job chopping romaine lettuce and saying, "Have a nice day" at Amberosia's.

"Stay here and help me," Amber argued in her you-can't-turn-down-this-deal, real estate voice. "We can hold this town together and help it grow and help it get even better. But I can't do it by myself."

She reached for our hands, but mine was holding my ale mug, and Merribeth was searching her purse for a tissue. Merribeth found the tissue and blew her nose, then said, "Amber, we've got our own lives now."

"Well, you're at least out there, saving those little kids, Merribeth," Amber said, "but why the hell does Wendy have to be off in La-la-land, writing about how to fry an egg? I thought you hated what you do, Wendomat."

I looked at Amber directly, then closed my eyes. I did hate my job, but it was easy, and it was far away. When I opened my eyes, Amber was smiling kind of tentatively at me. Star was grasping at the air. I think she was hungry, although she was reaching toward Merribeth and me, not Amber.

"I'm sorry, Amber," I said. "I just don't want to live here anymore."

Amber looked at me, unbelieving. "It won't take all that long to get it open again," she said. "Really."

"It's not my thing, Amber," I said, and signaled the waitress for the check.

"Fine," Amber said, as she unbuttoned her blouse to feed Star. "That's just fine, Wendy. If you want to give up the chance to have some real fun with your life, then fine." She looked at me. I felt horribly guilty, until she added, "You uncaring bitch." Then she laughed.

I knew she was joking, just being Amber, but I chose to react to the words, not the intent. I was fed up with her thinking, the way she talked, with this town, with my life. "Fuck you," I snapped at her and grabbed the check.

"No, fuck you," Amber snarled, snatching the check back.

Merribeth seemed shocked and turned her head as if to make sure no other diners were listening to us. And then Merribeth's eyes got really big and so did Amber's and mine, because somehow, Merribeth's father had sat down unnoticed at a table right across from our booth. And apparently, he'd heard every word.

"Well," Mr. Hartwell said, looking at us like a deer hunter about to blast Bambi with a double-barreled shotgun, "wouldn't you know Merribeth and her accomplices would be here, disturbing the peace?"

Merribeth just stared at him, her mouth wide open. I gaped at him, too, but my mouth was closed. Amber, who was nursing Star and partially concealing her actions with a plastic menu, said, "Well, look who's here."

Merribeth was still staring at her father and finally said softly but with the silvery intensity of a saber, "Father, that is no way to speak to me and my friends."

"I'll speak any way I choose to speak to you, Merribeth," Mr. H. replied. "Or maybe I won't speak to you at all."

Merribeth turned to us. "I thought we were just leaving," she said, like the adult and teacher she was. She grabbed at the check under Amber's elbow.

Amber grabbed Merribeth's hand.

"Not so fast, Merribeth," Amber said loudly. "I think your father owes you an apology."

"Amber," Merribeth warned, grabbing for the check but missing. Amber turned her face to Mr. H. "We think you burned down our restaurant, Jimbo," Amber said. "What do you have to say for yourself?"

Mr. H. flushed the color of the tomatoes on the Spats menu. He glared at Amber a moment, then turned to Merribeth and just about scalded the skin off her with his eyes. "You know, Merribeth," he said, his voice like bubbling lava, "Warren Caramel told me that's what you've been saying, that I was somehow responsible for that fire. But I told him he must be exaggerating. My daughter would never accuse her father of something like that."

Merribeth blanched as white as a death star. I'd never seen her looking so fierce. She stood up and took a step toward her father's table.

"I said it," Merribeth said, her eyes sparking like Kali's. "And I meant it." I jumped to Merribeth's side and tried to pull her away.

"You're just upset. Come on, let's go," I told her, surprising myself by playing the role of peacekeeper.

"I'm upset," Merribeth said, brushing me aside like a wool scarf, "because my father has no respect for me. But I just want him to know that respect cuts both ways."

"Come on, Bethy," I said, tugging on her arm. "Let's go."

Merribeth elbowed me and stood free. "Leave me alone," she said. "It's time I fought my own battles."

Mr. H. was studying Merribeth like a microbe.

"If you want to find out who burned down your restaurant," he snapped, "why don't you start with yourself and your girlfriends? Which one of you wanted to stop doing the dishes the most?"

Merribeth breathed in, then said as slowly as a sharp knife slicing a thick steak, "Just fuck you, f-a-t-h-e-r-r-r."

In the background, Amber cheered, "Way to go, Merribeth."

Mr. H. just stared at Merribeth, his mouth hanging as wide open as Amber's blouse. I tried to pull Merribeth away.

"Let's go, Merribeth," I insisted, but Merribeth held her ground like a tall pine with deep roots as she deliberated her next words. Then Mr. H. stormed again.

"Start with those playmates of yours. Or with that loon of a neighbor, Seal Whitby."

What? What was that?

"Just what are you saying?" I yelled at him.

"Come on," Merribeth snarled at me. "I thought we were leaving. Just let it go. You know your mother is weird." She towed me toward the restaurant door.

"Hey," Amber yelled after us. "You don't have to leave just because he's here."

Merribeth turned to Amber and yelled back, "Just shut the fuck up, Amber. Just stay out of my fucking business after this . . . And button up your fucking blouse."

Merribeth dragged me out of the restaurant.

I was stunned. "God, Merribeth," I said, "just calm down. She didn't mean any real harm."

Merribeth just glared at me and shoved me in the direction of Seal's car. "You can just shut the fuck up, too, Wendy," she said. "You all can just shut the fuck up." Merribeth strode to her car and blazed off. I stood waiting on the sidewalk and Amber and Star caught up in a minute.

"Boy, she's on PMS overload," Amber said.

And then I flipped out. "Just shut the fuck up, Amber," I popped off and stormed to Seal's car.

"Yeah? Well, you just shut the fuck up, too," Amber yelled after me. "Just go back to California where you belong."

As I slammed Seal's car door and peeled out of the parking lot, tears obscuring my view, I heard Star wailing and I thought I saw Amber wipe some tears off her own face with the back of a clenched-up fist.

Chapter 10

Dottie and Florence's Bridge Mix

6 Tablespoons butter
1 bag dried pineapple pieces
1 bag dried banana pieces
1 large bag M&M chocolate-covered peanuts or similar candy
1 bag chocolate-covered almonds
1 bag toasted coconut flakes
1 can salted peanuts

Have a large bowl handy. Open the bags and the can. Dump everything in the bowl.
Wash your hands and mix the ingredients. Or you could use a spoon.

Seal had her back to me and was curled in an "S" on the sofa when I stormed into the house from our ladies' luncheon. The door slammed shut before I realized Seal was sleeping. She turned onto her back, then struggled to sit up.

"Who taught you manners?" she snapped.

"Hi, Mom. Sorry," I mumbled on the way to my bedroom, as if I were 6 years old. I wanted to avoid all human contact for at least a couple hours.

"Just a minute," she said, and I halted, midstride. "How was Spats?" she asked. "I hear they've got a filthy floor."

It was strange, the things upon which Seal and I agreed. "You heard right," I said and continued toward my room.

"You shouldn't drink and drive," Seal said to my back. "Your face is red as a beet."

I strode the rest of the way to my room and heard my mother clumping after me.

"I hear that place is really popular," Seal said as I walked inside my own little space. "Much busier than Amberosia's. They must be doing something right."

I turned to close the door and glared at Seal.

"Dottie and Florence are raving about the place," she said.

"That's good," I said, pulling the door halfway shut.

But Seal had wedged her foot in the door. "They've got the kind of food people want," she said. "You're lucky your place is gone."

"I guess so," I said, looking pointedly at her foot, but she apparently wasn't ready to move it. I didn't know what she wanted and I didn't feel like chatting, so I decided to annoy her, which might get her to budge.

"I saw Mr. Hartwell there. He suggested maybe you burned down the restaurant."

That did it. Seal moved her foot. She moved both her feet inside my room. "What?" she said. "He said what?"

"He said that if we wanted to find out who burned down the restaurant, we should start with ourselves ... or you."

"That sounds just like the almighty James A. Hartwell," she sputtered. "He's just trying to pin the blame on anyone but himself."

"What do you mean?" I asked her, suddenly interested in a nice, long conversation.

"Well, you know he's not pleased with you girls for fighting his new hospital, and I'm your mother, so I guess I'm guilty by association. But maybe he was mad enough at you to burn down your restaurant, although it would surprise me if he'd be ambitious enough to plan a fire."

Seal looked suddenly startled, as if surprised to hear her own voice.

"Do you think he did it?" I asked.

"He could have," she said, turning toward the door. "I wouldn't put anything past him."

On her way out, she tripped over my suitcase. "One good thing," she said, "at least this is going to be out of my way soon."

"Sorry," I said and followed her to her bedroom door. "Why do you think he'd accuse you?" I persisted.

Seal darted inside her room.

"I already told you," she said, exasperated. "Because I'm your mother. You can't explain the ravings of a madman," she said. "Maybe he's still peeved I planted those raspberry bushes on the lot line. Maybe he thinks I helped turn Merribeth against him. He knows how I feel about the hospital. Jim Hartwell has always been an odd duck, as you should know."

Seal started pushing her door shut. "I need a nap," she said. "You woke me up. Thanks a lot." She closed her door, not gently.

Seal was hardly the one to be calling someone else an odd duck. I thought I'd wait until she emerged again and tell her what we'd discovered about Mr. H's financial dealings and see if she had any insights, but she said she wasn't hungry when I knocked on her door to announce supper, and by 8 p.m., she still hadn't stirred.

I was feeling rather restless. It's not as if I could just phone Merribeth or Amber and suggest we go to a movie or out for coffee or something. I was tired of reading. The TV offered few diversions. I headed for the garage and backed out the Olds before I'd formulated a plan for my evening's entertainment.

I drove randomly through the streets of Weewampum and found myself on the road that skirted the lake. The lake still was frozen over, held in place by plaster-like snow. There were tracks through the snow where ice fishermen had plowed their way to their small shacks on the ice. I saw at least one crack of open water. Pretty soon they'd be towing a car or a shack out of the lake, or a fisherman . . . or maybe not. The road continued out of town, but at Main Street, I turned left. Then I realized I didn't want to drive past Spats again, so I turned right after one block on Main, then left, onto Market Street, and down to the end. There, I turned right and found myself cruising past Dottie Wentzell's family's homestead. The car seemed to want to stop, so I obliged.

Dottie Wentzell had spent her whole life in this small, white frame house on Otter Avenue. African violets crowded each other in every window, and Dottie's house was like some obscure tropical island, not popular with tourists. Dottie kept the shades pulled three-quarters way to allow just a diffuse light creep its way over her plants like a vapor. Dottie was likely to be inside her humid house, wearing a long-sleeve cotton blouse tucked inside her red, forest green, or lavender stretch pants and with a sprinkle can in her hand. The concave lenses in her glasses magnified her eyes, so it seemed her head should be three times larger to maintain the proportions. Her hair was short, gray, mannish; her movements jerky, unpredictable. I'd always enjoyed watching Dottie hopping about, constantly moving.

She invited me in when I pounded on her door. She didn't seem all that surprised to see me, although it was dark, and I'd never visited her sans Seal. I wasn't sure why I was there; I was just hoping I could talk to her a little about my mother. I was leaving in two weeks. I guess I wanted some reassurance that Dottie and Florence would look after Seal in my absence. Dottie offered me some lemon sandwich cookies and raspberry tea.

We sat at a small wicker table near the shaded living room window, and I shoved some African violets to the back of the table so we could better balance our plates of cookies and teacups.

"Do you think Seal will be all right?" I asked Dottie. "I've got to go back home soon."

"Why wouldn't she be? You've been gone a long time. She's not used to having you underfoot," Dottie replied.

One thing about Dottie; she always called them as she saw them.

We talked about my job and about how Dottie rather missed being a full-time librarian, although she still helped out on the reference desk, but not really that often, and that was a good thing as far as she was concerned. She said she'd learned early on that working was not all it was cracked up to be and that, all in all, retirement made working for 45 years almost worth it. I told her that was music to my ears; she had given me something to look forward to. Dottie chuckled and poured me some more tea.

"Tell me more about Seal," I asked her. "Why are you friends with her?"

"First off," she said, holding me with those big eyes, "Seal's sure made a lot of sacrifices for you."

I ignored Dottie's answer and asked how long she'd known Seal, and she said all her life. They'd grown up one block from each other. Seal never had told me even this. I suppose I'd never asked my mother precisely how long she'd known Dottie, but when I'd ask her more general things about what she'd done as a young girl, Seal would just say something like, "You don't want to hear about that," if she answered at all.

132

Seal, Dottie said, had been a real high achiever in school, bound for success. She'd wanted to be a lawyer. No one in Weewampum could even conceive of a girl being a lawyer, but if Cecelia Dandridge said she was going to be a lawyer, then she'd be one, and everyone had agreed upon that. The summer after her freshman year of college, Seal had fallen hard for what amounted to almost an older man. Seal never finished her sophomore year because it didn't take much to get pregnant. She dropped out of school, started calling herself Mrs. Whitby, had me, found her secretary job at Weewampum State and devoted the rest of her life to raising me. It was an old story that Dottie told me, one I'd heard many times before. But it deviated quite a bit from Seal's version. For one thing, Dottie hadn't mentioned a wedding.

Dottie was collecting our dishes by now. She was amazingly agile for a woman in her 70s. We hustled into the kitchen, where Dottie ran steaming water into the sink for the dishes. The vapor obscured Dottie as she blithely plunged her hands into the near-boiling foam.

"Were you in Seal's wedding?" I asked Dottie. I knew Seal had been married. There was the picture on the wall to prove it.

"What wedding?" Dottie said. "Wendy, you know as well as I do that Seal's an old maid just like me. Only difference is, she had you. So I guess that makes her just plain old." Dottie cawed at her joke and passed me a wet saucer to dry.

"What?" I asked her. "What?" as if I couldn't spit out more than one syllable at a time. Then, finally, "What about the wedding picture on the wall?" I blurted.

"Oh, that," Dottie snorted, drying her hands on her pants and putting away the dishes. "A bunch of us went to the Dells one weekend, and they had one of those places where you can pose as whomever you like and they'll take your picture. I was an Indian princess in a buckskin dress. Seal roped this other tourist into posing with her in those wedding duds. I think she got the picture taken just to give to Jimmy to prove she'd look real nice in a bride's dress."

"Who's Jimmy?" I asked.

"Well, Seal's boyfriend, naturally. Your papa, darling," Dottie said, letting the water out of the sink with this giant sucking sound. Dottie seemed oblivious to the effect her words were having on me as she bobbed about the room. Now she was pulling the shades even lower.

Seal had told me my father, Rex, had been an Army officer, killed when a land mine went off in Korea, that he'd died before I was born. And I'd believed her as any trusting daughter would. What other lies had she told me over the years and what else was she concealing from me now? She hadn't told me about her cancer. Merribeth and Amber had been the ones to tell me that and summon me home. Who was Jimmy? Why hadn't he and Seal gotten married? Did Dottie know what she was talking about? Oh, my God.

Dottie interrupted my thoughts. "Do you want to see my cactus?"

"Uh, Sure," I said. Cactus? Sure, why not see the cactus as I tried to sort out my thoughts and emotions, whirling around like the Tilt-a-Whirl at the Weewampum County Fair.

Dottie led me into her bedroom. Unlike the rest of her house, it was exposed to the sun. The sun was down now, but the moonlight backlit the cacti like shadowy skeletons. Dottie flipped on the light and there were cacti everywhere. Pincushion, cholla, and prickly pear cacti and many I had no names for. She even had a Joshua tree in a big pot in front of a window.

"Dottie, tell me," I asked. "Why didn't Seal and Jimmy get married?" Dottie looked at me, her eyes bulging wider than I'd ever seen them.

"Lordy, girl. Haven't you heard any of this stuff before? What's Seal been telling you all these years?" I must have stared at her like a small house cat reflected in the spotlights of her glasses. "Get on home," she said. "You go talk to your mother. I know she's kind of cranky, but she loves you to bits, babe."

I was rooted in Dottie's plant room as she bustled about, checking on her cacti. "What about..."

"Naw, I've spilled the beans too much already," Dottie said. "You ought to get this stuff straight from the horse's mouth." Dottie handed me a cactus. "Here, this is for you," she said, grinning. "That's Margie. She's Mrytle's baby. That's Myrtle," she said, pointing to a plump and pleased-looking cactus. "I bet you never knew Seal gave me my first cactus."

"No," I said.

"No, I never did. Thank you, Dottie."

"You get on home now," Dottie said and aimed me at her front door.

I stumbled to the Oldsmobile. How could I have lived this long and not know anything about anything, about me or my mother or how we both had turned out so very, very odd?

I slowly headed for home, but I wanted to think how to handle Seal, how to get her to tell me what I wanted to know without provoking either a shouting match or another glacial epoch. The Olds seemed to be finding its own way, and I noticed we were passing Mellowwood Manor, the senior complex where Florence Schmidt, Seal's bridge partner, lived. I pulled to the curb.

Florence had traded her nice, big, colonial, brick house out on Hunter's Lane for a two-bedroom Manor apartment that was hers for life. All her meals were provided; there was a van that would take residents around town if they didn't want to drive. Florence liked this no-hassle lifestyle. I found it depressing, passing the elderly folks bundled in sweaters sitting in the lobby, staring at the smoke detector on the ceiling. I buzzed Florence's bell and told her who I was over the intercom. She seemed happy for a guest and invited me up to Room 514.

Florence's apartment was a contrast to Dottie's old-fashioned house. Florence had furnished the place with contemporary tables and an off-white sofa with blue and yellow accent pillows. It was mildly Swedish-looking. I imagined lots of sun poured in during daytime. I could see a three-quarter moon outside the balcony doors.

Florence said she'd held a big yard sale before she'd moved into the Manor. She'd decided to "downsize" her life and start over again and found it invigorating just to lounge in her living room and let the sun wash over her as if she were a stone.

I knew Florence had moved to town when my mother had been an adult. Florence taught eighth grade social science for years at Cedar Pines Junior High. Seal and Florence met at a bridge tournament and admired each other's understated skill. Then, Seal invited Florence to join her bridge club and they'd been partners ever since. I didn't know a fig about bridge and didn't want to, but I was forced to admit that if Florence could keep up with Seal in bridge, Florence was a pretty sharp cookie.

Florence was more regal than Dottie Wentzell. She was tall, thin, and wore cashmere sweaters, wool skirts, and her glasses on a chain of pearls. Her husband had owned a couple car washes around town, and I guess he'd done more than all right to keep Florence in all those sweaters. She answered the door with, "Ah, Wendy, I'm so glad you dropped in. I'm worried about your mother."

Florence then proceeded to tell me Seal had trumped Florence's trick three times the previous Thursday at the Manor's semiannual bridge tournament and that was so unlike Seal. What did I think was the problem?

I had no idea, but Florence was right, it was unlike Seal to flub a hand, to not pay attention.

"I don't think anything's the matter. Her doctor says she's fine. Maybe it makes her nervous having me around the house," I proposed.

"Oh, Wendy, don't be silly," Florence said, sitting beside me on the sofa. "She's thrilled to have you home. You're her whole life."

I must have looked at Florence kind of wide-eyed or shocked or something because she squeezed my right arm.

"Oh, don't you realize how proud she is of you?"

Florence then proceeded to tell me how Seal never failed to talk about me to her and to Dottie, with whom they also played bridge. Dottie, however, had a problem keeping a partner and was forever trying out someone new for the part. Seal had told them what a devoted daughter I was to just leave my job and come home and care for her while she was sick. Seal was so happy I was living in her house and hadn't rented my own apartment. She'd told Florence and Dottie about the amusing comments we made each night as we wrestled each other for the dictionary to look up words for our Scrabble games. I couldn't believe what Florence was telling me. Seal and I didn't play Scrabble that often and when we did, it was like the Cold War and there was almost no talking except for, "Pass the dictionary," or "Come on, hurry up."

It was hard to process what I was hearing, but I decided to play my big card.

"I know you might think this odd," I said, "but Seal doesn't really like to talk about it much. I was wondering if you could tell me a little about my father?"

"What do you mean?" Florence said, surprised, but seeming to welcome a chance for conversation. "She talks about him all the time. Well, not all the time, but now and then. Of course, I never met the man. He was killed by the time I moved to town. But I understand he was an Army officer. Well, for pity sakes, Wendy. You know all this better than I do."

"I'm sorry," I said. "I just never knew him. I just wonder about him sometimes."

"Oh, of course you do, honey," Florence said. "Well, I know Seal loved him. You know, Wendy, Seal's tried so hard to make a good life for you."

I tried to smile at Florence, but I knew I still was staring, semidazed.

"Honestly, Wendy. It's almost as if you don't know anything about your own mother," Florence said, looking at me and looking at me, as if trying to figure out if California had changed me in some permanent fashion.

"I don't think I do know her," I told Florence.

"Well, you've always been such a difficult person, Wendy. You just never gave poor Seal a chance. Do you think it was easy for her to defend you – and she did – when you took all those photos and made her and your little friends at high school look like such idiots?"

"They weren't my friends," I said, but I don't think Florence heard me; she just kept on.

"She tried so hard to understand you, and you always were hiding in your room or running off to your friends' houses when all your poor mother wanted was just to spend some time with you. You've got to start taking better care of Seal, showing her you love her. She deserves that."

I gulped and stared. Guilty child. Guilty middle-aged baby. But surely this wasn't my mother about whom Florence was talking. She smiled at me.

"You know that keychain Seal always carries around in her purse?" she asked me. I blinked at her. Of course I didn't know about any keychain in Seal's purse. "I have to laugh every time I see it," Florence continued. "Seal uses it as a lucky charm whenever we're playing bridge. She's so sentimental. She won't leave home without it. Though, come to think of it, I haven't seen it lately. I hope she didn't leave it behind when she was in the hospital. You know the one I mean, that little keychain you won at school when you must have been 6 or 7, that one with the little Oscar Mayer wiener whistle on it? The keychain's made of those pink plastic beads you girls used to play with. Weren't they called pop beads?"

What? I didn't remember winning any keychain. Oh, my God! That was Seal's keychain I found in the ashes? Could she really be the arsonist? How could it be the keychain? I couldn't remember ever winning it. Just what was my mother up to??!!

"Tell me, Florence," I stumbled on. "What did Seal think about our restaurant? Did she say anything, do anything, when it burned down?"

"Well," Florence said, eyeing me as if I were quite off-balance, "of course she loved Amberosia's. She was so pleased you were so resourceful, that you could find a way to express yourself and be happy in Weewampum."

"But, was she glad that it burned down?" I pushed again.

Florence looked at me, alarmed. "How can you even suggest such a thing, Wendy? Your poor mother has had to put up with just so much."

I thanked Florence for her hospitality and climbed inside the

Olds one last time that night. When I got home, Seal's bedroom door still was closed, which was just as well, because I needed time to put together the pieces of what Dottie and Florence had told me. I could have used a good heart-to-heart with Merribeth and Amber, but that wasn't likely, not tonight. Seal had warned me against the evils of alcohol, but I checked the refrigerator, just in case. It was empty of any revivifying liquids, unless you wanted to count skim milk. Which I didn't. I went to my room, sat on the bed, and stared at Seal's wedding picture. I don't know when I fell asleep, but sometime around 3 a.m. I woke up, sweating. I'd dreamed that Seal was taking an oath in some dimly lit courtroom, and I was the sole occupant of the jury box, but I also was wearing a drab, black judge's robe and was pounding a gavel against my head.

Chapter 11

Seal's Refrigerator Pickles

8 cucumbers sliced into rounds
1 cup sliced onion
2 cups sugar
1 cup vinegar
2 Tablespoons salt
1 Tablespoon celery seed
Mix the sugar and vinegar.
Sprinkle the salt and celery seed over the cucumbers and onions.
Pour on the sugar and vinegar mixture.
Let the mixture stand for awhile.
Then pour into a jar or plastic container and refrigerate.

– From Elizabeth Wilson

I couldn't get back to sleep. I kept wondering why Seal had been so secretive about who my father was and kept brooding about whether she was the firebug. I got up and caught the end of *Annie*. It was on the "Night Owls' Wee Hours Theater," or "Sunshine Early Good Morning Movies." I can't remember which. I'd always found Carol Burnett deliciously cynical in her role as Miss Hannigan. Who wouldn't be drunk or in a foul mood most of the time with all those cute little orphan girls running around with their hang-dog looks? It was Miss Hannigan's job to inoculate those kids with healthy doses of chutzpah, so they could survive in their hard-knock world. But who was there to pat Miss Hannigan on the back and encourage her to carry on? The orphans may have been trapped at the orphanage until they turned 18, but Miss Hannigan was facing a life sentence. It was enough to turn even Mother Theresa into a misanthrope. I liked Pepper the best, the scrappy orphan who told Annie to "blow it out your old wazoo." Just as I'd put up with Seal's strict rules, Pepper just stoically bore the orphanage outrages, unlike Annie, who kept running away while smiling perkily and singing about "Tomorrow." The movie really got on my nerves. I'm not saying Seal was Miss Hannigan. Far from it. Miss Hannigan's armor was black lace teddies and liquor. Seal didn't need armor. Seal was frozen solid.

Seal and I had been glaciers in the same house, never allowing a warm word or touch to melt us toward each other. Merribeth said Seal was weird. How weird was she? Consider this. When I was in third grade, she bought me five navy dresses with white lace collars. They were all slightly different and I hated them all, and I didn't know why she bought them since we didn't have to wear uniforms to school or anything. But that year, that's all Seal let me wear until I deliberately dumped oil paint on one and accidentally tore another on the chain-link fence around the baseball field and ripped the side seam on a third when I was shooting baskets.

Seal wouldn't allow the radio in our house to be turned to any station that played popular music because "I might get ideas." She wouldn't buy spaghetti noodles, any kind of bread other than white, or radishes, peppers, fish other than canned tuna, or such staples as brown rice, dried beans, basil, oregano, or spumoni ice cream because it was food "that foreigners ate."

She sent me to my room each night after we finished the dishes, and I couldn't come out until my homework was done. Some nights I'd fall asleep at my desk, and she'd just wake me up and make me keep working. When I'd finish, she'd check my work for errors, then make me rewrite anything that looked "too sloppy." Sometimes I did my homework over five or six times. And if I didn't get an "A," she'd make me do the assignment again until she determined I'd gotten it right.

Seal wouldn't let me wear fingernail polish, pierced earrings, or a Pixie haircut. One night after she caught me riding Merribeth's brother Joey's bike, she sent me to my room and wouldn't let me have supper, not because it wasn't my bicycle but because it was a boy's bike, not a girl's, and it was "unladylike." By the time I'd gotten to high school, I was doing everything I could to defy her, like getting my hair shorn to a near-butch, wearing black fingernail polish and never, ever, wearing a dress, except to school, where we were forced to. Seal retaliated by buying me Peter Pan collar blouses and a circle pin that I knew she'd spent good money on, and when she presented them to me like an unsheathed sword,

I backed down and wore them. She started picking me up after school during her afternoon coffee break, so I wouldn't be tempted to ride the bus to someone's house who might corrupt me further, or even worse, be seduced by the offer of a ride home in some friend's second-hand Chevy.

Every so often, I'd make a half-hearted overture to Seal in an attempt to try to create something resembling a happy American family. I guess I was overly influenced by Merribeth's seemingly happy home life and Timmie and Lassie. I made my mother breakfast in bed once but spilled the orange juice on her white chenille bedspread and spent the next half-hour trying to make amends as Seal grimly doused the spread in cold water and soap. I often thought if we could just get away, maybe take a trip, even just spend a few hours driving around Lake Weewampum, perhaps the change of scenery would make us more relaxed, slightly different people, and we could pretend for just a couple hours that we actually enjoyed each other's company. But Seal never wanted to go anywhere. She said it was a waste of gas. So I just went over to Merribeth's and played Monopoly with her and her brothers and sisters and pretended I owned some big hotels where I could spend my weekends, or I hid out in the tree house and dreamed of what my life would be like when I was finally old enough to make my Weewampum escape. Was Seal weird? I guess so. But then, I guess, so was I.

But these were my old grudges; I now had to revise them with my new insights into Seal's past. Why had she been so strict? Maybe just to be absolutely certain I didn't fall off the straight and narrow as she had. Why, when I reached high school, had she had such a dyspeptic view of my potential boyfriends? – not that there were legions of them. Her quickie, illicit romance with my father must have predisposed her to want to pour ice water on any smoldering young love, wherever and whenever it flared up. Consider this. I remember once in a tirade of cold, bitter words, Seal told me I definitely was my father's child. I'd taken that as a compliment, since I didn't want to be like Seal. Now, I could only wonder what she'd meant. Who was this Jimmy, and how had he burrowed his way into my mother's heart? Why hadn't he stuck around? What could he teach me? I wanted him to be an elegant gentleman, a diplomat or maybe an actor. Someone charming, witty, Seal's opposite, someone more the way I'd like to be if I ever felt like giving up my churlish ways.

That day when Seal told me I was a chip off the masculine side of our family block had been so peculiar. It was the summer when I was 14 years old and had just cut off some jeans into shorts, making Seal so mad that she forced me to pay for the pants out of money I'd saved from shoveling snow that past winter. As further penance, Seal sent me to the backyard to pick raspberries, a chore I tried to dodge, because there were always wasps hovering around the bushes, and it usually was hot and my fingers turned red and, well, it was hard work. I much preferred reading or working in the darkroom I'd rigged up or cutting out bird houses with the jigsaw I'd set up in the basement.

But that day, for some reason, the wasps were off-duty and I saw Joey Hartwell out mowing the grass next door. Joey didn't see me at first and he couldn't hear me because the mower was pretty loud. For some reason, I don't know why, exactly, I flipped a raspberry at Joey. He put his hand on his neck where it hit him but kept mowing.

I threw another one. It hit him on the right ear. This time, he turned around, but I crouched behind a bush, and he still didn't see me. He went back to his mower. I lobbed another raspberry at Joey. It dinged him on the back of his head. He turned around but I ducked behind another bush. Joey shut off his lawn mower and walked toward my yard. I threw another raspberry at him. It hit him on the lips. He still didn't see me. He ran toward the raspberry bushes. And then he saw me. I started laughing and ran toward my house, but Joey ran faster and trapped me against the back wall. He turned me towards him; he was laughing, and then he smashed a handful of raspberries against my face.

Well, I broke loose and ran to the raspberry bushes and we started flinging raspberries at each other. It felt so liberating watching all those raspberries flying through the air. Maybe we'd

144

get rid of them all, and I wouldn't have to pick them again for the rest of the summer.

Pretty soon we ran out of ammunition, and when we did, Joey said, "Come on over and wash up."

So I followed him to his backyard hose and we washed off our hands and I stuck my face under the hose and then Joey did and then I grabbed

the hose and squirted him and then he squirted me and pretty soon we were soaking wet.

I thought it was strange that Merribeth and the rest of her family weren't around, but Joey said his mother had taken everyone downtown, and their father was working. Joey had promised a week ago to cut the grass on Saturday, which was why he hadn't gone downtown with everyone else. So that's what he was doing now.

Then we both laughed because Joey wasn't making much progress on the lawn. I noticed it wasn't really as hot out as I'd thought, and I started shivering. Joey ran into the house for a towel and was out in two seconds with a giant red-and-white-striped one you'd use at the beach, which he wrapped around me like a mummy.

I couldn't move and he started patting my feet dry with the towel's edge and then he moved up to my ankles, to my calves, and when he got to my thighs, I said, "I can take it from here."

Well, I couldn't, really, because I still was mummified. But he laughed and said, "Well, all right. You know, I could use some drying."

So I untwirled out of the towel and wrapped him up in it, but the towel wasn't big enough to pin down his arms. I dabbed at his feet with the edge of the towel, then patted his calves and was trying to figure out what to do about the rest of his legs when he reached over and grabbed me by the waist and pulled me up until I was facing him. He winked, then hugged me against his wet clothes.

I was pretty surprised and just looked into his eyes. They had all kinds of lights in them and a brightness I'd never noticed before.

They were just glowing. I remembered you weren't supposed to stare into the sun and snapped my lids shut. With my eyes closed, his body beneath the wet fabric and his bare arms felt warm and soft as the sun on my back. Before I could think of something smart to say or slap him or run home, Joey's lips were on mine, and mine were on his, and we were breathing for each other, and I was wondering what I was going to tell Seal about my empty berry basket.

I needn't have worried because Seal saw everything from our kitchen window, and when I walked in the back door, she was so chillingly angry I thought I'd freeze into a pillar of rock salt and be banished to a spot in the garden near the raspberries until I washed away in the rain.

"You little bag," she said. "How dare you?"

I turned away as if she'd slapped me, but I wasn't totally sure what she meant. I mean, it was only Joey, Merribeth's brother, not some forbidden Romeo who wanted to ruin me forever. I didn't know if Seal was more angry at me for kissing Joey or for ravishing the raspberry crop. Both, I guessed.

At first I was devastated, crushed, not to mention angry that Seal had spied on us, but then I started thinking about that phrase – "little bag." The more I thought about it, the funnier and sadder it seemed. My mother saw me as some flimsy paper thing, insubstantial, to be used once, then tossed out. Well, at least with the raspberries decimated, she wouldn't see me as her perpetual raspberry picker. But just my luck, the berries grew back in a couple weeks, redder and thicker than ever.

From that day forward, Seal and I were more open about our animosity toward each other. She saw me as a tramp and guarded me like Cerberus protecting the gates of Hell. Sometimes, I tried to live up to her expectations, and sometimes I refused to play along and worked in my darkroom or with my woodworking tools, which infuriated her nearly as much as if I'd been out necking with some guy with a ducktail under our front porch light.

When I was in high school, Seal wanted me to be a social success – albeit a virgin – but except for Merribeth and Amber, I found most girls in my class too vapid for words, and the boys just hopelessly juvenile. I'd discovered Kerouac, Lenny Bruce, Leonard Cohen, Bob Dylan, Ken Kesey. They were about rebellion, black turtlenecks, and coolness. It didn't translate into Weewampumese. I also discovered photography in my sophomore year. That was Seal's big mistake, really. That Christmas, she gave me a Brownie Instamatic, along with the traditional white bobbie socks, and I started to take photo after photo and began to learn how I could frame reality to serve my purposes. I saved up my snow-shoveling and baby-sitting money and bought some darkroom equipment. I'd stuff towels around the door and the window in the bathroom and hole up in there for hours with my acrid chemicals, water dripping, and the paper that would magically change from a blank white into a rainbow of grays and the darkest black.

One day, I took my camera to school and shot roll after roll of my friends and acquaintances. I posed my pals pretending to drink out of chemistry lab flasks, flashing their legs like chorus girls while waiting in the lunch line, sitting behind a teacher's desk with their feet up. I shot them in shadow, I shot them in sun. It was an experiment to see how much I could change them.

When I developed those rolls, I felt like Dr. Frankenstein, Mephistopheles, a sorceress like Circe. I was mastering the art of transforming the truth to suit my own purposes. I shot Bobby Gilmore, the football captain – who had the brash manner of a mead-guzzling, steak-gnashing Viking – in a football crouch near the bicycle rack, surrounded by Schwinns. I shot him from a high angle, looking down at him amidst the forest of spokes and sparkling chrome. The photo was wonderful. It made Bobby seem like a tyke, trying to look like a tough guy, dwarfed among the big kids' wheels.

I persuaded blonde Darlene Abercrombie, valedictorian and head cheerleader – the absolute definition of high school success – to pose in front of a blackboard in Mr. Fiering's trigonometry class. There was a long, complicated problem stretching on the board in back of Darlene. I asked Darlene to stretch out her hands, like, ta-da, welcome to my math class. The photo made it look as

147

if the trig problem was going in one of Darlene's ears and out the other. Her hands were spread as if the matter were hopeless; she was the quintessential airhead. I loved it.

I had a few shots left on the last roll when I came home from school, so I surreptitiously shot Seal in silhouette, gazing out our paned kitchen window as she scrubbed a pot in the sink. Her hands turned out blurred like a fast-moving machine. That was the only photo on the roll that I hadn't planned before shooting. I loved the way it caught her eyes looking steadily and longingly out the window while her hands were a flurry of motion. It transformed her into someone softer than I recognized, someone I'd like to get to know better.

As I saw my work develop in my plastic trays, I was elated by my accomplishments. As soon as the pictures dried a little, I ran over to Merribeth's to show her my handiwork. Merribeth couldn't stop laughing at the photos, which drew her mother and sisters and brothers to come and admire what I'd done.

"Take me, take me," the twins begged. But I'd used up my last roll, so I just promised I'd shoot them some other time. Joey, who was a senior that year, came down from his bedroom to see what all the noise was about.

"Wow!" he said. "Cool. This is really something, Wendy."

I could tell he truly was impressed, and I felt proud. Joey did some photography himself and had a fancy Nikon, so I knew I must have done something right if I could get him to blink. He asked me if he could borrow the photos for a day or two. He said he wanted to study them more carefully, see how I'd used shadow and light. He said I had a real eye for photography. Of course I said yes. If I could serve as an inspiration and a guide to Joey, who was two years older than I was, then I thought that was pretty neat.

The next day at school on my way to French class, Barbara Nudelman, who was best friends with Darlene Ambercrombie, blocked my way into the classroom.

"Boy," she said, "you've really got balls." I had no idea what she was talking about and told her so. "That photo of Darlene. How could you?" she said and stormed to her desk across the room.

What was she talking about? How could Barbara know about Darlene's picture? Joey. What had Joey done?

I tracked Joey down to the band room, where he was first trumpet in the concert band. When he looked at me, I knew he'd done something he wished he hadn't.

"Hey, Wendy," he said, stretching both arms out to me. "Now, don't get mad. I just wanted to show your photos to Mr. Kendall. I just thought they were really professional." He said Darlene was in Mr. Kendall's art class, too, but Joey hadn't shown them to her. But Mr. Kendall had thought the photos were so good, that he'd shown them to the whole class. Joey said he was really, truly sorry. He hadn't really been thinking; he just thought Mr. Kendall should know how talented I was.

"Oh, great, Joey. You've just ruined my life," I said. And that was pretty much true. Bobby Gilmore backed me against my locker between sixth and seventh hours and probably would have strangled me if Darlene Abercrombie hadn't walked up and told him not to waste his time.

"Don't get yourself in trouble over a little scumbag like her," Darlene yelled at Bobby. "We'll get her. But not the way she thinks."

I cut gym that day, my seventh-hour class, and walked home from school. I took the long way. By the time I got there, Joey, Merribeth, and Amber were sitting in the kitchen with Seal, waiting for me. The photos were spread on the table. Merribeth immediately hugged me.

Amber snorted and said, "You're a real Picasso. Oh, never mind, he's a painter."

Seal said, "How could you?"

Joey just looked sheepish.

"How could you, why would you, make me look so crazy?" Seal demanded, then stood up and grabbed a scissors and sheared her photo in half. She stomped out of the kitchen.

I felt as if she'd cut my head off from my heart, but strangely, it didn't hurt all that much.

Merribeth hugged me again. "It's OK, Wen," she said. "Really. It's OK."

Amber said, "Anybody gives you any lip, they've got me to deal with."

"Me, too," Joey said. "I'm really sorry."

"It's going to be OK," Merribeth said over and over. "It will blow over soon."

It was nice having friends to support me, but it never really did blow over. I was pretty much the high school pariah after that. Darlene and Bobby made sure of it. Eventually, I came to enjoy my outcast status. It wasn't so bad. Merribeth and Amber stood by me the best they could, but my enthusiasm for photography scurried behind the wastebasket in a corner of my makeshift darkroom and refused to come out. It seemed I was playing with fire, and I didn't want to get burned again, at least until I could leave town for good. I started writing mournful poems, instead. They seemed more private to me, and I made sure I found ways to hide them from Seal and all my friends. Seal became even more of an iceberg, and that was just fine with me. All I had to do was serve my time, finish high school, then break out of Weewampum for good.

Although I was much older now, I still felt like a misunderstood adolescent every time I visited Weewampum, where people like Emma Swanson and Florence Schmidt still passed on the story of how I'd betrayed my mother and my friends with my photos. I'd only returned to Weewampum – it hadn't been easy – to take care of Seal while she was recovering because I was her only child, and somehow she'd succeeded in drumming some small sense of obligation into me.

After *Annie* ended and the little orphan girl found her Daddy Warbucks, I wondered if I had one, too, but just didn't know where to find him. I walked out on the porch to fetch the *Weewampum Bugle*. Warren Caramel was parked outside in his red pickup, so I waved. He pretended not to notice, and I walked back inside.

I was on my third cup of coffee and reading a story about the ground-breaking ceremony of the new hospital when Seal walked into the kitchen. She was wearing a pair of navy-blue, belted pants, a plain white, long-sleeve cotton blouse buttoned up to the neck and a matching navy blue jacket, one of the suits she'd worn when she was the secretary to Dean Pritchard at Weewampum State. She looked determinedly businesslike.

"Finish your breakfast," she ordered. "We've got things to do."

I looked at her, surprised. Whatever she had in mind, she was resolute about it. "What's up?" I asked.

"Just hurry up," she said. "We're going for a ride."

I told her she'd better have some breakfast, that I was ready when she was, but she needed to eat to start her day right. I poured her a cup of coffee. She took a sip, then poured it into the sink.

"Let's get going," she said.

I shrugged and set down the newspaper, which she grabbed and scanned and then observed, "It says here the hospital's going to cost $95 million and be the most state-of-the-art medical center in the area. There will be a special nephrology wing and they'll be doing kidney transplants. La-de-da, la-de-da."

She slapped the newspaper down. "That's progress, I guess," she said, sounding unconvinced. "Come on. The day's a-wasting." She went to the closet and pulled on her camel-hair coat and a white wool toque. She grabbed her purse and strode to the door and stood, waiting for me.

The day was gray and misty. If we were lucky, it might hit forty degrees. The snow had turned to that slushy, sludgy mess of ice and mud of late March. But the sidewalks and roads were bare. We pulled out of the driveway. It was hard to see around Warren's truck but we eased out into the quietness of Hubbard Street. Warren started up his truck and followed us to Clyde's 76, where Seal directed me to stop. I topped off the tank and then headed north along the lakeshore road that skirted Lake Weewampum, following Seal's instructions. Warren tailed us to the city limits. Seal told me to keep going north. Warren made a U-turn and headed back into town.

"Where are we going?" I asked, but Seal told me to just keep driving. We passed the exits for Otterton, Pearville, Sinsippee. If we continued north, we'd end up in the town lost to football – Green Bay. Seal gestured to turn right, skim the top of Lake

Weewampum and head south. And then the road opened up. There were miles of open land. It was flat and the snowbanks were capped by a crust of ice. Sometimes, the road ran through a pine forest, but other times, we could look down upon Lake Weewampum. On this side of the lake, there were sand dunes that wind, water, ice, and glaciers had built into mounds about 30 feet high. They were covered by snow at the moment, but in summer, they were locally famous. The lake looked more wild from this side, not nearly as frozen here. The ice was breaking up, and small floes were heading for shore. They pounded into each other and against the beach. As we drove, it started to drizzle. There was little traffic; we were in our own gray world.

"Well, I guess I might as well tell you," Seal said, as the sleet clung to our car like melting plastic. "The cancer is back."

I slammed on the brakes and our car fishtailed. "Watch it! Are you crazy?" Seal hissed.

"But Mother! How do you know? I thought Dr. Bill said you were fine," I pleaded.

"I saw him one day when you were out. I've been feeling tired," she said.

After I got the car moving again, Seal's voice was as even as the yellow line in the road, not scared, sad, worried, just Seal, just Seal telling me the facts. "Where is it? What are you supposed to do?" I asked.

"It's in some lymph nodes," she said, as if giving dictation. "More chemo, radiation. The works. It all starts up again on Monday."

"Oh, Mother," I said. "I am so sorry." And I was.

"Me, too," she said. We drove a couple miles in silence; the sleet was turning to wet snow. It made the day considerably brighter as we drove through the whiteness, all alone. We could hear the ice slamming the sand on our right. We passed a sign that said "Cranberry County Park, 1/2 mile," and as we approached the turnoff, Seal said, "Pull in."

So I did. The park road was slick from the snow and we slipped a little as we drove slowly along a cliff overlooking the lake. There was a little parking area on a ledge and Seal motioned me toward it. I drove the Olds into the whiteness and stopped. From this parking lot we could look out on almost the whole lake. Across the water we saw lights and some smoke.

"That's Weewampum, right over there," Seal said, nodding. And then she did a very uncharacteristic thing. She put her gloved hand on my hand, which was encased in a white mitten.

"It's not been easy for us, has it?" she said, her brown eyes moist like the changing patterns on our car windows.

"No, Mom. No, it hasn't," I said. And I was really sorry for both of us, that we had so stubbornly avoided each other for so many years.

"Mom, I'm really sorry."

Seal patted my mitten.

"Dottie and Florence phoned while you must have been driving home last night. They said you paid them a visit."

I should have known they would, but I don't always think ahead, and really, what of it?

"That's right," I said. "They told me some things."

"I know," Seal said. I waited for her to begin, but she was quiet. We watched the snow fall for a while as the ice ground away at the shore. Finally, I couldn't wait any longer and started the spark of conversation, hoping to avoid a conflagration. I told Seal the Threesome was trying to find out who'd burned down the restaurant because Warren Caramel seemed eager to pin the fire on us. Seal said Warren was just trying to take the easy way out, and she knew we hadn't done it. Our voices rose and fell like the ice, sometimes loud, sometimes a whisper over the crashing.

I pressed on. I told her about the wiener whistle on the pink-plastic-bead keychain that I'd found in the rubble and how Florence Schmidt had told me that Seal kept a wiener whistle of mine in her purse.

Seal's eyes hardened into anthracite and blazed up. "Surely you don't think I set the fire?" she said, her eyes reducing me to rubble.

"Well, Jim Hartwell did suggest it, and I did find the keychain," I said.

Seal turned her head from me and stared at the snow. And then

I noticed a tear pushing its way down her left cheek like melting runoff. She turned to me, her mouth kind of stuck open, and then she touched my hand lightly again.

"I'm sorry, honey. I'm sorry you would think that," she said, softer than usual. "But didn't I invite the Weewampum Secretarial Association Bridge Club to Amberosia's that one Wednesday afternoon? I thought enough of the place to bring my friends there, didn't I? Why on earth would I want to burn it down?"

I looked at Seal and her eyes were soft again, not really pleading but like fine, tillable soil. Yes, she'd brought the bridge club to the restaurant once. I'd won her nod of approval and hadn't even noticed. But what about the whistle?

"That whistle?" she said. "Don't you remember when you won it in Mrs. Carruthers' room for having the neatest penmanship? And those are your pop beads that make up the keychain. It's like I can take you with me wherever I go."

I still couldn't remember winning that whistle and especially I couldn't remember the part about ever being neat. And then I dimly recalled how proud I'd felt that afternoon long ago when Mrs. Carruthers gave me the whistle, back when I still was eager to make my mother think I was the smartest girl in the world.

"Well, how did it wind up in the ashes?" I asked. It just didn't make any sense.

"I don't know," Seal said. "I have no idea. It's been missing from my purse for a few months. Maybe I left it on a table in the restaurant, maybe on the restroom sink. I really have no idea."

Then my eyes melted. Whistle or not, answer or no, I knew there was no way Seal had burned down Amberosia's. I pulled her to me and we cried for a while as the snow fell. But crying didn't come easily to Seal or me, especially when we were together, so we stopped. Seal still wasn't talking. I just couldn't wait any longer, so I asked her to tell me about my dad.

The snow still was falling, and we couldn't see across the lake anymore. Seal opened the car door and got out. I followed her around to the front of the car. She leaned against the hood, and so I did, too.

"I wanted to be a lawyer," she said. "But this view turned me into a mother."

She stared into the snow in the direction of the lake, and I stared, too, trying to see a day many summers ago when the water gently lapped against the sand and the wind fanned the pine trees and robins warmed their nests.

Seal said she'd been engaged to a young man named Rex Whitby, and he was in the Army, off in Korea, and she'd missed him a lot. It was a beautiful afternoon in June, the day of the summer solstice, and she was on her front porch reading *Gone With the Wind* for probably the fifth time. A neighbor drove up in his new red DeSoto. He wondered if she'd like to go for a ride. She said, "Yes" because it was such a lovely day. They drove halfway around the lake. When they reached this point, the sun was going down.

The sun on the lake was like coral, ochre, and burnt orange oil paints flowing into each other. She kissed the neighbor man because the water looked like a living painting, and then they kissed some more and did some other things, too. Nine months later, there I was. My father wasn't the Army officer she'd told me about because that man had been away in Korea and yes, he'd died when he'd stepped on a land mine. The neighbor man with the red car was my real father, but Seal had never gone anywhere else with him after that. The neighbor man still was our neighbor man, Merribeth's father, Joey's father, James "Jimmy" Allen Hartwell, member of the American Institute of Architects and major Weewampum asshole.

"Oh, my God," I said.

"Exactly," Seal said. "Come on, let's get in the car."

There was plenty more I wanted to ask her, but Seal seemed tired. We were covered in snow, like abominable snow women. I caught her gloved hand and then her arm and pulled her to me. She resisted but yielded enough so I could hug her for a moment, then she broke away.

"I love you, Mother," I told her, the warm tears turning to ice the further they trickled from my eyes. "I love you more than you know."

Seal just looked at me with her skeptic's eyes, but then she smiled enough to show one corner tooth.

"I love you, too," she said so quietly that I almost didn't hear her, but I saw her lips moving so I know she said it.

And then we hurried to get back inside the car. The snow was really starting to come down. I couldn't get the car to go forward; we were stuck in the snow. I got out again and opened the trunk and waved the emergency blanket at my mother and she smiled. I laid down the blanket in front of the car and Seal slid into the driver's seat. She gunned the car and I pushed against the Olds as hard as I could. Suddenly, the car spun forward and was free. I picked up the blanket and jumped back into the car, and we made our way onto the main road. Then Seal insisted she wanted to drive us the rest of the way home. We talked maybe once or twice more, which was OK with both of us. When we got home, we lit a fire in the fireplace and sat there and I read a book. I think it was a new translation of *Beowulf* and Seal did a crossword puzzle, and we were as content as we could be. Warren Caramel pulled up in front of the living room window around 9 p.m. He just sat outside our house in his pickup and never once knocked. We had a last cup of Sleepytime tea about 11. Warren still was there. And he was still there when the fire died out around midnight and Seal and I said, "See you in the morning."

Chapter 12

Seal and Wendy's Oatmeal

1-3/4 cup old-fashioned oatmeal
1 cup water
1/2 cup brown sugar
1/2 cup chopped walnuts
One apple, washed, cored, and diced
Milk

Boil water.
Pour the oatmeal into the water and stir with a wooden spoon.
Turn heat down to low.
Simmer uncovered until all the water is absorbed and the oatmeal looks good enough
to eat.
Turn off heat.
Cover and let stand a few minutes.
Put about 1/4 cup or less brown sugar in the bottom of each of two cereal bowls.
Dice the apple and put half in each cereal bowl.
Chop the nuts on a cutting board and divide between the two cereal bowls.
The oatmeal should be ready.
Scoop half into each bowl.
Drown in milk.
Enjoy.

I awoke at dawn. I thought I might take a walk along the lakeshore road and try to process the fact that Jim Hartwell, not Daddy Warbucks, was my father. I started my day in the usual fashion, retrieving the *Weewampum Bugle* from the front porch. Warren Caramel was in his pickup, drinking from his thermos. I nodded, but he chose to pretend he didn't notice before I ducked inside.

Five minutes later, though, he was rapping at our door. I invited him in just as Seal walked into the hallway to see what all the noise was about. She didn't nod at Warren, just walked into the kitchen. Warren and I followed her. Seal got some coffee perking, and I made oatmeal. But Warren said he'd already had breakfast.

He wouldn't even take the cup of coffee Seal tried to pour, nor would he remove his navy wool jacket.

Warren poured himself some more coffee from the thermos that he'd brought inside. He had a clipboard with him and a legal pad, and he sat on the edge of Seal's oak captain's chair with his back as straight as a fire pole. Seal asked him if he had any suspects yet, and he said, "Everyone's a suspect until proven otherwise," which seemed a rather unconstitutional attitude, but at least encouraging, in that Warren actually might be considering either Lars Hunssen or Jim Hartwell, aka Daddy, as potential arsonists.

So I asked Warren if he'd found out where Lars and Mr. H./Dad had been the night of the fire. Warren said that was his business, not mine. I told him about the research Amber, Merribeth, and I already had done and what we'd found out about these two Weewampum statesmen, and Warren seemed quite put out.

"What makes you think you have the right to investigate a private citizen just as if he were some common, ordinary criminal?" Warren asked, setting his thermos lid full of coffee on the table and trying to stare me down.

"It's a free country," I said. "You just said everyone's a suspect."

Warren picked up the lid of his thermos and drained the coffee, then screwed this cap back on as tightly as possible.

"Invasion of privacy is a serious matter," he threatened, "especially from someone who's a prime suspect in an arson case."

Seal had been slowly eating her oatmeal but now set her spoon down carefully and braced her hands on either side of the bowl.

"We invited you into our house for breakfast, Warren Caramel," she said, her voice an icicle. "And first, you refuse the perfectly good oatmeal we offer you, and now, you insinuate that my daughter caused that fire."

Warren leaned back confidently in the wooden chair until I thought it might tip over, but he didn't seem concerned.

"Now, Seal, I didn't say that precisely," Warren said in a tone that I'm sure he intended to be soothing but that was like Muzak playing while the dentist drills your molar. Warren picked up his legal pad. "I have just a few questions, if you don't mind."

Seal stood up, her hands still braced on either side of her bowl. She glared at Warren. "It just so happens that I do mind," Seal said, coldly. "We have nothing more to say to you."

Warren sat up in his chair, surprised. Apparently, not that many people refused to cooperate with Weewampum's foremost and only fire marshal.

At first, Warren didn't move. I just hoped Seal's gaze wouldn't freeze him permanently to the chair, so I said, "You can go now, Mr. Caramel. We won't be needing you."

To my surprise, Seal laughed a short, "Ha!"

Then Warren stood up from the table and Seal walked towards him and Warren backed towards the door.

"You may be interested to know," he said, as he stepped onto the porch and glared at me, "that I've narrowed my investigation." We followed him out the door just to make sure he left. "I've got a pretty good idea of what happened that night," he said. "You might be interested in this."

He pulled a photocopy of a photograph out of a pant pocket. He shoved it at me. At first I couldn't make it out. It looked like abstract patterns of black, gray, and white waves. I studied it more closely; it looked like a Rorschach blot. It could be footprints.

"What's this?" I asked.

Warren looked at me as if he looked long enough, he could read my thoughts. Then he looked at my feet.

"I see you wear those little boots. Not real boots, not suited for here, kind of sawed-off. What do they call those things?"

I looked down.

"Chukkahs," I said.

"Chukkahs," he said. "We found some chukkah tracks in the snow. You'll be hearing from me soon."

What? Surely he didn't think. . . . It was only then as he turned toward his truck that it struck me. He was wearing a pea coat. I glimpsed one of the buttons. It had a little anchor on it. Warren walked away too quickly for me to see if one of the buttons was missing. Could he have burned down Amberosia's? Why would he? To prove he could solve a case by pinning the blame on me or Merribeth or Amber? That didn't make any sense. The button probably had fallen off his coat while he was investigating, if it was his at all.

Still . . .

Warren ground his truck into gear and chugged down the street.

"He never had many brains," Seal said when we returned to the kitchen. "He should have pumped gas for a living."

I took this as an opening to ask her to tell me more about her childhood. She and Warren must have grown up together. But Seal apparently had talked herself out the day before, or maybe she just was in a hurry.

"I'm meeting Dottie and Flo for a bridge game at Eunice Shroeder's," she said in response and went to her room, changed her clothes to a gray pantsuit and was out the door in under 10 minutes.

I was at loose ends, as I'd frequently been since returning to Weewampum. The prospect of a walk along the lake no longer seemed appealing. I wasn't ready to wave an olive branch in Merribeth's or Amber's direction. Let them make the first move, I thought.

The *Beowulf* translation was interesting as far as it went, but it wasn't calling me this morning. I could have used a good gossip magazine, but Seal, of course, wouldn't deign to subscribe to any, and really, I had to admit, I didn't either, so I really couldn't hold it against her. The game shows on TV seemed too complex for me to grasp. It seemed too much effort to turn on my laptop. In just a few more days I'd be safely ensconced in my condo with all my diversions, my jazz and classical CDs, my work friends and other friends, my multiplex movie theaters, cappuccino bars, and the oddity gift shops just a few stops down the freeway. But really, how could I leave Seal, just as she faced a new slew of doctor visits and medical tortures? It was hard to know what she wanted from me. More than anything else, I wanted to talk to her for long, long hours. But she wasn't making it easy. Maybe I should schedule an appointment to talk with her, but she wouldn't go for that. How I longed to dissect the whole thing with Merribeth, my sister.

In a drawer near the kitchen phone, Seal kept used paper. Any printed material that entered the house she'd flip over to see if there was a clean side. If there was, the paper made its way to the drawer – we never ran out of scratch paper. I grabbed some sheets that Seal's insurance company had sent, explaining the benefits of adding accidental death coverage. I flipped the sheets over and drew a line down the center. On one side I listed what I knew about Jim Hartwell, Merribeth, Joey, and all the rest of the Hartwells. On the other side, I listed the questions I wanted to ask Seal.

Like, why had she stayed living next to Jim all those years? Hadn't it been humiliating? Like, why hadn't she told me any of this stuff before? Around the margins I wrote the questions I wanted to ask Jimbo but that I wasn't sure if I ever would. Like, why had he stayed living next to Seal all those years? Like, had he ever felt remorse at just loving and leaving her? Like, why had he never told me once that he was my father, or at least smiled at me on occasion and given me a nickel or a pat on the head?

When Seal returned, I tried pressing her for more details. She said, "Not now," but when I wouldn't give up, she just said this was her family's home and Jim's was his, so why should either of them have moved? She said she hadn't planned for me, but then after I was there, she just got on with her life. I was feisty and strong and had kept her busy for quite a long time and after a while, she just didn't think about Jim – or Rex – anymore.

It seemed to me she had given up so much for the dubious distinction of being my mother, so I asked her if there hadn't been some way she still could have gone to law school. She had settled into a corner of the sofa, crossword puzzle in hand. She sighed and said with some exasperation that together with Rex dying in Korea and my arrival, she hadn't felt like doing much for quite a while. She tapped her pencil on the puzzle.

"Stop picking scabs," she said. "Just leave it alone and whatever you do, don't tell Merribeth . . . or Jim."

She looked at me as if to seal the agreement. Then added, "Have you seen the dictionary?"

I wanted to talk into the night with her, but that apparently was out of the question. I wanted to talk to Merribeth, my sister, but Seal's edict now was banishing me to the land of silence. I could defy her but I knew, somehow, she'd find out, and then I'd feel I'd stabbed a sick woman in the chest, then ripped out her heart.

It's not as if I were speaking to Merribeth anyway, so it wouldn't be a problem keeping mum. And I wasn't sure how Merribeth would handle another revelation about her/our father. I did wonder if there were any genetic traits she and I shared. I could think of very few, except that we both once had liked climbing trees. I wondered what would have happened if Joey and I'd pursued our sudden passion by the raspberry bushes, which we hadn't. I hadn't wanted Seal spying on us anymore as she had that day of our berry fight.

Mostly, I wanted to know why Seal and Jim had a fling when Jim was already married. It must have been hard, living next door to each other all those years, pretending they were just neighbors. I wondered when Seal planted the raspberry bushes, whether it was before or after her summer solstice drive with Jim. I wanted to talk to him and find out what made him tick. Did Mrs. H. know about me? I didn't see how she could and still be so warm and friendly. I thought how ironic it was that I'd envied Merribeth her happy family for so long, when all along, I'd been a member of it. Well, sort of.

Since I wasn't going to get any satisfaction from Seal, at least, not for a while, I told her I was going for a ride.

"Get the car back by 2:45," she said. "I'm the volunteer in the bookbinding room at the library today."

I slid into the car. I wondered where it would take me today. It puttered along the lakeshore. The lake was pocked by big rifts where the ice was splitting up, and choppy, gray waves moved back and forth like impatient sharks. The ice-fishing shacks had disappeared. The car turned a few corners. I wasn't surprised to find the Olds idling in front of Merribeth's apartment. I didn't feel I was ready to apologize for the luncheon episode, however, so I decided to drive on. The car coughed, then stalled, though, so I got out and rang Merribeth's bell.

She opened the door almost immediately, although she didn't instantly hug me as she always did, but gazed at me warily.

"Look, Merribeth," I started saying, not knowing where this was going to lead. "You're my best friend. I need you to not be angry with me. I'm sorry."

I guess I was as surprised I'd said this as she was. And then I hugged her. It was one of the few times Merribeth had seen me contrite. She hugged me quickly, then took off toward her kitchenette. I didn't know if she still was angry, but she picked up a cookbook and handed it to me.

"Help me pick a menu," she said. "I thought I'd make up with you and Amber by having you all over for dinner. I was going to call you in about an hour."

And then we both laughed.

So we chose cream of spinach soup, tossed greens, shrimp creole, and key lime pie for our reconciliation dinner. Amber could bring the wine. Merribeth was worried that she had only two chairs for her table, so I said, why not have the fete at Seal's? Then we phoned Amber at her office.

Amber was on the phone with a customer but because of call-waiting, picked up our call on the fourth ring.

"I'm really sorry, Amber," I started out.

"Hey, Wen, how's it hanging?" she said, seeming to be not at all fazed by my apology – or our argument, for that matter.

"I was going to phone you and Merribeth after I wrap up this $450,000 deal," she said. "It's a steal. Five bedrooms, lake rights."

"Can you be at Seal's at six?"

"That's cutting it pretty close."

"You know Seal doesn't like to eat late."

"How would I know? She never wanted me to come over when you lived here before. Oh, all right. Catch you then," she said. "Got to go."

She hung up. It was as if our luncheon had never happened. So Merribeth and I went shopping for our dinner provisions and the Oldsmobile started right up. We wound up toting seven bags of groceries into Seal's. My mother told us she'd never bought more than four bags at once, that extravagance is nothing to be proud of.

"You're right, Mrs. Whitby," Merribeth said and smiled, while unpacking the potato chips, cola, and double chocolate chip cookies we'd purchased, just in case we still were hungry after our four-course dinner.

Seal looked at me and shook her head.

"You could learn something from Merribeth," she said. "She doesn't do what I'd do, either. But at least she does it with a smile."

I looked at my mother and tried out a smile. I could be just like Merribeth. I smiled and smiled. But Seal wasn't buying my act. She was more than a little irritable.

I'd forgotten to bring the car back home for her volunteer stint at the library, and, instead, had brought home a dinner guest and was making work for us all and Amber would be coming, too. Honestly, sometimes it seemed like I didn't think at all. Then, Seal smiled a begrudging half-smile. It was fleeting, but I did glimpse it.

Chapter 13

Merribeth and Wendy's Shrimp Creole

1 large onion, chopped
2 ribs of celery, chopped
1 green pepper, cleaned and chopped
1 red pepper, cleaned and chopped
4 cloves garlic, diced
2 Tablespoons vegetable oil

Saute the vegetables in oil until the onion is transparent.
1 15-ounce can tomato sauce. If you want to choose the seasoned kind, that's fine.
4 plum tomatoes, chopped
1 Tablespoon instant chicken bouillon granules
1/4 teaspoon Tabasco
1 Tablespoon Worcestershire sauce
1 teaspoon thyme
1/2 cup fresh chopped celery or parsley leaves
1/4 teaspoon cumin
1 medium jar green olives
2 bay leaves
1 pound or more of shrimp. Choose the size you like and clean them.

Add everything except the shrimp to the vegetable mixture and simmer 10-plus minutes. Then add the shrimp. Simmer 5 to 7 minutes. Serve over rice.

Amber was late. It was nearly 7 p.m. and Seal was getting more ornery with each passing minute.

"Just go ahead and eat," I told her. "Here, I'll dish up a plate for you."

"I'm perfectly capable of dishing up my own dinner," Seal snapped as she poured herself another cup of coffee. "It's just that it's rude to say you'll be somewhere and make people wait for you and. . . ."

"Hey, ho," Amber called, breezing in like the northwest wind, Star strapped to her chest like a parachute pack; all Star needed was a little red scarf and a leather baby helmet to look just like the Red Baronette.

"Look what I found," Amber said, shoving two grocery bags at me. I pulled a pineapple, some Mallomar cookies and two bottles of a cheap, but effective, asti spumante from one bag; the other was filled with bags of pretzels, barbecue- and vinegar-flavored potato chips, and a can of cashews.

"Some of our top-10 comfort foods," Amber said. "Well, maybe not the pineapple."

"Dinner is ready," Seal said, acerbically. "It's getting cold."

Amber just shrugged, not really aware she was late. Soon she was complimenting Merribeth and me on our culinary finesse.

Seal sniffed at the shrimp creole but ate it, nonetheless. "I don't understand why you feel you have to take perfectly good shrimp, then ruin them with all that Tabasco sauce," she said as she polished off everything on her plate.

I just smiled at her, and so did Merribeth. Amber was preoccupied with Star, who was lying on a blanket near Amber's feet.

"Warren Caramel came to see me," I told my friends. "We threw him out." I smiled at Seal again. This time, she smiled back. "I think I'm his main suspect," I told Merribeth and Amber. "He's got a photograph of my bootprint."

"There's no way he can pin the fire on you," Amber insisted. "I'm the owner. His first bullet's got my name on it."

Merribeth shook her head and sighed. "I think he suspects me," she said. "You know, the evil daughter, who wants to blame everything on her father."

"Well, what do we do if he actually arrests one of us . . . or all of us?" I asked them. "Maybe it's time we started taking Warren Caramel's incompetence seriously."

"Now, Wendy," Merribeth interjected, "you can't really say it's incompetence. We haven't been able to figure out who set the fire, either, have we?"

"No, Merribeth," I said, exasperated. "No we haven't. But in case you haven't noticed, it's his job, not ours."

Merribeth pursed her lips, then bent down to pick up Star. She baby-talked to Star while Amber said, "Oh, hell, he can't touch us.

166

He's got no real evidence. Does he?"

Seal got up to slice the key lime pie.

"So why should that stop him?" I asked. "It will look bad if he doesn't wrap up the case."

I helped Seal bring the pie slices to the table.

"Who wants this?" Seal asked, looking disdainfully at the pie slices. Merribeth and Amber both grabbed one. "Everyone likes apple," Seal said and sat down. I set a piece of key lime pie in front of her and she reluctantly sank her fork into it.

"Good stuff," Amber said. Seal chewed slowly and was silent. Merribeth put Star down and sampled the pie.

"So what are we going to do if we go to jail?" Merribeth asked.

"Prison," Amber corrected. "Jail's just for small stuff. Firebugs go to prison."

Seal had finished her pie. She set down her fork. "You are not going to prison," she said. "If you're arrested, you hire an attorney."

"Let's face it," I said to Seal. "There's nobody else except us whom Warren's investigating."

Seal looked at me as if she could see right through a window in the back of my head. "If you didn't do it, then you won't go to prison," she said. "I won't let it happen."

Merribeth, Amber and I all looked, surprised, at Seal, who seemed as determined as a boulder blocking a highway. She just looked at us and didn't smile but didn't flinch, either.

"Thanks, Mom," I said. "We appreciate your support."

"Oh, Mrs. Whitby," Merribeth said, "don't you worry about us. Everything's going to be all right. Isn't it, Wendy?"

"Oh, yeah, just peachy," I said. Merribeth patted my arm.

"Don't worry about it, Wendy," she said. "It will be all right."

Amber pushed away from the table. "I don't know about you," she said, "but I could use a walk."

"You never walk. You drive," I reminded her.

"I could use a walk," she insisted.

Amber quickly bundled Star up and slung her trench coat around her own shoulders.

Merribeth and I found our coats. "Don't think I'm going to do the dishes," Seal said, huffily, then walked into the living room and picked up a crossword puzzle.

"Ready?" Amber asked.

We followed her into the early April evening. A mist was hanging in the sky like a cough, and the air was as cold as Warren Caramel's handshake.

"Where are we going?" I asked.

"How the hell should I know?" Amber replied. "Let's go."

So we all walked around the block.

"This could be one of the last times we're together like this, eating, walking, having a good time," Amber said.

Merribeth sighed. "Do you think Warren Caramel will ever solve the case?"

"Who cares, really?" I asked. "We need to move on."

"We're not moving anywhere if we're locked up in Waysippee Women's Farm and State Pen," Amber pointed out.

We returned to Seal's driveway.

"Too bad my father destroyed our tree house," Merribeth said. "We used to do some of our best thinking up there."

And then we looked at each other. We were still the Fearsome Threesome, weren't we? The tree house was gone, true. . . . But there were other trees.

"Come on," I said, and led my Fearsome confederates into Seal's backyard. Two maple trees stood there. One, tall and slender, reached toward the moon. The other spread its ample branches as if it preferred the company of the raspberry bushes to that of the other maple and was trying its best to just blend in with the bushes. We walked over to that tree. It's where I would have built my tree house if Seal had allowed it. The branches were low and there were plenty of crooks where we might sit if we were silly enough to try it.

"Want to go up?" I asked. "You bet," Amber said.

"That would be nice," Merribeth said.

"There's a ladder in the garage," I said.

We headed into the garage, but the ladder had a couple rungs broken.

"Maybe it's a bad idea," I said.

"No, wait," Merribeth said. "I know my father's got a ladder."

So we tiptoed through the backyard, squeezing past the raspberry bushes and into Merribeth's parents' backyard. We sneaked into the garage, and there, against one wall, a sturdy aluminum ladder seemed to be just waiting for us. It was kind of difficult turning the ladder from vertical to horizontal without dinging Mr. H's silver BMW, but we managed this maneuver. Amber was toting Star in the baby sling and wasn't much help carrying the ladder, but Star was as quiet as a first-rate cat burglar, with her eyes wide open, as if memorizing how to do this for when she was a little older. Merribeth and I silently cleared the doorway with the ladder. Amber tripped over the lawn mower on her way out and yelled, "Jesus Christ," then slapped her hand over her mouth.

Merribeth giggled. I don't know what got into her. Star chortled, too. Merribeth and I trotted across the hard ground with the ladder, and Amber and Star trailed with Star laughing merrily. We had trouble slipping through the raspberry bushes with the ladder, so we dropped the ladder on Seal's side of the bushes and it clattered. Merribeth and Star giggled some more. Then we all slid through the bushes, grabbed the ladder, and ran to the maple tree. I set the ladder against the broad trunk so it ended at a commodious, scooped-out crook.

"After you," I bowed to Amber. Then it dawned on us that perhaps Star was too young to become airborne.

"She'll be fine. Really," Amber insisted and clambered her way into the crook with Star still in the sling. Amber really didn't seem any more uncoordinated than she had been 30 years earlier and managed to make it up the tree with just a couple "damns." Amber sat in the tree, facing me. "See. Easy as key lime pie," she said and we all laughed.

Merribeth picked a spot and climbed up easily. I found a perch on a limb that was as broad as a swing seat.

"Who-hoo," Amber yelled, "isn't this great? It's Star's first taste of the Fearsome life."

Then Amber's eyes got as wide as her daughter's.

"Do you think we should initiate her?"

"What do you mean?" I asked.

"You know," Amber said. "What you did for me. The Pepsi. The brownies. . ."

"We don't have Pepsi. Or brownies," I said.

"Well, there's plenty else. It's not an exact science," Amber said.

I looked at Merribeth. She shrugged.

"OK, wait here," I said and climbed out of the tree. Inside the house, I grabbed the remaining half-bottle of asti spumante and the Mallomar cookies.

"Where are you going with that?" Seal asked, as she scoured the sink after having washed the dishes.

"Oh, Mom," I said. "We would have washed them."

"And someday we'll go sunbathing in January," she said. I hugged her quickly and dashed out the back door. The logistics of initiating Star into the Fearsome life while in a tree and without a tree house were daunting. I handed the asti spumante to Amber.

"Hey, she's not even on formula yet," she said.

"You said you've got to start them young," I told her.

"Oh, yeah," she said.

Amber really couldn't handle Star and a bottle of asti spumante at the same time, so Merribeth slid out of her cranny and inched down a branch until she was near Amber, and Amber passed the bottle to her. I stood on the ladder near them.

"Like you said, Merribeth," Amber remarked, "We could use a good tree house just about now. Why was it again your old man wrecked it, Merribeth?"

"Oh, you know," Merribeth said quietly. "Just because."

***

The day of Joey Hartwell's funeral, I'd been up in my bedroom, changing out of my funeral clothes, when I heard this thwacking sound. I looked out the window and wasn't surprised to see Mr. H. chopping our tree house down. He'd always thought the tree house was some kind of he-man fort for Joey, although the Threesome had taken it over right from the start. And who knows, maybe

170

that was part of Mr. H's reason for destroying it. I know that's what Merribeth thought.

It was almost as sad for me to watch Mr. H. demolish that piece of our childhood as it was to think that I'd never see Joey again. He'd given up a scholarship to the University of Wisconsin to go to Vietnam because his father, our father, said that boys who got 2-S deferments were cowards, and Joey had wanted to make his father proud.

Joey was stationed near Ke Sanh. I looked it up once on a map in the Weewampum High School library. He was just an infantryman, and that was such a waste because he really was a smart boy. But I knew he wanted to prove to Jim that he could take the heat, stay in the kitchen, that he truly was his father's son.

Merribeth told me that she and Joey had been talking once, and he asked her if she weren't a girl, would she go to Vietnam? And she said she didn't know, but she didn't think so. Mr. H. overheard them and said, "You're lucky you're my daughter and not my son."

I know Joey wrote to his family just about every day from Vietnam and never complained about the rain or the food or anything, even about all the blood and death and senseless loss. He saw a lot of his friends die in combat – or from accidents – or get a leg blown off or leave part of their faces behind in the jungle weeds. Merribeth couldn't understand how her brother could stand to see all these things and worried about him constantly. And so did I.

I wish Joey had realized he really didn't have to do this, that he just could have gone off to the university and become an architect like his father and lived happily ever after in some more cosmopolitan place than Weewampum, Wis., U.S.A. But Joey wanted his dad to be proud of him, and slapping mosquitoes and shooting rifles at strangers in some far-off land seemed the most direct route to winning his father's respect.

Joey wrote Merribeth about how some nights when he had sentry duty, he'd be standing out in the middle of the jungle, trying to sort out the sounds of birds and bugs from the more sinister noises like the tiptoeing of boots. He'd sniff the air for the smell of gunpowder or sweat mingling with the odor of the wet, heavy leaves and constant mud, and he'd try to peer into the black, muggy night to spot he wasn't sure exactly what.

It was an Army sergeant who told the Hartwells, and then, Merribeth, who eventually told me, how one hot muggy night no different from the others, someone sneaked up on Joey. There were soldiers down the line on either side of him, and they heard nothing at all. Someone sneaked up on Joey and split his head open like a melon, using the pointed end of a bayonet. The sentries did hear Joey scream once before they heard him slump to the ground. They shone a flashlight, spotted a teenage Vietcong and shot him; he was just another young man, doing his soldierly job. He screamed once, too, as he fell into the mud. Then all they could hear was the buzz of the bugs. You can't say the war effort was helped much on that clammy, black night in June near Ke Sahn.

Joey came home in one of those plastic body bags, or at least I assume he did. I never really inquired about the details, and Merribeth didn't tell me this part. She did say her father broke down and cried all night the day the soldier came to the Hartwells and told them their son and brother was dead.

You could tell that Mr. H. was proud of Joey by the way he carried the flag they gave him at the funeral, like a bouquet of Fourth of July lilies and blazing zinnias and bachelor buttons. Merribeth said her father ordered everyone in the family not to change a thing in Joey's bedroom.

So you would think that Mr. H. would have wanted to leave everything the way it was – including the tree house. I know when he built it, he probably figured it would be Joey's hideout, his sentry post, but when the Threesome took it over, Mr. H. never said a word to us about it. Maybe that afternoon of the funeral, he was thinking that if Joey had had a chance to get some early lookout training in the tree house, that if we girls had not stolen the tree house from Joey, then maybe Joey would still be alive. Maybe chopping down the tree house was a way for Mr. H. to release his anger that it was us girls, not his son, who could still walk and talk and laugh and climb a tree if that's what we really wanted to do. I didn't really know, but I just wasn't surprised when I heard the steel ax sinking into the old yellow bathroom door that had been our private deck. Mr. H. splintered the tree house into seven pieces like stakes from some jagged picket fence. Then, he started on the apple tree, itself, and that's when I started screaming.

My mother flew up the stairs to see what was the problem and ran to the window and looked out.

"That bastard," she yelled and opened up the window and screamed at Jim Hartwell, but no one really heard her because Mrs. H. and Merribeth had run into their backyard and were screaming at Mr. Hartwell, too.

For a moment, Seal and I stopped our yelling. We couldn't help but just stand there and watch the neighborhood drama play out.

"Stop it! Just stop it, Jim!" Mrs. H. screamed. "That tree is a friend of this family!" But Mr. H. just chopped all the more.

"Stop it, Daddy, stop it!" Merribeth screamed and ran to her father's side. Mrs. H. ran after Merribeth, screaming, "Stop it, Jim! You can't bring him back. Now don't destroy another living thing!"

Mr. H. paused with the ax in the air, then turned and faced Mrs. H. and Merribeth, glowering like a bull. His face was so red it seemed it would burst open. I couldn't just stand there and watch him chop Merribeth and Mrs. H. in two.

I raced down the stairs and out of the house and Seal tore after me. We charged through the raspberry bushes and into the Hartwells' yard, but by the time that we got there, Mrs. H. had somehow wrestled the ax from Mr. H.'s hands. She was marching into the garage with the ax and she must have flung it at the car because we heard a loud DING. Mr. Hartwell was crumpled into a ball at the base of the tree, sobbing, as if life were too horrible for him to bear.

My mother took my hand and led me home, and there she pulled me into her arms. She was crying, and I was crying, and it was something we never did.

***

So now, as Merribeth, Amber and I were about to make the

173

Fearsome Threesome a Foursome, we were trying to adjust to changing times and tree accommodations and only partially succeeding. Merribeth couldn't reach Star with the asti spumante from where she perched, so Amber pulled the wriggling baby out of the sling and held her in both hands.

"Hurry up," Amber said, nodding at the bottle. "Just do it."

Merribeth leaned toward Amber, but the angle wasn't quite right and some wine hit the ground and not our newest member.

"Let me get closer," Merribeth said and gingerly inched toward Amber and Star. "OK, I think this will work," she said and raised the bottle, but just then Seal yelled, "Stop! What on earth are you doing?!" My mother had sneaked up on us and was standing under the maple tree, next to the ladder where I was still perched. "Have you lost all common sense?" she screamed.

Merribeth lowered the bottle and balanced herself on the limb. Amber tried to hold Star still in her lap. I just looked down at Seal. What was she doing here?

"Get out of that tree right now!" she insisted. "Put that baby in that sling and get down here this instant!"

You'd think we all were grade-school girls whom Seal had caught stealing birds' nests, and I guess we looked pretty stupid for women who were supposed to be grown-ups. Amber, Merribeth and I looked at each other sheepishly.

"Oh, Mother, it's . . ."

"Get down here. NOW!" Seal demanded.

Merribeth, Amber, and I glanced at each other and shrugged. OK, maybe Seal had a point. Amber picked Star up to tuck her back into the sling. And she would have, but all of us were distracted when we noticed a pair of headlights and then a car pull into the Hartwells' driveway. It was Mr. H's car, the sporty one, the red Alpha Romero. The lights flicked off. The door opened. Jim Hartwell stepped out. We thought he'd walk into the house, but instead, he headed toward the garage. He looked around cautiously, peeked inside the garage, then pulled its service door shut. Apparently, we'd forgotten to close it. He looked around the side of the garage suspiciously; he glanced toward Seal's yard.

And then he must have glimpsed the aluminum ladder, or maybe he saw us first.

He strode to his side of the raspberry bushes and yelled, "Who's there?"

We didn't answer.

He pushed through the bushes and into our yard and up to us. "Well, wouldn't you know," he said. "It's Merribeth. And Seal, too. And, uh . . . Wendy. And your little friend with the baby. And it looks like you've got my ladder, too."

"We borrowed it," Merribeth said.

"I told you to stay away," he said to Merribeth. "We don't want to see you. We don't want to have anything to do with a traitor."

Then, Seal amazed us. She walked right up to Jim Hartwell, hands on her hips, eyes blazing like kindling. "Get out of my yard, James Hartwell," she snapped. "If you don't know what a good daughter you've got, then you're a fool."

"She's a traitor," he growled. "And you and your daughter have turned her against me."

Then he pushed Seal aside as if bending back a twig and marched right up to me.

"Get off my ladder now, you stupid idiot," Jim yelled at me, looking more furious than was called for, almost as angry as the day he'd chopped down the tree house.

"If I'm a stupid idiot, then I guess I inherited it from you," I yelled right back.

I've said it before and I'll say it again. I've never quite mastered the art of thinking ahead. With just a few words, I'd betrayed my mother's secret, and now all I wanted to do was crawl under a raspberry bush and hide there and hope the sun would come out in the morning.

A shock wave seemed to ripple across Jim's face, and then he backed up and started to turn for his yard. But before he could take more than a step or two, Merribeth yelled at her father like an avenging archangel, "You come back here right now and apologize to Wendy. You come back here right now and apologize to my sister."

Seal gasped. So did I. Merribeth seemed to understand exactly what I'd said. How long had she known? Amber shrieked, "What did you say?"

Mr. H. stopped in his tracks. I started climbing down the ladder; I was getting dizzy. Seal grabbed my hand.

"You just bring me back my ladder," Mr. H. rumbled.

"What's going on here?" Amber yelled.

"Stay out of our business," Merribeth and I yelled at Amber at the same time. Amber involuntarily reached her hand toward her mouth, and somehow Star squirmed out of her mother's other hand and in an instant was rocketing headfirst toward the ground.

Amber screamed. Seal and I both dove for Star. I almost caught her, but she slid through my hands like Silly Putty and crumpled in a heap amidst the tree roots. I bent to her. She was still breathing. I was afraid to touch her.

"There's no time for 911," Mr. H. yelled. "I'll get a piece of plywood. We can lift her that way." He ran through the raspberry bushes toward his garage. "I'll drive us to the hospital."

Chapter 14

Seal's Fried Egg Sandwich

2 pieces of sprouted wheat bread (Wendy makes me buy this. I used to use white and I don't see what the big deal is.)
1 fried egg, easy over
Mayonnaise (Salad dressing works just as well)
Ketchup
Salt
Pepper
Cooking oil

Warm up the oil in a frying pan and crack open an egg and drop it into the pan.
Fry it on one side.
When the white starts becoming visible in the yolk, flip the egg over with a spatula.
Let it get crispy brown on the edges but don't let it burn.
Meanwhile, put two pieces of bread in the toaster and toast.
Spread mayonnaise or salad dressing on each piece of toast.
Shovel a fried egg onto one piece of coated toast.
Pour on some ketchup.
Wendy likes to use salsa but I can't be bothered with that.
Put the other piece of toast on the top and you're ready to go.

It was less than a mile from Seal's house to Our Lady of Perpetual Need Medical Center. When the new building opened, it would be at least five. Amber sobbed about what a bad mother she was on the ride over; Merribeth just kept patting her arm. Star didn't make a sound, and neither did anyone else.

The hospital staff started working on Star immediately when we carried her in on the plywood. I have to commend them on their swiftness in springing into action, although their policies about visitors need to be revised. A nurse told Amber she couldn't follow Star into the examining room.

"I'm on the hospital board. You've got to let me in," Amber screamed. A nursing supervisor and two orderlies sprang out of the supervisor's office.

"Rules are rules," the supervisor said. "We have to get her

stabilized."

An orderly flew to each side of the supervisor. There was no way Amber was getting past this defensive line.

They had other plans for Amber, anyway. She had to fill out insurance papers. I guess Amber must have learned a lesson about having no insurance for Amberosia's. She had a top-of-the-line, Blue Cross policy for her daughter. She frantically tore through her purse three times before Merribeth helped her find Star's insurance membership card.

But after the papers were in order, there was nothing to do but wait in a corridor the color of veins on hard, orange, molded-plastic chairs.

Amber alternated between sobbing and closing her eyes as if praying, while biting big gashes into her lips.

"God forgive me," she cried over and over. "God forgive me."

Merribeth and I took turns hugging her and telling her there was nothing to forgive.

"God forgive me," she cried. "God forgive me."

Finally, a surgeon in a scrub suit appeared. He said Star's spleen and gall bladder had been shredded. They'd removed the gall bladder and tried to stitch the spleen back into place. Her spine was fractured in three places. She had a brain concussion. She was alive – for now – but unconscious and would be in intensive care for quite some time. They couldn't predict if there would be brain damage. They couldn't say for sure if she'd even pull through. But we should all go home now; Amber included. They wouldn't allow Amber to see Star until tomorrow, when she'd be more stabilized.

"I'm not leaving," Amber sobbed. "I've got to see my baby." The surgeon just sighed and hustled off to the room where surgeons go.

"I've got to see her. I've got to see her," Amber cried.

"There, there," Merribeth tried to comfort her. "You can see her in the morning."

"I have to see her now," Amber insisted. "She needs me. She can't go to sleep without me."

Merribeth and I hugged Amber and cried along with her but

178

there was nothing we could do. Finally, my mother, who'd been unusually silent, even for her, walked up to Amber and touched her shoulder.

"Why don't you spend the night with us, Amber?" Seal suggested. "It would do you some good to get some rest. You're going to need it."

Amber just howled, in her own world of pain.

"I've got to see her. I can't leave her. I almost killed her. I've got to see her," she repeated like a rosary, as if by saying these words over and over, she could somehow will her daughter to stay alive.

My father, who was sitting several chairs down, joined our little huddle.

"There's nothing more we can do tonight," he said. "She'll be so full of drugs she won't wake up for days. We should go now."

I shot a look at Mr. H. I didn't know how to feel about him at the moment. Merribeth looked at him, too, almost calculating her risks, then grabbed his hand and laced her fingers between his.

"I'm glad you were there for us, father," she said shakily. It couldn't have been easy for her to tell him this after the way he'd been treating her.

Mr. H. studied his hand a second, then pulled Merribeth to his chest. I noticed he was crying.

"I'm sorry, baby," he said, his voice breaking. "Please come home and stay with us tonight."

I was feeling pretty carried away by this father-daughter reunion until I remembered that he was my father, too. I guess he must have been thinking along the same lines, because he pulled away from Merribeth a little and extended his hand to Seal. To my knowledge, it was one of the first times in years he'd acknowledged that Seal existed.

"I'm sorry about a lot of things," he said, his voice softer than I'd ever heard it. I even saw some tears forming in Seal's eyes. She'd only been waiting to hear those words about half a century. She took his hand and glanced at him briefly, but then turned her full gaze on me.

"Don't be sorry," she said, rather clipped. She didn't smile but she didn't frown, either. And then Jim Hartwell stretched out his hand to me.

"I'm sorry I didn't get to know you better, Wendy," he said softly, and I didn't have any words to say back. I just looked at my hand in his and then into his eyes and he looked back.

I tried to smile but I didn't have any left, so I just willed that the Great Eternal Manipulator in the Sky or all of our collective good wishes were enough to force Star to stay alive through the night.

I'd been so wrong about Star. It was when she'd been slipping through my fingers that I realized how right Amber had been. Star was our light, the one to carry on our tradition. She was what we'd needed, even if we hadn't known it. Amber had been wise to go ahead and have her. If I could have traded places with Star and been the one with the brain concussion, I would have done it in an instant.

"Let's go home," Jim Hartwell told us. "The baby's in good hands."

"I can't leave," Amber cried quietly.

"I'll stay with Amber," Merribeth said.

"Me, too," I said.

So Jim Hartwell offered his arm to Seal, and she gingerly took it but kept her distance, and they slipped out the emergency room doors and into the murky night.

Before we even had a chance to try to get more comfortable in those unforgiving chairs, I spotted a body running down the hallway, blond hair flying like thunderbolts and with a physique like a Greek discus thrower. Oh, shit. It was Lars.

I saw him before Merribeth or Amber noticed and tried to motion him to turn around and disappear. But he kept on coming. I couldn't distract him. And then he was on us, shaking Amber and yelling, "Jesus Christ! What did you do to her?"

Amber screamed. So did Merribeth. "Get off her," Merribeth shrieked and kicked Lars and pulled him back by his hair.

I clasped my arms together and whammed him in the stomach. He stumbled, Merribeth let go and he hit the floor. The same two orderlies materialized in the hallway but Lars waved them away.

"I'm OK," he groaned.

We stood panting, waiting to see what he'd do next.

"Just stay away," I yelled.

"I will, I will," Lars said, slowly crawling to his feet. "Just tell me what happened to her."

So we told him as he caught his breath in one of those plastic chairs.

We told him how we'd substituted the maple tree for the apple tree and how we missed our tree house. He didn't stop us and tell us to hurry up and get to the point so we pressed on. Merribeth and I stressed how well Amber seemed to be protecting Star as she sat up in the branches, and that Amber was a very good mother, and that we'd just wanted to initiate our youngest member into our tree-house sorority. We told Lars how Mr. H. distracted us just before Star tumbled out of the tree.

"That is so stupid," he said.

I thought Amber might rally and argue with him at this point, but she just cried.

Merribeth picked up the cudgels, however.

"It is not that stupid," she said. "We had a lot of good times up in the tree house. We just wanted to share them with Star."

"Couldn't you be doing something more useful," I shot at him, "like finding out how she is?"

Lars just stared at me kind of incredulously. "Don't you understand anything?" he said, his voice shaking. "Don't any of you understand anything? We don't know how she is. No one knows anything. Everyone is so stupid."

And then Lars Hunssen, rapist, gynecologist, Fabio imitator, and Star's father, sat on a hard orange plastic chair and cried.

I don't know who cried the loudest. Amber and Lars drowned out Merribeth and me pretty quickly. Finally Lars stood up.

"I'll let you know if anything changes," he said, sounding as professional as he could under the circumstances. He looked at Amber, who still was crying.

"It just was so incredibly stupid," he said.

"Oh, just shut up," Merribeth said.

He looked at us all and sighed.

"I'll keep you posted," he said and turned and strode down the long hall.

Amber just cried.

***

The next morning, it was snowing in great wet clots as we cracked open our eyes. We'd been dozing off and on all night in those chairs and the surly weather matched our moods. The day-shift nurse who started at 7 told us Amber's pediatrician had just arrived. He'd be evaluating Star this morning; he was the one who'd make any visitation decisions. It shouldn't be too much longer before we could see our little girl, the nurse said.

She told us we should move to the fifth floor, where there was a more private lounge for the families of I.C.U. patients. So we grabbed our purses and one of the *People* magazines from a formica-covered coffee table and wound up in a room as cozy as a dentist's office, even less welcoming than the hallway outside the emergency room. The maroon indoor-outdoor carpeting here was almost scuffed through in spots. The orange plastic chairs were tethered together. I don't know who they thought would want to take one home as a souvenir.

Finally, Doctor Vernon Rose towered over us.

"How is she? How's my little Starlight?" Amber cried.

"We don't know yet. She's had a nasty spill. She's unconscious and will need surgery but her vital signs are good. Her breathing's a little labored. How did this happen?" he intoned, as if reading from a medical chart.

We told him.

"Children are not toys," he said with a little more emotion, a stern man in his early sixties.

"I know that, doctor," Amber wept. "When can I see my daughter?"

He looked at Amber more intently and her remorse apparently ignited some small glimmer of compassion. "Later," he said. "Possibly this evening. I want to observe her for a little while longer; make sure she's stabilized. It will be good for her to have you with her later, but right now, she just needs to rest."

"I've got to see my little girl," Amber insisted.

"I'm sorry, Ms. Moore," Dr. Rose said. "But that's just not possible."

I reminded him, "She's on the hospital board." Dr. Rose patted Amber on the shoulder as if she were the same age as her daughter.

"Just take her home," he told Merribeth and me. "Bring her back around 7 tonight."

He disappeared before we could argue.

"I've got to see her," Amber cried.

She was becoming so unglued I thought she might have a stroke. Merribeth and I weren't faring much better, although we sat numbly while Amber cried and fidgeted.

Finally Merribeth said, "I think we should go home. There's nothing we can do here right now."

"I can't leave my baby," Amber cried like a reflex.

I knew how she felt and I wasn't one to eagerly follow doctors' orders, but I also had a backache that these chairs weren't going to help.

"Let's go home for a little while, Amb," I said more softly than I was used to hearing myself speak. "We can come back in a couple hours."

With both Merribeth and me prodding her, we managed to get Amber to agree to leave temporarily. We stepped outside into the clots of snow and then remembered we didn't have a car.

I phoned Seal. She was over in minutes, then drove us all to our house, where my mother insisted that Amber take her bed and Merribeth said the sofa would be fine with her and I fell into my own bed and we all woke up four hours later.

Well, actually, I woke up first and walked into the kitchen, where Seal was working on a crossword puzzle in the *Bugle*. I glanced at the banner headline: "Quicksand Quandary Bogs Down Hospital Plan." I read the story. It said construction workers at the new hospital had hit quicksand as they dug the foundation. No one was sure about the implications. They might have to stop construction completely, scrap the new building. Or maybe they could just shift everything over a few feet. At this point no one was sure.

I looked at Seal, who was looking up a word in the dictionary.

"Do you think we still have a chance to save the old building?" I asked her.

"Well, aren't we Miss Pollyanna?" she said without looking up. She wrote a word in the puzzle, then looked hard at me.

"Good thing the hospital was where it was and not out on the highway last night," she said.

"That's for sure," I said. She entered another word into the puzzle.

Merribeth walked into the kitchen silently, then asked if we had any orange juice. I poured her some. Seal told her she'd make her a fried-egg sandwich.

"No, Mrs. Whitby. I really don't want one," Merribeth said. "Yes, you do," Seal said, and started making sandwiches for all of us.

Then Amber stumbled into the kitchen and Seal fired up another egg.

I helped Seal serve the sandwiches. No one felt much like talking, except Seal, which was unusual.

"You can't see her until tonight? That's ridiculous. The sooner she knows you're there, the faster she's going to heal. That's just the way it is," she said, polishing off her sandwich before anyone else had taken more than a bite or two.

"Oh, God, what am I going to do?" Amber cried, starting up her first tears of the day.

Merribeth put an arm around Amber. "You've got us, honey," she reminded our friend.

"Not for long," Amber reminded her back.

"Eeaaahh, she's a scrappy kid, just like you," Seal said. "She'll fight her way out of it. You'll see."

Amber snuffled at Seal and tried to smile.

"What am I going to do if she doesn't . . . doesn't . . . ?" Amber sobbed.

"She's going to get better. She's got to get better," Merribeth tried to reassure her.

"She'd better get better if she knows what's good for her," Seal told her. "But tell me, have you thought about who's going to take care of her if Warren Caramel sends you girls to the slammer?" my mother asked, matter-of-factly.

"What?" Amber shrieked. "What?"

"Well, it's just something to think about," Seal said and shrugged, getting up and walking into the living room.

At that moment, I thought Seal was one of the most insensitive creatures this side of the Mississippi, but I knew better deep down. So I like to think maybe she said that just to get us to stop focusing on something we couldn't fix and thinking about something that maybe we could.

"Oh, my God. Who'll take care of my little girl if I'm locked up?" Amber ranted. "Oh, God. What am I going to do?"

"Now, look," Merribeth said. "We've got to stay calm. We're doing the best we can for Star. But maybe we should think about what Seal said. We still don't know who burned down the restaurant. Maybe there's a stone we've left unturned."

"What do you mean, Beth-a-weth?" I asked her skeptically.

"Well, it wouldn't hurt to go over everything one more time, you know, retrace our steps," Merribeth proposed.

Amber bawled and mocked, "Oh, sure, Merribeth. Just like on 'Columbo.'"

"That's it," I yelled. "That's what we should do."

Merribeth and Amber looked at me glassy-eyed.

"What?" Merribeth asked.

"Let's get in the car and go over to Amberosia's and look at what's there and go through everything we did the day of the fire, and maybe something we've overlooked will just pop to mind."

"That's a good idea, Wendy," Merribeth said. "What have we got to lose?"

"I'll get our coats," I said and jumped up. It beat sitting around watching each other bawl.

"I can't go," Amber cried. "What if the hospital calls?"

"You've got a cell phone. Come on. It won't take very long," I urged.

I found her trench coat in the front closet and the jaunty purple scarf she had stuffed inside a sleeve and draped them around her.

"I don't want to go," Amber said. "You go alone."

Seal was standing in the kitchen doorway. "You'd better go, too," she told Amber. "You might remember something they don't. If you don't go and you wind up in the slammer, you'll have only yourself to blame."

Amber looked at Seal for the longest time, then her eyes got wide.

"I guess I do have a cell phone," she said. "Mrs. Whitby, will you promise to phone if the hospital calls?"

"Cross my heart and hope to spit," Seal said.

***

The snow was hurtling down even faster now, determined like pigment flying from a paint gun. We pulled up in Seal's Olds at Amberosia's corner of soot-covered soil, now being whitewashed by snow. Empty fast-food wrappers and plastic containers whipped about in the wind.

"OK," I said. "Let's think carefully about what happened on the day of the fire."

"All I remember," said Amber, her voice quavering, "is that we shut down early so I could go have Star." And then she started crying all over again.

"We should try to be methodical," Merribeth said gently. "Let's try to start with when we opened up and try to mention everything that we can remember."

"All right, then," Amber gulped. "Well, I remember I poured the punch and smiled and wished everyone Happy Holidays."

"Did you notice anything suspicious?" I asked.

"Well, other than Lars and Jim showing up, uninvited . . ."

"Amber," Merribeth pointed out, "you know we didn't invite anyone. It was open to everyone."

"Well, who needed them?" Amber cried louder. "They wrecked everything. It was going along so perfectly until they showed up."

"Did you notice anything else?"

"Well, I felt all crampy. I was looking forward to closing because I was getting tired."

I guessed if Amber had noticed anything out of the ordinary, she would have mentioned it by now.

"Merribeth," I asked, "what time did you get to the restaurant and what were the first things you did?"

"I remember you were the first one there, Wen, and when I walked in about 8, the turkey was roasting and the hams were in the ovens and the pumpkin pies were baking and it all smelled so heavenly."

She said the Schaum Tortes had not fallen. The mincemeat and pecan pies were cooling on the racks, everything was flowing, and it was just like "Santa's kitchen." She wished she hadn't already eaten breakfast and had saved room for a piece of pecan pie.

She walked through the kitchen doors to the dining room, where the bright morning sun through the front window silhouetted the Christmas tree. We'd decorated the tree with popcorn and cranberry chains, cutout cookies, paper chains, and Seal's antique bubble lights to make the artificial evergreen seem quaint and old-fashioned.

When she turned on the lights, she saw what a good job our waitresses had done the day before, setting up. The green and red placemats were festive, and the live poinsettias on every table "added such a special touch."

We'd draped fake holly garlands from the ceiling and she paused to admire them. Then she straightened the chairs and asked Jennifer, one of the waitresses, to Windex the windows one more time. At Merribeth's request, Tony, the dishwasher, spent an hour vacuuming the dining room. Then, Merribeth, herself, went out and shoveled a light powder of snow and sprinkled sand on the walk.

By 10, everything seemed in order. We weren't opening until 11:30 so there was a lull during which Merribeth helped out in the kitchen, deviling eggs. She wondered if Amber was feeling well because our friend had said she'd be at the restaurant at least by 10, but by 11, she still hadn't made an appearance. Merribeth thought about phoning Amber, but then decided that Amber would phone if something was truly wrong.

"I was hunting all over the house for my Santa's cap," Amber snuffled. "Somehow, it wound up under my bed."

Sometime mid-morning, Merribeth wasn't sure precisely when, Henry filled the steam table with water and turned on the heat, and later, dumped ice into the salad bar well. Around 11:15, we started bringing out the food to the buffet line. At 11:20, Merribeth brewed the coffee, and by 11:25, we were all ready.

"Merribeth," Amber asked between snuffles, "how on earth do you remember all those times? You'd think you worked for an airline or the bus company."

Merribeth just smiled. "It was an important day for us," she said. "Some things just stick with you."

Merribeth said she turned on the CD player with its six discs of holiday music at 11:25. The first disc – her favorite – was all Christmas carols played on a hammered dulcimer. She looked around the room; everything seemed to just glow and she felt so proud we'd created this special place. Then she noticed something streak by the steamed-up front window, maybe the flash of a red scarf. At 11:30, when she unlocked the door, she was overwhelmed to see a line of people waiting to get in. The line stretched down the sidewalk and wrapped around the corner.

She walked among the throng, wishing everyone, "Happy Holidays," then invited the first ones to come inside.

"I felt so bad that people were standing out in the cold, but they just all wouldn't fit in the entry," she said. "But the line moved along pretty fast and I was so pleased at how well everything seemed to be going."

Merribeth said Amber walked in at 11:45, wearing her Santa cap, her fake leopard coat, and a flowing, red gauze top over an elasticized white gauze skirt.

"I wondered if she'd be warm enough," Merribeth said, but Amber assured her she would be fine. Merribeth found a chair for Amber, and Amber sat behind the buffet table, ladling out punch into paper cups right before the customers reached Merribeth at the cash register.

Then, it had been just nonstop people, and the restaurant still was packed at 1:30, when Amber started having contractions and we'd sent everyone home.

I remembered running to the kitchen and turning off the stoves, the ovens, the dishwasher, and the lights. I distinctly remembered we'd shut down everything in the kitchen and had quickly wrapped up the food and put it inside the walk-in. In fact, I'd asked Henry to double-check the kitchen and he said everything was A-OK. I wondered if Warren had interviewed Henry and the rest of our staff.

I'd sent everyone home without doing the dishes or finishing the cleanup. I didn't think it would be fair to make others stay after we left on Christmas Eve. And, all right, why take chances? I felt that it would be best if we, not an employee, were the last ones to leave.

Merribeth said after we'd shooed everyone out of the dining room, she remembered to shut off the coffee makers and the CD player and was sure that as we locked the front door she'd turned off the lights.

I remembered I'd almost forgotten to turn off the steam table. I was at the front door and Amber had her arm around me and was quite heavy and was moaning, and I asked her to try to stand by herself for a minute, so I could run back to turn off the steam.

"Do you remember that, Amber?"

"Naw," she said. "All I remember is the pain." And then she started crying again.

Merribeth patted Amber's hand but asked me, with some concern, "Do you remember I turned off the lights?"

And then I remembered that she had, because I remembered thinking as I pulled the door shut, locked it, and we left for the hospital, how quickly the restaurant had transformed from a party scene into a silent room and how still everything was.

"Oh, you know what?" Merribeth asked, as the snow covered our car windows in patterns, like crocheted doilies. "I remember 'Silent Night' was playing when I clicked the CD player off, and I remember thinking how magical that was."

"So where does that leave us?" Amber cried. "It doesn't sound like anyone noticed anything suspicious."

"I didn't," I said.

"Me, either," Merribeth said.

"Oh, that's just great," Amber sobbed. "Well how in hell did the place burn down?"

We looked at each other, blank. We had no idea. Then I had an idea.

"Maybe we should get out, walk around. You know, actually retrace our steps," I said. "Have you ever noticed how sometimes you get ideas when you're walking?"

"No," Amber said.

"It couldn't hurt," Merribeth said and opened the door.

I trailed Merribeth onto the long, narrow, rectangular lot. We thought Amber was going to stay in the car, but then we saw her stumble out. When she reached us, she said, "Oh, hell, I guess we're standing in the kitchen right now."

The snow clung to her hair and eyebrows like lost mashed potatoes. Amber took a few steps.

"Here's where the dishwasher and the ovens were. Here's the walk-in cooler." She walked through a pretend kitchen door and faced the street. "And here's the dining room."

She looked at me uncertainly. The wind was picking up and it was getting hard to hear each other. The snow was really coming down.

"I can't do this," Amber said, breaking into tears again. "All I can think of is Star." She grabbed inside her purse for her cell phone, dialed, then screamed into it, "Did they call yet? Did they call? Oh, OK. I can't hear you either. It's the wind."

She shoved the phone into her purse. Tears were freezing to her face.

"This is really stupid," she yelled. "I don't want to do this."

"Yes, I think we should go now," Merribeth agreed.

I was ready to call it quits, too, but I shouted, "Well let's just try to remember those last few minutes."

"Oh, Wen, let's go," Merribeth shouted.

Amber was already starting for the car but suddenly she paused, grabbed her stomach and cried, "Oh, my God."

"What is it?" Merribeth and I shouted, running up to her. She looked at us wild-eyed. "Oh, nothing," she shouted. "It's just the baby." The wind was howling and Amber's purple scarf flew almost perpendicular to the ground. Her hair lashed her face, which was contorted as if she were the wind, herself. Merribeth and I glanced at each other. Our friend looked quite demented. Merribeth reached for Amber, but Amber pushed her away.

"Stay away, you bastard," Amber screamed at Merribeth as if she were Lars. "The rest of you, Merry Christmas. Now, all of you go home."

Merribeth and I grabbed Amber's arms.

"Amber, stop it," I screamed.

We couldn't let her go mad right before our eyes. We started tugging her toward the car, but when we reached where the front door of Amberosia's used to be, Amber dragged her legs.

"Stop," she screamed. "We've got to lock up."

So Merribeth and I stopped and turned. The wind was whipping us. We were being buried alive by snow. Merribeth pretended to turn off the wall panel of lights and I locked the door; then, we turned to make a dash for the car.

"Wait, wait," Amber screamed. "I want to see the tree one more time. See, there it is," she pointed. "All lit up in the window. That's something I can tell my daughter about next Christmas Eve."

Merribeth and I glanced at each other. Poor Amber.

She started sobbing even louder, but her last words rang in our ears like Christmas bells clanging. Then we all looked at each other, even Amber. And we screamed, "The lights! The bubble lights!"

We'd forgotten to turn off Seal's antique tree lights! Maybe they'd shorted or frayed or something. Maybe we'd burned down Amberosia's after all.

We dove for the car and raced back to Seal's.

"We burned down Amberosia's," I yelled to Seal as we trooped in.

Her mouth fell open. "What?" she said.

Amber ran into the kitchen to phone the hospital, shrieking to Seal as she ran past her, "Did they call? Did they call?"

"Sit down," Seal ordered. But Amber phoned the hospital and demanded to speak to Dr. Rose, but he wasn't there. Then she asked for Lars, but he wasn't on duty. Amber darted back into the living room, where Merribeth and I were too nervous to sit down. Seal perched on the sofa, as if watching us on TV.

"What did you do to Amberosia's?" she demanded.

"We think we burned it down," I told her. "We think the bubble lights shorted out."

A smile broke across Seal's face like the one she got the time WMPM-AM 98 radio station pulled our name out of a hat and delivered an avocado-colored refrigerator.

"Well, what do you know?" she said, still smiling. "I hadn't thought about that."

She got up and planted herself in front of Amber. "Amber, go to bed. You look like you just saw a ghost."

"I think I did," Amber whispered.

"Well, go get some sleep now. We'll wake you up in plenty of time," Seal said. "Now, get in there if you know what's good for you."

"I can't," Amber said. "I have to go back to the hospital."

Merribeth and I glanced at each other. Amber was right.

"Come on," I told them. "Let's go."

Chapter 15

Our Lady of Pepetual Need Cafeteria's Gluten-Free Lemon Bars

1/2 cup white rice flour
1/2 cup butter, cut into pieces
1/4 cup powdered sugar
1 cup sugar
3 tablespoons white rice flour
1/2 teaspoon baking powder
1/4 cup lemon juice
2 eggs

Mix the first three ingredients in a food processor until crumbly and press into a greased 8" x 8" pan. Bake for 15 to 20 minutes at 350 degrees. Cool slightly.

Mix the rest of the ingredients and gently pour over baked crust. Bake at 350 degrees for 20 to 25 minutes longer. Take out of the oven when lightly brown on top and dust lightly with powdered sugar. Cut into squares while warm. Serves 9.

– From *Ann's Cooking From Scratch: Cookbook and Anthology* by Ann B. Moser

They finally let Amber in to see Star at 7 p.m., just as Dr. Rose said they would. Merribeth and I waited in the lobby because the I.C.U. lounge was full. It was Saturday night, the middle of a long weekend. The rose-colored marble floor was nice in this building we'd been trying to save and so was the statue of Jesus, but the 20-foot-high, acoustic-tiled ceiling gave this vestibule the warmth of the Weewampum Greyhound station. The hard plastic chairs were lined up in rows like soldiers who'd just finished a 50-mile hike but still weren't about to let down their guard. We watched the people come and go; the husbands with flowers and puzzled-looking children in tow; the older women by themselves, occasionally an older man, looking lost. Young mothers and stressed-out, middle-age women; nurses rolling patients to the door in metal wheelchairs that went thunk-a-thunk-a-thunk over the marble floor in this more-than-a-little shabby lobby.

"I hope she'll be all right. Don't you think she'll be all right?"

Merribeth pleaded.

"She'll be all right. She's a scrapper just as Seal said," I remarked, surprising myself by repeating my mother's words.

"She'll be all right," Merribeth said like a prayer.

"She'll be all right," I said like an incantation. She had to be all right. I'd just begun enjoying my aunt role. Why hadn't I cuddled Star more and allowed the smiles she so freely gave to force my own lips to curve up more often? Why hadn't I memorized her giggle, engraved her soapy smell after a bath onto my brain so I could replay this at will like a reliable CD? I'd underestimated how strong a pull one tiny, trusting face could have on an unsuspecting heart. I glanced at Merribeth, who looked as pale as a hospital sheet. She glanced at me and took a harder look. I must have looked the same way she did.

Finally, around 9, Amber exited the elevator and looked around, dazed. We scurried up to her.

"She's still unconscious," Amber said, her voice like rain glancing off gravel. "I touched her toes, her face. She didn't even blink. They said she's in a coma."

Amber fell into Merribeth's arms, sobbing.

Oh, my god. What had we done to our little girl?

"Will they let you stay with her?" Merribeth managed to whisper.

"I can stay with her," Amber said in great sobs.

"Can we see her?" I asked.

"No," Amber cried. "No, you can't. No visitors. Maybe sometime. Not now. I've got to get back."

She broke away from Merribeth's arms, darted to an elevator door that was just closing and was gone.

"A coma?" Merribeth said.

"Oh, my god," I said. And then we cried for our stupidity and our helplessness and because our lives couldn't go on, not really, if Star wasn't part of them.

We spent the night in the drafty lobby in the uncompromising plastic chairs, using our coats as tents. Around 5 a.m. Amber shook us awake. She looked scared, beaten, beyond tired.

194

"They hooked her up to a respirator," she cried, as if the words were glass on her tongue. "She can't breathe on her own."

"Have you eaten?" Merribeth asked. "Have you slept?"

Amber nodded, shook her head, shrugged. She neither knew nor cared.

"Amber, listen," Merribeth said. "You've got to hold up. You've got to sleep and eat so you can be there for her when she needs you. I'm taking you home for just a couple hours. I'll bring you right back. I promise."

Amber just looked, lost, at Merribeth.

"I can't," she whispered.

"You must," Merribeth insisted.

Amber looked to me.

"You've got to, Amb," I said.

And then with Amber crying, Merribeth and I bundled her up and got her into the Olds. I dropped them off at Merribeth's and helped Merribeth tuck Amber into bed. We agreed to meet at the hospital at noon, or sooner, if something changed.

Then the Olds found its way back to Seal's and I crawled into bed before my mother woke up. Around 11, while Seal was working the Sunday crossword puzzle and looking for a four-letter word for "sea lettuce," the Olds and I crept back to Our Lady of Perpetual Need.

Merribeth was already there. She said the I.C.U. lounge still was packed and that Amber was with Star and faring as well as could be expected. Star's condition hadn't changed.

Merribeth and I passed the afternoon in the lobby, and then the evening, and then the deep of the night. People came and went but not Amber. We mostly sat silently with our wishes that we could change the past and prayers that we could influence the future.

While we were sitting as still as the statue of Jesus, Amber slipped up to our chairs around 1:45 a.m.

"She's coughing in her sleep," she choked out. "They gave her something to stop the cough, but it hasn't kicked in yet. You guys better go home."

"We're here for you," Merribeth told her. "We're not leaving until you do."

Amber tried to smile but couldn't, then hurried back to the elevator.

A long metal bar kept Merribeth and me from pushing the chairs together to form makeshift beds. We lay across the chairs anyway. But of course we couldn't sleep.

In the morning around 8, when a new wash of visitors was vying for the empty seats around us, Amber appeared at our chairs with a smile like a field of new snow sparkling in the sun.

"She moved her foot when I touched her," Amber said. "I think maybe she recognized me. She's not coughing as much."

But Amber admitted, under our gentle questioning, that Star still was unconscious and her foot movement could have been a reflex. But we rejoiced with Amber at this small change.

"When can we see her?" Merribeth and I both asked.

"I don't know. Not for a while. A few days, maybe. I've got to get back," Amber said and disappeared behind an elevator door.

After another 10 minutes in the chairs, Merribeth said, "Maybe we should go home, take a shower. I'll stop over at Amber's and pick up some fresh clothes for her and some things."

That sounded like a good idea. We asked the I.C.U. nurse to tell Amber we'd be back in a few hours.

When I got home, Seal wasn't there. The house was cleaner than the hospital, and the refrigerator was stuffed full of casseroles. And then I remembered. It was Monday morning. Seal was starting her next round of chemo and radiation. She must have been thinking she'd be so sick afterwards that she wouldn't be able to do anything or that they even might hospitalize her. And I'd let her down again. I turned the Oldsmobile's nose in the direction of the hospital and let it find its way back.

I found Seal sitting next to a man with what seemed like Tourette's syndrome, on a hard plastic chair in the outpatient waiting room. The man was yelling, "The devil knows your name," at Seal, but she was working a crossword puzzle and seemed to be doing an exemplary job of ignoring him. When she saw me, though, her eyes welled up, but she blinked away the tears and said, "I could have used the car."

I hugged her and then asked the receptionist how long it would be before Seal had to report for her bout on the rack. The receptionist said about another 15 minutes, so I walked Seal outside and we leaned against a brick wall.

"I'm sorry, Mom," I told her. "I forgot. Star moved her leg a little." Seal patted my hand.

"That's good. Babies are tough," she said. "And thank you for coming."

I took Seal's arm and we walked inside, and four hours later, I took my mother home.

I put her to bed, pulled the shades and let her sleep. She seemed rather nonchalant about her experience, although she was exhausted. I was a total wreck.

What if the radiation didn't fry every single cancer cell? What if the chemotherapy didn't poison every last invader? How could I lose Seal now that we were finally starting to talk to each other? Why had it taken so long? Why were we so stubborn?

And Star? Why did these things have to happen? She was an innocent. Why were we not punished, not her? Come to think of it, why did anyone have to be punished? Why couldn't there just be a universal force that let us live and let live?

While Seal slept on, I dug through the closet of the room that used to be mine and that I still occupied. Although Seal had transformed this eight-by-ten space into a beige desert, I got lucky and found my Barry McGuire single in a stack of records she hadn't thrown out.

The only stereo in the house was part of the TV console in the living room. I tiptoed to the record player and dropped "The Eve of Destruction" on its spindle. Because I can be considerate every now and then, I kept the volume just barely audible, then curled into a snail position and cried for all the world's lost souls, especially mine.

I wanted my mother to be healthy and to live to be at least 125. I wanted Star to grow up to be a strong, smart woman, with a lot more sense than the Threesome combined. Before I could play the record for the fifth time, the phone rang. It was Merribeth.

She'd found some clean jeans and a fresh sweatshirt for Amber. She couldn't get anything done. All she could do was think of Star. Did I want to go back to the hospital now or wait until after dinner?

I told Merribeth I wanted to get back and find out if anything had changed, and I wanted to stay and take care of Seal but she was resting.

"What do you think I should do?"

"I don't know," she said and paused, then suggested, "Well, there is one thing we could do that might be kind of positive."

Oh, great, I thought. I hoped she wasn't going to propose anything that involved smiling or any physical effort.

"What's that?" I asked, without enthusiasm.

"Well, we could go tell Warren about the lights," Merribeth said. "That might give us some good news to tell Amber."

So I picked Merribeth up and we drove to the fire station. Miss Trumble, Warren's new secretary, who had transferred to the job from the Department of Public Works, had gray hair and granny glasses. She must have been pushing 65. She asked if we had an appointment, and when we said we didn't, she said we'd have to leave. But we told her we'd wait, that perhaps she could find a way to work us in. Miss Trumble sighed and went back to pecking at her computer keyboard, ignoring us. I'm not sure what was going through her mind. She could have advised Warren that we were there and given him the opportunity to sneak out a window, or she could have phoned the Police Department, which was just down the hall, and it wouldn't have been a big problem for an officer or two to stop by and escort us out the door. But at 4:45, when Merribeth and I were thinking that we should be leaving, Warren sauntered out of his inner office. Miss Trumble didn't even look up; she just kept typing.

Warren did a double take when he saw us. "What brings you here?" he asked. Miss Trumble stopped typing.

"We know who set the Amberosia's fire," I said. Warren raised one eyebrow, then continued toward the door.

"Stop!" Merribeth said in the commanding voice of a teacher breaking up a fist fight.

"We know who did it, and we've been waiting here for hours to talk to you, and we want to do it now."

Warren stopped with his hand on the push-bar that opened the door. "Is that right?" he said.

"Yes," Merribeth said. "We'd like to speak with you in your office."

So, Warren Caramel headed into his office and Miss Trumble's eyes were question marks behind her glasses. Her eyes followed us into Warren's room, but then Warren shut the door.

Warren sat behind his desk, his upper lip pulled into an unsteady sneer, like a baby bat trying, for the first time, to master the concepts of aerodynamics.

"We know who did it," I told Warren, pausing for emphasis. He was barely making eye contact, but I knew he was listening.

"We did it," I said.

Warren's mouth fell open and his eyes flew wide. He fumbled for a notebook and pen, ready to take our confession.

"It was the bubble lights, really," Merribeth amended. "An accident."

Warren squinched his eyes and glared at us while we filled him in on the details of how we'd forgotten to turn off the old-fashioned tree lights. Warren set down his pad in obvious disgust and stood up and aimed himself at the door. We stood up, too.

"If I need you, I'll call you," Warren said. He didn't say, "Thank you," or "Way to go," or "How clever of you to figure this out," or "How could you be so stupid?" or even "Get lost." Just, "That will be all."

Merribeth and I stared at each other. Warren hadn't written down anything we'd said or really even paid attention. He hadn't taken us seriously.

"Look, Warren," I said, "that is what happened. You can either accept it and close the case and give us all a rest, yourself included, or you can keep barking up the wrong tree, but you'll just go hoarse."

Warren sucked in his cheeks and squeezed his mouth so it looked like a prune.

"You'll be hearing from me," he said, flinging open his inner office door as if wishing it were a rock he could hurl at us. Then he stomped past Miss Trumble and out the main door.

Merribeth and I looked at each other. This encounter wasn't exactly going to perk Amber up. We nodded at Miss Trumble.

"Thank you," we both said. She nodded back. "Good luck to you," she said.

***

At the hospital, we asked an I.C.U. nurse to send Amber out to the lounge. Amber said Star was coughing slightly less. Whatever was attacking her daughter had to be stopped now, before it turned into pneumonia. We gave Amber the jeans and sweatshirt. She thanked us and set them on an empty chair. She was barely functioning, couldn't process things. Merribeth picked up the clothes and walked Amber to a restroom, insisting she change. Amber just numbly did as told. When they returned, Merribeth had stuffed Amber's soiled things into a plastic bag. Amber hurried back to be with Star.

The I.C.U. lounge was nearly vacant now. It was strange how the population here ebbed and flowed. I didn't want to think about the implications of that but couldn't help it. The *People Magazine* on the end table didn't distract me enough to take my thoughts off Star and Seal.

Around midnight, Amber returned and seemed slightly less distraught. "Go on home now. Nothing's happening," she told us. "She's not coughing as much."

Amber managed a slight smile and then ducked behind closed doors.

Merribeth and I capitulated and decided we needed a night's rest in our own beds. We went home and fell asleep, exhausted. Then we got up the next day and headed back for the orange plastic chairs.

And so our days went. To the hospital. Home. Hospital. Home. At home, Seal was getting sicker and sicker as a result of her treatments. She was completely bald again. She had dropped to 93 pounds and walked bent over like a 93-year-old woman. I could almost tell time by how often she threw up. I wanted to help her, make it better. I brought brown rice to her bedside, 7-Up. And then she threw that up. But some days she'd get up and sit at the kitchen table. On those days she'd say, "The bathtub needs cleaning. The carpet is filthy."

I tried to keep things shining to her exacting standards but there always was something else. "Did you vacuum the venetian blinds yet?"

I'd pull out the vacuum and just before I'd get started, she'd say, "Oh, never mind. You'd better go see Star."

So I'd oblige her and go and wait for nothing. Because nothing changed.

We were waiting. Waiting patiently. Waiting impatiently. Waiting was something that Merribeth, Amber, and I didn't do well. Seal was waiting, too, to see if all her vomiting and sweating and exhaustion from her treatments was going to pay off this time. Merribeth probably did the best job of waiting and Seal was a trouper. Amber hung in there. I complained the most.

Sometimes, as Merribeth and I squirmed on the plastic chairs, we'd talk about how hard it had been for Merribeth to keep it a secret all these years that her father was really mine, too.

"How could you not tell me, not even once?" I asked her.

"My mother made me promise," she said. "She wanted to keep our family together, no matter what. She thought it would be easier for all of us this way."

Merribeth said her mother had told her one night when she was in eighth grade.

"She told you voluntarily?" I asked her, even though I'd heard what she said. "Why would she tell you?"

"Because of Amber. I felt so bad you were spending so much time with her and not with me that I guess my mother just wanted to assure me that you and I would always be close."

"Oh, Beth-a-weth," I said. I felt like a jerk, even though it was 30 years ago that I'd dropped Merribeth like a hot potato when

Amber flared into my life. But then my oldest best friend next door had shown my new best friend our tree house, and we'd been a threesome ever after. Still, I couldn't puzzle out how even though Merribeth and I were half-sisters, we were as different as dawn and dusk. I never could have kept this secret all these years.

"Weren't you ever tempted to tell me?" I asked her. "Not even once?"

"Oh, sure, every day," she said. "But I made a promise to my mother not to tell anyone. Anyway, it wasn't so hard. I just felt like your older sister, who had to keep this secret so our families could do what they thought was best. In some ways, it made me feel closer to you, kind of special, that I was sort of protecting you."

Oh, god. I loved Merribeth, although I'd probably never understand her. But instead of telling her how much I appreciated her, I asked, "Well, what do you think we should do now? You know, now that everything's out in the open, more or less."

"What do you mean?" she replied. "Nothing's really changed."

I thought about this for a while. Nothing had really changed. Seal and Mr. H. weren't about to become an item. Maybe I could give him a birthday present and a Father's Day, card but I didn't want to upset Mrs. H. if she happened to see them. I wondered if Merribeth's brother and sisters knew.

"Everyone knows," she said. "Everyone? Did Joey know?"

Merribeth paused and looked at me in a funny way.

"You know. Maybe he didn't," she said slowly but wouldn't comment further, even when I asked her what she meant. Anyway, she wasn't much help in suggesting how I should act toward our Dear Father. And really, none of us had any experience in these matters, so how could she know what to do?

"Just act natural," she'd say if I ever mentioned I felt uncomfortable about the situation. Maybe it was just that she'd had a lot more years to get used to the idea that we were all just one big happy family.

We waited and waited. Seal was sick. Star slept in a coma where, with a whole lot of luck, her young bones and brain were knitting and purling away, trying to put themselves back together. Amber

202

seemed manic-depressive. Merribeth was like Our Lady of Perpetual Sorrow. I was a basket case and wondering what I should do about returning to my job. I kept phoning and postponing my date of arrival by a few days, a week, whatever I could get away with.

I don't believe in predestination or anything, but sometimes you just have to do your part and then wait for others to do theirs. It's kind of like the Fates take over, and you might as well just go cruise the aisles of Wal-Mart or sort though your linen closet until those sisters stop gabbing with each other and get around to spinning and snipping the thread of your life. Merribeth, Amber, and I didn't have the energy for a Wal-Mart visit and cleaning the linen closet was beyond our powers. We were waiting, going through the motions, of what it took to push one day into the next and inch closer to hearing what we might not want to hear.

The only thing we didn't have to wait for was news on the fate of Our Lady of Perpetual Need Medical Center. A story in the *Weewampum Bugle* said that construction workers digging a hole a few feet from the quicksand broke a drill bit when they hit bedrock. Now, it seemed the hospital could be built just a few feet over from the original hole.

The morning I read this story in the *Bugle*, I grabbed the newspaper and headed for the recycling pile in the garage. I wanted to get it out of the house before Seal saw the news and it sent her to bed for the next three days.

As I was shutting the garage door, who should be getting into his red Alpha Romero next door but my dear darling father? I nodded at him. He was grinning. That was a little odd. Usually, he seemed so stern. He walked over to me, his *Bugle* tucked under his arm.

"Nice morning," he said. There was nothing nice about it. Heavy clouds hung over our heads like mallets. But my dad was smiling as if there were a rainbow somewhere I couldn't see. I nodded at the newspaper.

"Looks like you won," I said and took a step toward the house.

"Wendy, wait," he said, so I waited. "I was just heading over to the site. Why don't you come along?" he proposed.

I turned to look at my father. His dark eyes, usually severe, seemed more relaxed today. There were wrinkles around his chin where he'd creased in years of smiles and frowns, although the frowns held the edge. His face seemed well-worked, much used, and now he was using it to show how much he would like for me to come along with him.

For a brief moment, I could understand how Seal might have been tempted to put down *Gone With the Wind* one hot summer day and take a spin with Jim.

"I'd like to get to know you better," he said and smiled in a way that zoomed in under my sincerity radar.

So I got into the Alpha Romero, and Jim tooled over to the new hospital site, where bulldozers and ditch diggers and all manner of modern-day earth-eating equipment were plowing and pushing the soggy red soil into huge mounds.

"Aren't you jumping the gun?" I asked. "Don't you have to get some kind of official approval?"

"Let's say I'm optimistic," he smiled while shouting over the din. "We'll have to modify the plans a little. But the size and shape of the basement will stay the same so we might as well get started."

I watched the digging and plowing. I didn't have much to say. Nice to know my father was such an important person that he didn't have to bother with permits and zoning ordinances and all the other little regulations that were supposed to bind a town together.

"I hope it's a good idea," I finally managed.

"It will be," he said. "Come on."

We hopped back into the car and my father drove us to the drive-up window of the McDonald's along the interstate, where we both ordered coffee. Then we zoomed along the highway for a couple of exits.

"Sometimes, I just like to get out of town, take the car out, see what she can do," he said.

"Uh-huh," I said. Finally, I had to ask him, "So, how come you never gave me any inkling who you were?"

He didn't answer. Just kept driving. Typical male. Finally, he took a Pearville exit, drove a couple blocks and pulled up to a bakery. He stepped inside and reappeared, smiling again, with a white bag. Inside the bag were two giant, powdered-sugar-covered, custard-filled rolls.

"These are the best in the Carp River Valley," he said and got into the car and aimed it back at Weewampum. He ate and drank as he drove, which was interesting to watch. He obviously had done this more than a few times. A paper napkin on his chest and one on his knee fended off rogue droppings of powdered sugar. I wasn't anywhere nearly as adept keeping the sugar off my jeans and turtleneck sweater.

But there was no way he was going to buy me off with one breakfast roll.

"I could have used a father when I was growing up," I persisted. This time, he turned his eyes on me.

"Seal did a good job," he said. "She never asked for any help."

"Well, of course she didn't," I said, exasperated. "She never would ask. You should have offered."

"I did," he said. "She told me to keep to my side of the bushes and concentrate on my own family."

"So you did," I said.

"So I did," he said.

I wasn't going to let him off the hook this easily.

"Would you have left your own family for her if she'd asked you to?" He took a big gulp of coffee and swallowed.

"Look," he said, a little testily. "That's really between your mother and me."

"No," I said. "I really think it's a family issue. Only I just never was consulted. Didn't you ever want to just talk to me, give me some hint who you were?"

"You really didn't need me," he said, evading the question like the shrewd Weewampum string-puller he was. "You're so much like your mother. Self-contained. Self-sufficient."

"I would have liked to have known about you," I said, not about to be diverted by flattery, if that's what you wanted to call it. "Maybe

I would have turned out differently if I'd known who you were."

"I doubt it," he said, smiling.

OK, I'd give up this line of questioning for the time being. I wasn't going to guilt-trip him into anything, at least not this time.

"So what now?" I asked.

"What do you want?" he asked. I thought for a second. The powdered sugar was sticking my fingers together in a most annoying way. If I asked him, would he stop building the hospital? Not a chance. Would he give me money? Maybe. But I didn't really want that. Would he give me love? It was too soon to tell. Would I return it? Hard to say.

"Promise me," I said, not processing the words before they flew past my lips, "when I get back to California, you'll find a way to take care of Seal."

He looked at me as if I'd trapped him, asked the one thing he couldn't deliver – well, other than stopping the hospital.

"Promise?" I asked.

He gulped some coffee.

"How is she?" he asked, not betraying any emotion.

"OK. Not well. Getting better. I don't know," I said and started crying.

He wiped his hands, first one, then the other, on the napkins, crumpled the tissue and hurled it into the back seat. He kept his eyes on the road.

"Seal will be fine," he said evenly. He looked at me then and his eyes softened. "I promise you, Wendy."

I tried to look at the road, too. I wasn't sure if it really had started raining or if it was just me.

"If I go back to Santa Dolorosa but Seal gets worse, will you promise you'll call me?"

"I promise," he said.

We drove the rest of the way without speaking, but when he dropped me off in front of my house, he turned to me. "I doubt if she ever told you, but I asked Seal to marry me before I ever asked Clare. Seal was going out with me and Rex Whitby at the time. She wanted to be a lawyer. Seal said she had better things to do than get stuck in a small town with a small-time architect. That hurt. So I married Clare."

"So what about me?" I asked him. I wasn't sure I was buying this explanation.

"Joey was older than I. So's Merribeth, a little. How did I figure in?"

"Your mother is an interesting and most unusual woman," was all he said. "Don't underestimate her."

And then he smiled and drove into his own driveway.

***

In late April, we finally got our first piece of positive news from Seal's doctors. Although Seal was sicker than a dog who's eaten a football field of grass, it was possible the chemo and radiation were doing what they were supposed to do. It looked as if maybe the cancer cells were being held at bay, that they hadn't made it past her lymph nodes.

I phoned The Boss Lady yet again and pleaded for another two-week extension. "You're pressing your luck," she said and hung up. I took that for "Yes."

Star still was unconscious. Her bones were mending. Whether she had brain damage or not, no one could tell until she woke up, and she didn't seem in any hurry to do that.

The second bit of news came first by a phone call, on the Tuesday of one of the many weeks that I was supposed to be back at work. Miss Trumble was on the line.

"Mr. Caramel wants to see you and your lady friends," she said.

I picked up Merribeth, and then we went to retrieve Amber from the hospital.

"I can't leave," Amber said.

"Yes, you can," Merribeth said.

"What if he arrests us?" Amber asked.

"How can he?" I replied.

"What will Star do?" Amber asked.

"She'll keep on getting better," Merribeth said.

Amber looked at us. Her eyes filled with tears. Amber seemed so doubtful, so hesitant, so unlike Amber. It was painful to see.

"Uh, right," Amber said slowly. "That's what she's going to do."

"Come on, Amber," I said, my throat catching as I pulled her toward the hospital door. I loved this big, noisy, careless woman who had more love to give than she received. "In case we need to tell Warren Caramel to go to hell, you can do it best."

Amber looked at us wearily. She was not sleeping, not eating. She tried to smile and said, "I can't leave her."

"Yes, you can," Merribeth insisted, as commanding as a general. "There is no one else but you who can tell Warren off in just the right way, so you are coming with us and that's final."

Amber just shrugged in resignation and we tugged her and pushed her into Seal's Olds.

***

When we arrived at Warren's, Miss Trumble told us to take a seat. The chairs were as unwelcoming as the ones at the hospital. I tried to clear my mind and prepare for whatever was coming next, but the top of the chair was poking into my spine, and all I could think of was the good old steno chair that had never given me any problems, waiting for me back at the *Santa Dolorosa Advance.*

As I was crossing my legs for the thirteenth time, Warren's inner office door swung open and Warren stuck his head out.

"You may come in," he said as formally as a Supreme Court justice. We tried to keep our faces blank as we followed him into his room. He gestured for us to sit on more hard chairs. I wondered what kind of chairs they'd made the victims of the Spanish Inquisition sit on while they were interrogating them. Or maybe they just made them stand, which had its plusses. Warren reached for a manila folder on his desk and opened it. There were lots of typed pages inside. He picked up some forms and gave one to each of us.

"You may find this report interesting," he said, boring his eyes first into Merribeth's, then Amber's, then my personal space.

My eyes swept the form. It was a fire report. The date, place, times, and number of trucks that responded to Amberosia's fire all were spelled out. One line said the fire was reported by an automatic alarm. On a line for the owner of the restaurant, Amber's name sat like a lone sparrow on a telephone wire. There were three lines where it said, "Narrative description:" and someone had typed: "Building fully engulfed when Company 1 arrived, 24:01. Smoke pouring from windows; roof gone, rafters exposed. Company 2 arrived, 24:10. Fire extinguished, 1:07. Two firefighters remained at scene until 10:00."

On the line where it said: "Estimated damage:" someone had typed, "Total loss." And then finally on the line where it said, "Cause of fire:" someone had typed, "Suspicious. Undetermined origin."

The three of us finished reading the report. We looked at Warren for a further translation.

"Well," he said, "that about does it."

We stared at him for a moment and then I asked, "What do you mean, 'Undetermined origin'? We told you we did it. It's not undetermined at all."

"Who's the fire marshal here?" he asked, locking his steely eyes on mine while tucking his papers inside the manila folder and flipping it shut.

"You can keep those reports. I made you each a copy," he said. And then he swept past us and handed Miss Trumble the folder.

She toted it to a file cabinet, wedged it inside, then resumed her typing. Warren walked out the office door to his red pickup truck and drove off.

Merribeth, Amber, and I just stared at each other. "Well, we're free women, I guess," Merribeth said.

"But the report's wrong," I said.

"It doesn't matter, Wen," Merribeth said. "We're at least free now to go about our lives."

"Woohoo," Amber whispered as she folded her report and stuffed it inside her purse, then started to cry. Merribeth pulled Amber into her arms and our flame-haired friend cried and cried because the only thing that would make her happy was knowing that her daughter had a future.

"Come on Amber," I said, patting her back and stroking her hair. "Things are starting to look up. We're free now to open Amberosia's

II.''

As I've said before, sometimes I speak before I think through what I'm saying. But I've learned to think of this as a positive trait, something that defines who I am.

Amber stopped sobbing long enough to take in a big breath of air. She turned to me and fell into my arms.

"Woohoo," she whispered, and then we flooded Warren Caramel's office with tears. Miss Trumble brought us tissues, and I think she wondered whether she should phone the Police Department down the hall to remove this disturbance of the peace from her office, or transfer back to the Department of Public Works, where they were better equipped to drain off storm water and dry out flooded buildings. But I think she decided that, for the moment, staying where she was made the most sense. It was where she could be the most help, where she was most needed, and probably, in the grand scheme of things, that counted for something.

Chapter 16

The Main Ingredient's Schaum Torte

8 eggs, separated
2 cups sugar
1 teaspoon baking powder
1 teaspoon vanilla
1 teaspoon vinegar
Topping of your choice:
Fresh or frozen strawberries
Fresh cherries or cherry pie filling
Other fresh, frozen or canned fruit
Chocolate sauce
Ice cream
Whipped cream

10-inch greased, spring-form pan

Heat oven to 500 degrees. When the oven reaches 500 degrees, turn it off.
Mix sugar and baking powder. While beating egg whites at a slow speed, add
the sugar/baking powder mixture. Continue beating and add vanilla, then
vinegar. Beat egg whites until stiff. Transfer mixture to spring-form pan.
Place the pan in the oven and allow torte to bake until the oven is cold. (This
usually is over night.) This is a good way to keep the marshmallowy center
up high. The meringue will sink, but you can top off the dessert with
strawberries or the fruit of your choice, chocolate sauce, ice cream,
whipped cream, or a combination.

From Esther Weber

I'd like to say everything worked out for the best. And if this
Schaum Torte looked less like a pile of crumbs that someone
dropped on the floor and then tried to cover up with strawberries,
I might be more inclined to say I am grateful to be cooking this
morning for 300 people on a Christmas Eve day when much
of the rest of the world is out shopping or sipping rum-spiked
eggnog. I'd like to say everything unfolded according to the Great
Goddess' plan – or, at least, ours. But the only plans I ever knew I
actually was witnessing being revealed were the ones for the new
Our Lady of Perpetual Need Medical Center, and those should

have just self-immolated right on the spot. Well, maybe I'm being too critical. My father assures me the new building will have a bronze fountain of stylized doves in the lobby and a solarium with Weewampum's biggest collection of tropical ferns. I suppose I should wait for the grand opening before passing final judgment on my dad's edifice.

I'm not ruling out that divine intervention brought me back home, and some would say that's definitely why things turned out as they did. I guess if anything has been revealed to me, it's that I truly like feeling pastry dough or freshly chopped romaine lettuce beneath my fingers and watching people eat the food I prepare for them. It beats sitting on a steno chair, comfortable as it might be, and writing about someone else's spritz cookies. And OK, it might not be totally trendsetting, intellectually admirable, or on the cutting edge of ushering in a new era of social and political change, but I admit I enjoy being within driving distance of my friends and just a room away from my mother.

We opened the Main Ingredient on Labor Day in the former Marilyn's Bridal Boutique, right next door to where Amberosia's went up in smoke a year ago. Marilyn gave up on downtown and moved to a mini-mall along Highway 11 over the summer. I don't really blame her. It was tough running a business that caters to hope next to a burned-out corner of charred wood chunks and errant burger wrappers. If The Main Ingredient goes over, we may even expand onto our old lot. Even though Amber financed just about everything for our new venture, she insisted we come up with a more globally encompassing name than Amberosia's II. Merribeth, who did chip in to pay for the dining room furnishings from a savings account she had tucked away, and I, who cashed in my *Santa Dolorosa Advance* IRA for some chef's knives and a waffle iron, as well as Amber, were all stumped about what to call our eatery, something that would indicate what we were about. "The Fearsome Threesome's" sounded more like a bar and grill for pirates than a cozy dining establishment. So until we come up with something better, we've settled on "The Main Ingredient," hoping to convince our customers that we've got just the main ingredient they need, or else that they're the main ingredient and they're doing us a favor by using our restaurant as their special clubhouse.

I'd like to say that everything worked out for the best, and, as far as Seal goes, things aren't too bad. She finished her round of chemo and radiation. Her hair's even starting to grow back in clumps. No one can say if she's licked the cancer yet, but she has booked the four back tables at The Main Ingredient for the next two years for the Wednesday afternoon meetings of the Weewampum Secretarial Association Bridge Club. I haven't moved out of her house yet, and that surprises both of us. But we're getting along by ignoring each other a lot, which suits both of us just fine. We talk some, too. I learned just yesterday, for instance, that when she and Dottie Wentzell were 9, they sliced their fingertips with a razor to become blood sisters, but Seal shaved too much off and had to go to the hospital for stitches. We do manage to get in at least three Scrabble games a week. Seal's still champ, two to one.

I'd also like to say that everything's worked out for the best in the matter of my father, and I guess things could be worse down that thorny avenue. So far, we've mostly kept our distance, although he did ask me if I wanted to go along when he took the family to a Brewers' game. It was a Thursday night and we were shorthanded at the restaurant, so I declined in a manner I thought was fairly gracious for me. I still feel awkward when I think about how I should relate to the Hartwells, even though they've always welcomed me as Merribeth's best friend. Perhaps if I knew that Seal definitely was going to outsurvive us all, and perhaps if I had assurances that Star was going to lead a long and happy life, I'd find it easier to pick open all the scabs with my mother and father and let them air out and dry up to just a few, slight, silver scars. For right now, I'm doing just fine keeping one door away from my dad.

More than anything, I'd like to say that everything's going to be all right with Star, that she's flying around the house like a comet and laughing and swearing like a little pirate. It was the first of June when the hospital staff finally let Merribeth or me alternate in visiting Star for 10 minutes each hour. Star's hair was growing curly and long by then, and she looked like a little Raggedy Ann doll. All she did was sleep, and we couldn't rouse her. But I sang her nursery rhymes and oldies but goodies. I read her stacks of children's books, Shakespeare, comic books, and books about child development so she'd know what she was supposed to be doing. I held her, counted her toes, crawled into her bed to be close to her, but she barely moved.

By the end of the month when the summer heat had set in and everything was slowing down, the hospital relaxed the rules so that Merribeth and I could visit together and whenever we wanted. On the evening of the Fourth of July, Amber, Merribeth, and I sat around Star's bed, watching what we could glimpse, through the windowpanes, of the annual fireworks glittering above Lake Weewampum. Amber held Star's hand through the whole show, but Star didn't seem to notice. It wasn't until they shot off the 21 boom salute at the end and lit the sky with a sparkling American flag, that Amber screamed, "Oh, my god! Oh, my god!"

We looked at Amber, who was gazing at Star with a look of wonder that it didn't seem likely that the fireworks flag had produced. Then we noticed that Star was looking back at her mother with the same look of amazement. And then we all cried. We scooped up Star and hugged her and hugged each other and screamed and shouted. It took two full weeks after that, though, before Our Lady of Perpetual Need released our little girl into her mother's care.

Star still sleeps a lot but she's crawling. Although many kids her age are walking and talking and creating bragging boors out of their parents, Star seems to be taking it a little easy, although I don't want to say she's slow; she's really been through a lot. Still, when we call her name or show her teddies or zip a toy Corvette under her fingers, it seems to take her a while to react. Maybe she's just trying to puzzle out why so many people are trying to get her to do so many things that she really has no interest in. It's just too early to tell how much we injured her; that's what the doctors say. Or maybe we didn't hurt her that much at all. Kids are resilient,

214

they keep telling us.

Lars drops in at Amber's every weekend to visit Star. Amber makes sure her housekeeper Marta, Merribeth, or I are there with her when he comes by. From what I've seen, Lars seems quite smitten with Star. He's constantly attempting to get Amber to try new ways to get their daughter to walk and talk and engage with her world. Amber usually tells Lars off, but so far, she hasn't barred him from seeing his child, and I think that's to her credit. I can't predict whether Lars will want to stay in the picture if Star doesn't develop as quickly as other kids. All I know is that Amber, Merribeth, and I love our little tyke to pieces, and we will smile for hours at a time, well, at least for several minutes, whenever we hear her squeaky laugh.

I also know I've got enough work today basting the turkeys to a golden brown and popping in the dinner rolls around 11:15 a.m. to think much further ahead than lunch. Amber is thinking ahead, though. She's confident Star will make a full recovery. And when she does, Amber says we should start concentrating on developing a plan to turn this downtown around. Amber says if we start circulating petitions and looking for private funds, then we can put together a proposal to turn downtown Weewampum into a cute day-trip destination for the residents of the greater Carp River Valley. No one else, surely not the City Council, has as much foresight as we do, she insists. Perhaps she has a point. It's a rather small and bourgeois dream, but at least Amber has one, and, as always, she's willing to share it with us.

The City Council and hospital board did approve construction of the new medical center upon the bedrock portion of the land along the highway. By the time they got around to voting, the basement was in and the workers were starting to put up the steel girders. Things are pretty much the way they've always been in Weewampum, and my father continues to play a role in seeing that they are. But I guess you could say the Threesome are becoming part of the establishment. Our holiday buffet is now an annual event.

I've not had a twinge of regret about no longer being food editor.

I think Merribeth misses being a teacher now and then, but she says she's not looking back. And if she really wants to, she could always substitute-teach for Weewampum Unified.

We realized that with Amberosia's, we had built something up and burned it down all with our own six hands. And that's more than we'd ever accomplished before on our own. The power of three (or six, depending on how you count it) is greater than the power of one, we discovered.

Amber's still Amber. She's hardly ever here. And when she is, all she ever does is eat and talk, but that's OK. She's spending most of her time with Star, so much that I'm beginning to worry about her. She's not had a date since before the accident. One of these days, she's got to get out and circulate.

Of course, Merribeth and I are hardly the social butterflies of Weewampum, although Merribeth's been dating a dentist, Carl Demler, who recently moved to town. We all like him because he seems to like us, although he's a bit too serious for my taste. Me? Still solo. What can you expect if you live in Weewampum? Look at Seal. But my mother, who keeps up with the town gossip, says she's heard that Randy Seccombe's left the ministry. He's opened a dance school in Minneapolis. "And he's not homosexual," she tells me at least twice a day.

"Gay," I tell her.

"Well, whatever."

I don't know why she's so hung up on Randy.

"He's coming home for the holidays," Seal says. "Maybe he'll come to the buffet."

Oh, great. That's just what I need. Maybe Randy and I can polka around the dining room to the Barking Dogs' version of "Jingle Bells."

For this year's buffet, we decorated The Main Ingredient with gold and silver snowflakes strung from the ceiling. We've got a new, fake Christmas tree in the window and, for our Christmas gift, Seal gave each of us a string of up-to-date, small, blinking tree lights.

I've still got to finish the gravy and it's about time to pop these dinner rolls into the oven. Amber, Merribeth, and I are taking bets about whether Lars Hunssen and Jim Hartwell will make a return holiday appearance. We kind of think they will. Mrs. H. told Merribeth she's bringing the twins and Billy, so my father probably will show up with the family. Lars might drop in to see Star, whom Amber is bringing by for a while; mom and daughter will be decked out in their new, matching, red velvet dresses. Seal, Florence, and Dottie have reserved a booth next to a window.

Seal asked me for a complete rundown of the menu and sighed when I told her we were adding tamales this year. She said there was no way anyone in town would eat those things. I must have looked a little disappointed, so she amended her declaration.

"Well, all right. But I'm not going to eat more than one."

I took this as a small but important step toward promoting world peace from Weewampum, Wis., U.S.A.

I wish I could say I know more than I do and that all of us will live happily ever after until we're 303. I guess one of the few things I can say with any certainty is that my room grew noticeably larger when I finally unpacked my last suitcase.

The Main Ingredient

What does it mean to love? How does one defy death? And will people pay good money for your Friday night fish fry?

These are some of the mysteries facing West Coast food editor Wendy Whitby when she reluctantly returns to her childhood home in Weewampum, Wis., to await her mother's demise. But cantankerous Seal (Cecilia) refuses to pass into the Great Beyond according to schedule. While Wendy waits for Seal to expire, Wendy begrudgingly helps out her two high school pals, flamboyant Amber Moore and reticent Merribeth Hartwell, who have opened a restaurant in downtown Weewampum.

Wendy and her friends soon are embroiled in their hometown's political feuds. Some of the well-heeled citizens, including Merribeth's father, have decided they want to close the town's hospital downtown and move it to a spiffy building along the interstate. But the women feel the downtown will deteriorate even further if the old hospital shuts its doors, so their restaurant, Amberosia's, becomes the headquarters of the Stop the Hospital Move campaign.

After Amberosia's burns to the ground, the women are convinced someone set the fire to scare them off because they oppose the hospital move. However, Fire Marshal Warren Caramel suspects the women torched the place to collect the insurance money. The threesome realize they'll have to solve the arson case themselves to avoid spending the best years of their lives in Waysippee State Prison for Women.

As their arson investigation opens old wounds, causes new ones, and reveals secrets that maybe should have been left concealed, the women are forced to grapple with such issues as: How much does a friend do for a friend? How far does family allegiance go? What is the price of family, and especially, mother-daughter love? What are the magnetic and repelling forces of one's hometown? And, of course, how much will someone pay for a plateful of fried lake perch?

About Margo Wilson

When Margo Wilson was 3, she thought an elevator operator was about to squish her imaginary friends, Keke and Frick, in a department store's elevator doors, so she screamed for the operator to free them. The operator complied, while Margo's mom shook her head, and Margo beamed like a superhero. The incident still is the ultimate example of how Margo's imagination influenced reality, and it helped hook Margo on the power of inventing her own world.

But the daughter of a police officer and elementary school teacher is nothing if not practical, so Margo chose to be a journalist, a career in which facts and information, presented in compelling ways, often have a chance to influence others' actions. Margo worked as a staff writer and editor at nine newspapers, ranging from the Spruce Grove Star, in Edmonton, Alberta, Canada, to the Los Angeles Times. Her words led to the defeat of a racist school board member, the resignation of some greedy community college administrators, and publicity for an unknown recording artist who later became one of Margo's best friends. Margo learned that words have power.

She also learned that words have beauty. So she returned to school (Goddard College) to polish her creative writing skills and as a result, landed a job teaching writing at California University of Pennsylvania and snagged a book contract with Ramsfield Press.

These days, she's working on a memoir about travel and taking a journey, and a series of novels about a dog who ... well, let's leave that a secret.

Although she grew up in Wisconsin, Margo has lived in Indiana, Canada, and California. She makes her home in Southwestern Pennsylvania, with her flat-haired retriever (Well, maybe that's what she is. The vet is not sure.) Moosie, and her cats Oreo, Lucy, ChaCha, and Mimi. They are forever using their imaginations to devise new ways to persuade Margo to feed them or pet them.

Contact Margo Wilson at www.margowilson.com.

Ramsfield Press

Ramsfield Press is an independent publisher dedicated to finding, publishing, and promoting books by new and emerging authors.

Our Goals

To publish the best narrative fiction we can find - and the occasional
special project.

To give authors an outlet that treats them with respect.

To collaborate with writers to 'get the word out.'

Ramsfield Press' **Publications:**

You Are Here: Romville Stories, by Joe Boland

Ann's Cooking From Scratch, by Ann Moser

A.C.T.I.V.E. A Mindfulness Based Program for Helping Cancer Patients and Their Families, by Timothy W. Pedigo, Ph.D.